MY NAME WAS JUDAS

C.K. Stead was Professor of English at the University of Auckland until 1986. In 1984, he was awarded the CBE for services to New Zealand literature. He is the renowned author of novels, of poetry, of literary criticism and of short stories. *My Name Was Judas* is his eleventh novel.

ALSO BY C.K. STEAD

Fiction

Smith's Dream

Five for the Symbol (stories)

All Visitors Ashore

The Death of the Body

Sister Hollywood

The End of the Century at the End of the World

The Singing Whakapapa

Villa Vittoria

The Blind Blonde with Candles in her Hair (stories)

Talking About O'Dwyer

The Secret History of Modernism

Mansfield

Poetry

Whether the Will is Free

Crossing the Bar

Quesada

Walking Westward

Geographies

Poems of a Decade

Paris

Between

Voices

Straw into Gold: Poems New and Selected

The Right Thing

Dog

The Red Tram

Criticism

The New Poetic

In the Glass Case: Essays on New Zealand Literature

Pound, Yeats, Eliot and the Modernist Movement

Answering to the Language

The Writer at Work

Kin of Place: Essays on 20 New Zealand Writers

Edited

Oxford New Zealand Short Stories (second series)

Measure for Measure, A Casebook

The Penguin Letters & Journals of Katherine Mansfield

The Collected Stories of Maurice Duggan

The Faber Book of Contemporary South Pacific Stories

Werner Forman's New Zealand

C.K. STEAD

My Name
Was Judas

VINTAGE BOOKS

London

Published by Vintage 2007

2 4 6 8 10 9 7 5 3 1

Copyright © C.K. Stead 2006

C.K. Stead has asserted his right under the Copyright, Designs
and Patents Act, 1988 to be identified as the author
of this work

First published in Great Britain in 2006 by
Harvill Secker

Vintage
Random House, 20 Vauxhall Bridge Road,
London SW1V 2SA

www.vintage-books.co.uk

Addresses for companies within The Random House Group Limited
can be found at: www.randomhouse.co.uk/offices.htm

The Random House Group Limited Reg. No. 954009

A CIP catalogue record for this book
is available from the British Library

ISBN 9780099501381

The Random House Group Limited supports The Forest Stewardship
Council (FSC), the leading international forest certification organisation.
All our titles that are printed on Greenpeace approved FSC certified paper
carry the FSC logo. Our paper procurement policy can be found at:
www.rbooks.co.uk/environment

Mixed Sources
Product group from well-managed
forests and other controlled sources
www.fsc.org Cert no. TT-COC-2139
© 1996 Forest Stewardship Council
FSC

Printed and bound in the UK by
CPI Cox & Wyman, Reading, RG1 8EX

Acknowledgements

MY GRATEFUL THANKS ARE DUE TO CREATIVE NEW ZEALAND for the award of the Michael King Fellowship, 2005, for the completion of work on this novel.

And to Paul Morris, Professor of Religious Studies at Victoria University of Wellington, who, when I told him I was thinking about writing this novel, and feeling uncertain, replied, 'These are our stories. They must be constantly retold.'

CHAPTER 1

THIS AFTERNOON MY GOOD FRIEND AND BROTHER-IN-LAW,
Theseus, called down to me. There was something he wanted
to show me. I went at once, up the steep path through the olive
grove, and he took me out on to his terrace which looks over
the top of my house, and my family's houses, and out to sea. It
was unusual weather, the view clear all the way to the horizon.
He had already told me his thoughts on this view but now there
was a chance to show me more exactly what he'd meant and
let me judge for myself.

I grew up inland, in the region of Galilee, and there we were
used to clear days and very long views. From Tiberias, for
example, where my father had a house, you could see across the
lake towards Golan, or north, all the way to Hermon, its snow-
white peaks clear against blue sky. Here on the Mediterranean,
especially in hot weather, everything becomes hazy in the far
distance and it's often hard to be sure where sea ends and sky
begins. It's all one long gradation of blueness, receding into
distance, blurred and obscured at the horizon.

But today the air had cleared and everything was outlined sharply.
As I stood beside Theseus on his terrace, there, sure enough, was
the horizon he needed me to see, a line so clear it was as if a
draughtsman had put it in, determined there should be no mistake.

Now, Theseus insisted, I could see for myself what he had talked about a few nights ago. Why, he asked first, was there so sharp a line? If we were looking out to the limit of human sight, the view would fade and become indistinct. But that was not what was happening. We were *seeing* that line, *seeing* that limit. What did it mean? Not that the world stopped – because we know that ships sail great distances and don't come to an end, an edge. They can sail on, it seems for ever. Theseus had watched ships sail out to that limit and vanish; and when that happened they seemed not to go out of sight, but to *sink* from sight. He repeated the word. *Sink*. That was what excited him. It wasn't that human eyes failed. It was that ships went *out of sight*. Where had they gone?

Our senses, he insisted (he was in full flight now) provided the answer; and he told me I must follow that horizon line, first to the extreme left, then to the extreme right. Wasn't it true that there seemed a faint curve, a very gentle but just perceptible bowing of the line, so that it was higher in the middle than at either end?

I stared hard, followed the line slowly to the left, then to the right. I've always prided myself on excellent eyesight, but I'm no longer young. Without being anything like certain, I said that yes, I believed there was a very slight curve.

'And there', he said, 'is our explanation. Everything is curving away from us. When we look straight ahead and see that clearly defined line it's because the surface has curved away, *down*, out of sight. This is something we can only recognise when we look out over the sea, a calm sea as it is today – because only then do we look across a perfectly flat surface. Perfectly flat, except that it's curved!'

At this point in his exposition we had, once again, the disagreement (though I lacked conviction, and he was full of it) that we'd had a few days before, sitting under the stars drinking wine, when he had expounded what his friend, an astronomer, had explained to him, that the surface of the earth was curved, and that ('therefore') it must in fact be a gigantic ball – unimaginably large, but a ball.

Now, as then, I expressed my doubts and then fell silent.

'Isn't the sun a sphere?' he persisted. 'And the moon? Why should not the earth be the same?'

Were the sun and moon spheres? I supposed he was right, they must be; but that idea, too, took me by surprise. I wasn't sure, even, what I'd thought in the past, or whether I'd thought about it at all. The idea of the sun as a great burning disc, thin and flat, sliding into a slot in the western ocean at nightfall, seemed real enough – but also, on reflection, improbable.

But then everything was improbable – the sun, the stars, the earth itself.

Long ago Theseus and I made a pact, that we would look at the world as it is, and try to understand only what seemed to be confirmed by common sense and observation. We would look carefully at, and take due note of, everything around us – plants, animals, seasons, weather, and above all the behaviour of our human brothers and sisters – and we would draw from that our 'philosophy'. That was what he was doing with this observation of the curve of the horizon. He had been assured the world was a sphere, and his learned friend the astronomer had shown him a way of demonstrating that it was. I couldn't quite follow him there; couldn't be sure it was true, and thought the fault probably mine, the lack of a sufficiently agile intelligence.

But whether right or wrong didn't matter; it was all in accord with our promise to one another, that we would accept as 'true' only what could be confirmed by our senses and by reason. We didn't reject out of hand the mystical, the mysterious, the numinous, even the magical; but we would not accept them, either, on the say-so of others. Perhaps there was one God who heard our prayers and appreciated our sacrifices, as I had been taught in childhood; or many gods as the traditions Theseus inherited would have it. Perhaps the air was full of angels, and dead men walked in the night. But perhaps equally there were none of these things. We were resolved that we would need to see them and hear them, feel their presences and their powers, before we would believe in them again. And what we had found, over the decades of our friendship, was that the less we believed in these forces, in that 'other world' and its creatures, the less they gave us reason to. Gradually life, consciousness, the very air we breathed, the sky, sea, rocks and desert sands – everything – was cleared of 'emanations'.

It was like a mist lifting, a veil being torn away. Strange sounds in the night were strange sounds in the night, and had discoverable causes. The fiery chariot of God's wrath in the sky could be turned at will into something less ominous – a golden camel, a white stallion, a giant carp – and finally into nothing but cloud and sunlight. When my mule dropped dead it was old age, not a curse, that had done for him. There was a comet in the sky, or a shooting star? Very well, it was a comet or a shooting star. Why did it have to 'mean' something? A sacrificial cow gave birth as its throat was cut (this happened recently, not far from here, causing fear and panic in the region)? So it had been about to calve and should not have been chosen for the sacrifice. A neighbour's barn burned down, destroying his store of grain? No it was not, as he believed (beating his breast and weeping) a punishment because he had sinned and neglected prayer and sacrifice. Much more likely (though we didn't tell him) it was the work of his drunken and disorderly son.

4

We would no longer pretend we could 'read' these things, nor accept that anyone could. They were the world going about its business, paying us no attention.

Even the bolt of lightning which, all those years ago, had struck the ox cart bringing my few worldly possessions from Tyre and set them burning – I saw that, now, as a natural event, because I had been given no cause, then or since, to see it otherwise. If God existed and wished to speak to me, then He must speak and I would listen. I listened even when He didn't speak; but I would not pretend I heard His voice in a silence, or in the fact of an ox cart of prized nothings inconveniently set alight.

The mysteries remained. Why is life as it is – so valued, so rich, so imperfect, so full of contradiction and of pain? Why must it end in death, and why must we know that it does and yet have no cause, except in the untested words of prophets and scriptures, to believe that there is anything afterwards? What is 'out there' among the stars and beyond the stars?

It was not the mystery we rejected, but the explanations, which seemed, most of them, weak stories made up to pacify or to frighten small children. We aspired to be rational men, and practical men, unafraid of the dark. There was reason enough to fear what was visible and tangible, without adding fears of what might be there, invisible and intangible. I had lived all my life with fear of my fellow men (and not just of the Roman overlord, though I feared him most) – of wild animals, sudden storms, drought and famine, disease and what it might do to my children. And of death. That was quite enough fear for any man, and I was determined there would be no more, and no other, unless reason could be shown for it.

I had rid my consciousness of gods, ghosts and demons. If they came back I would try to deal with them; but once gone it seemed (the deathbed may prove me wrong!) they were gone for good.

But of course I have made it all sound too easy. When his child grows ill what does a loving father do but abase himself and pray? When that infant dies, as two of mine did, what does he do but search his mind for fault, for reason, for what he has done 'wrong' to bring about this calamity? When I feel an intimation of the illness that will one day kill me, what do I do but pray? Not *for* anything, not even to be saved. Just pray.

'Please . . .'

'Please what?' the great God might ask if He were there and listening – and what could I reply, since I know I will not live for ever? Just 'Please' – that's all. It's not natural to be always rational; but it is wise always to try.

The resolve to live in this way, rejecting the faiths and fantasies of our upbringing, came to me less easily than to Theseus. He too had old gods and monsters to reckon with, and old habits of prayer and propitiation that went with them. I know that he still can't resist trying to read his future in the alignment of the stars; and sometimes when we go fishing together I see his lips moving and know that he is praying to some Greek god of the waters, probably only that the fish will bite, but perhaps also that no sudden storm will strike. But his path towards reason and scepticism has been easier than mine. As an educated Greek he inherited a tradition different from mine as a Jew. I felt I needed his help, and he has given it over many decades. My debt to him is very great.

Forty years ago I came to this coastal village just south of Sidon to escape from Judaea, from Jerusalem, from what had happened to me there, and from everything that my home region and the holy city (as we called it) had come to represent. I wished to escape my childhood, my race, my religion, my mistakes; to escape my own story; to begin it again; to rewrite it by reliving it, giving it what might be something like a happy end.

Like my father before me I became a trader in foodstuffs – mainly olive oil, dates, balsam and salt, and sometimes also, when the season was good, wheat and barley. I prospered, married (a second marriage, my first wife having died in Galilee while I was still in my early twenties). I am now a father of two adult sons and three daughters, and a grandfather many times over. I have reached the age of seventy, which the Psalmist tells us is the upper limit of our claim on life.

Certainly I never expected to reach such advanced years; and when the birthday came last year, I felt relief, as if there was no longer any need to struggle, or to hold tight to anything. I have had my life. My story, duly revised, has told itself. There have been mistakes, and waste (there is always waste), but the outcome has not been unfortunate. If anything is to follow I will see it as a coda, and (while I still find life enjoyable and full of interest) a bonus.

But I am not yet dead, or even dying, and cannot quite detach myself from the world or from my past. As the news comes to me of violent happenings in Jerusalem, of revolt, civil war and, most recently, the advance on the city of four legions – 24,000 foot soldiers – under the command of Titus, son of the new emperor, who will surely inflict terrible punishment for these Jewish challenges to Roman rule, I have found myself going back in my thoughts to the past which, until now, I have wanted only to put behind me.

My dear wife Thea, Theseus' sister, died three years ago, an event which has tested and, at times, severely challenged my

7

'philosophy' and my claim to have made myself the 'rational man'. She used to say, gently mocking my determination to reject stories about ghosts and resurrections, that if there should be a life after death she would come back and whisper something in my ear that would take me by surprise. At night I often take a walk before bed, along the shore, and in the darkness I speak to her, telling her I love her, saying the things one should say and never does until it's too late. My ears are always open for her replies, but alas, Thea is silent, and I suppose must remain so.

My children have asked me sometimes (though never as if it's a matter of great importance or urgency) to tell them about my past; to explain how Judas of Keraiyot, as I was for the first thirty years of my life, became Idas of Sidon, as I have been for the subsequent forty. I have given them only scraps, anecdotes, random reminiscences, but never the part that seems to me most significant. This is not because I'm ashamed of what I think of as 'the real story'. There are reasons for keeping it secret, although I know the secret would be safe enough with them. But I suppose I have preferred they should know me as I've made myself, not as I was before the important lessons of my life had been learned.

Perhaps now is the time to fill the gaps.

Our world a
ball or a saucer – these
questions matter.

Under my window
I hear my grandchild
Hector ask,

'Mummy, why
does Grandfather talk
in that funny way?'

She explains
it's the accent
of the land of my birth.

No sign of
the rain I need for
my orchard garden.

Out of my dark
past I conjure the
barren fig tree

that Jesus cursed
on which it's said
I hung like ripe fruit.

CHAPTER 2

WHEN I FIRST KNEW JESUS I THINK WE WERE SIX OR SEVEN years old. His father was a carpenter and mine a successful trader, so there was a social divide between us. My father was not only prosperous, he was also of a priestly family, a family of Sadducees originally from the Judaean town of Keraiyot; and in the years of my discipleship, when my eleven brethren wanted to mark out a difference between themselves (good earthy Galilean stock) and me, they would refer to me as Judas of Keraiyot. The fact that I'd never lived there made no difference. I was the one who was different – not of their region – and also from a privileged family, another difference that was held against me. On the other hand, though I was not the closest to Jesus in love, nor the one he felt safest with, I was the one who had known him longest.

My father's father and grandfather had been rabbis, and his brother was a senior priest attached to the Temple in Jerusalem. My parents were proud of the status this connection conferred; but I had the impression, acquired in the way children do get hold of such things, without ever having it confirmed or explained, that my father had given some offence to his family, possibly by marrying my mother, who had no priestly connections, and that he was determined that I, his only child, should regain the lost approval. He'd chosen a learned man whose name was Andreas to be my teacher, or tutor, and I went to his house four days of the week, together with another boy, Thaddeus, whose parents could also afford to pay for their son's tuition, and with Jesus, whose parents could not. Our tutor had discovered Jesus quite by chance, and offered to teach him because he was exceptionally quick and clever – an *Ilui*, Andreas said, a child genius. Jesus also had great charm and good looks. In fact I sometimes thought (without ever doubting Jesus' cleverness, of which I saw daily demonstrations) that it was the charm and the good looks as much as the scholarly promise that had won him his place with us. I, by comparison, was an ordinary-looking boy, straightforward in manner, but somewhat lacking in grace.

When I think back to those lessons my image is of Andreas with a languid arm around Jesus' shoulders, talking to us in his high, excited voice, as if simultaneously protecting and teaching his favourite. Sometimes, when we pleased him by learning difficult things, he would kiss us on the cheeks. Jesus was kissed more often than I or Thaddeus. He learned more, and more quickly, so the kisses were deserved. But we knew Andreas loved him in a way he didn't love us.

Andreas was to teach us, first, to read in our own language, and then to write. As time went on we were to learn Hebrew as well, to study the holy texts, to learn the history of our race, and whatever other history he considered it might be useful for us to know. We were to spend a great deal of time copying, and also memorising, significant passages. Andreas was a Syrian whose first language was Greek; but he was a fine scholar and an excellent linguist, and considered his own Aramaic superior to ours, because he'd learned it in Jerusalem. He told us our accent, of the Galilean region, was 'bucolic', chided our 'country consonants', and made us correct them when we read our texts aloud.

There again Jesus earned kisses. Even as a child he had a beautiful voice and could soon read the most difficult texts aloud, at sight from the scrolls, with astonishing competence, seldom making mistakes. His singing was good too; but we were all good at that, and sang four-part folk songs with our tutor.

We also learned some Greek from Andreas, and something about his own Greek traditions. Much of what we learned I've since forgotten; but I remember once there was a lesson about the philosophy of Diogenes, whose followers, called the 'dog philosophers', rejected ownership and attachment to things, and went about the world in a state of poverty, wearing ragged clothes, taking food and shelter where they could be found. There was a story about Diogenes outside Corinth, walking the dusty roads in bare feet, carrying only a staff and a bag over his shoulder, encountering Alexander the Great, who was setting forth to conquer the world, something which the philosopher (so the story went) thought 'unnecessary' since, as he saw it, *his* world – *himself* – he had already conquered. The great king, wearing a shining breastplate and helmet and backed by military retainers carrying spears with scarlet and black pennants, looked down from his magnificent horse at the philosopher in rags, and was impressed by his keen, intelligent face and his strong presence. Was there anything he could do, the king asked, to assist a man whose reputation for wisdom went before him in the world?

'You could move back a little,' Diogenes replied. 'You've come between me and the sun.'

I remember this story, not so much for itself but because of the reaction of the boy Jesus on hearing it. He laughed raucously, with his mouth open wide like a peasant, and banged his open hand repeatedly on the desktop. His eyes shone with a strange crazed light.

I was embarrassed at his lack of self-possession, and hissed at him that there was no need to put on such a show for our teacher. But Andreas kissed him. 'Jesus recognises wisdom and delights in it,' he said, 'and so should you, Judas.'

Many years later, when we were travelling the roads on foot together, preaching and practising poverty and abstinence, Jesus reminded me of that lesson.

'We are the dog philosophers of the modern age,' he said.

We were both hot and tired, and I was in no mood to flatter. 'And you,' I said, with some little edge of sarcasm, 'I suppose you're our Diogenes.'

'Since you say so,' he replied. There was something intransigent and self-satisfied in that answer, a tone that would later enrage both the Roman authorities and the Jewish priesthood; but in those early days his self-assertions were always tinged with humour, a hint of self-mockery.

We'd been arguing, as we often did, about how much it was possible and desirable to go without. He'd told us – his twelve disciples – that we should wear only one jellaba and carry only a wallet-bag on a shoulder thong with a very few items, including just one loose coat for warmth in the evenings and cold weather. He'd also ordained (one of his sudden edicts, which seemed to come without thought or warning, this one later allowed to lapse) that we should travel without walking staffs. Why, he asked, should we need protection from brigands if we carried nothing worth their taking? And in any case, he was teaching us that we should give whatever was asked of us, if we had it to give. There ought to be nothing to protect.

I wore the one jellaba and carried the required one-only bag, but I'd refused to give up my staff. It was like a friend. It made walking easier when we had to make our way over stony uneven ground, and I felt safer with it in the open countryside.

'Don't make me choose between my two friends,' I'd said to him, and he'd laughed in the way he did when we were alone together, implying that he was prepared to be patient with me.

On this occasion there were just the two of us together (he often divided us up to work in pairs) on a rough track, coming down towards Capernaum where we were to meet at evening with the others. Hot and bothered, on the edge of quarrelling (we'd found no ready ears that day, gained no new followers, and had even been stoned by small boys), we came over the brow of a small hill and found ourselves confronted by a pack of wild dogs.

'Here they are,' Jesus said. 'Our brethren dog philosophers.'

It was a nice try, and it's quite true he didn't look in the least afraid – but there was going to be no miracle transformation. These were wild dogs, not philosophers, and they were hungry.

They were nervous of us, but held their ground, crouching, snarling, curling black lips back and baring fangs. I could see the pack mind asking itself, 'Can we do this? There are only two of them. Are they weak or strong?'

I went into action at once, straight at them, swinging my staff, laying about me. They cringed, yelped, scattered, and in a moment were gone over the hill, leaving one so seriously wounded I finished him with a blow to the head.

As we walked on together I waited for Jesus to say something, to make some acknowledgement, commend me for what I'd done, but he said nothing. At last I couldn't hold my tongue any longer. 'You told me I should go without a staff,' I said.

'I did,' he confirmed.

'And do you still say so?'

'I do.'

14

'But if I'd not had my staff we might have been mauled to death. Torn to shreds and eaten.'

He smiled – more a grin than a smile. 'But you *did* have it,' he said.

As boys we got on well and became friends. He was clever, but I was by no means stupid, and we enjoyed learning, playing word games, competing to memorise great tracts of scripture. Those texts were like a loam laid down in the mind. They remain with me now – not as a source of faith, but as an enrichment. And I was to see Jesus, in his great days as a preacher, make wonderful use of them. For me the language of the scriptures was (and is still) a source of beauty and comfort; for him it became a source of power.

That was what made us friends. Though he was later to accept the admiration, and even the discipleship, of some men whose minds were, to say the least, ordinary, as a child he was keen, competitive, impatient and easily bored. If I had been dull and boring, as we thought Thaddeus was, Jesus would not have been interested in me. He showed no sign, ever, of seeking me out because I had good toys and lived in a handsome villa. If anything, he held those advantages against me, forgave them because I was a companion who could compete with him, and sometimes match him.

We played mind games which we invented ourselves. Some were attempts to communicate thoughts silently. One of us had to think very hard of a colour, or a number between one and twenty, or an animal, and attempt to send it by thought to the other, who concentrated, eyes closed, trying to receive it. We kept count of how often these transferences of thought occurred, and compared that count with the chance (which in the case of the numbers was, of course, one in twenty) if the outcome had been merely random. Always our success rate was so far ahead of the numerical chances, we were convinced that in some degree we were gaining the power of silent communication.

And because there was, even at a very early age, an intellectual bond, we also did together all the more ordinary things that small boys do to fill their days. We roamed the countryside, wrestled and played hide-and-seek in the barley fields, explored caves, climbed rock faces, often falling and hurting ourselves and receiving reproaches and punishments for straying too far outside the limits of the village. In the hot weather we bathed in the stream that ran through the valley. We became expert, as every boy should, at throwing stones. I was at least his equal, or slightly superior, with a sling; but I couldn't match Jesus in throwing by hand. We were about even in size and physical strength; but when it came to throwing he had a way of twisting and flicking his wrist at the last moment which seemed to give greater distance. And his eye was deadly. I have seen him knock a bulbul off a tree branch at a hundred paces.

Sometimes I would visit his home, a small flat-roofed house in a narrow street, where he lived with his parents and his four or five younger brothers and sisters. It was a rough, overcrowded household, nothing like my own, smelling of food, human bodies and one or two dogs. His father, Joseph, was a burly, quiet man, with a warm smile. When he wasn't working Joseph liked to sit up on the flat roof, or on a stool outside in the street, playing a reed pipe. I never heard him say very much, and he seemed uncomplainingly dominated by his wife.

The mother, Mary, was a skinny, intense woman who concealed a steely quality under appropriate appearances of meekness and submission. She waited on her husband, as a woman should, served his meals first and ate only when his was finished. There was nothing overtly 'different' about her. And yet somehow you were made to feel that in her slightly crazed way she was the ruler of the roost.

When she met me in the street she would take me by the upper arms and stare into my eyes, telling me what a 'nice little fellow' I was. She had tearful eyes, and at close quarters it was as if a drowned soul was looking up through the water. 'Here's Jesus' little friend,' she would call to anyone and no one when I appeared at the door. 'How are you Judas? You're looking lovely today, darling. And isn't it a nice day? Where did your mother find that beautiful shift? Did she make it herself? No, but of course not – one of the servants would have done that, yes? How is your mother? And what about your father? Is he back from Tiberias yet?'

I didn't have to answer any of these questions, because each was followed immediately by another, and then she would go, without a break, straight into telling me about Jesus, her 'little *ilui*' (she'd snatched the word from Andreas), her wonderful first-born, her miracle child – what he had done this morning, what he'd said last night, what he'd made for his younger brothers.

When I first knew the family, Jesus would blush and squirm at these praises she heaped on him. As he grew older they produced impatience and irritation which he did nothing to hide. 'Mother, will you please shut up?' I heard him say that many times, but it was as if she didn't hear. She was living inside the fortress of her own head, sending out messages, but not receiving any back. When I was small I found her spooky. Much later, when Jesus became a famous preacher and prophet and I saw how cruelly he rebuffed her attempts to claim him and to give him love and advice, I felt sorry for Mary. At the end, at his death in Jerusalem, she was far away, still in Nazareth with her family.

Once, probably in the second year of our lessons with Andreas, we read together with Thaddeus the story about the birth of Moses – the passages in Exodus that tell how the Jews were increasing faster than the Egyptians, and how the Pharaoh, who ruled over the Jews, worked them harder and harder, trying to wear them down and check their increase. But this was unsuccessful, Jewish numbers went on rising, so the Pharaoh ordered the killing of every newborn Jewish male. To avoid this fate for her child, Moses' mother, when he was born, set him afloat on a little raft among the bulrushes, where he was found by the Pharaoh's daughter, who saved him and brought him up as her own.

We both liked this story of the child saved to become the great patriarch of our race, but there was something unusually intense in the way my friend responded to it, and when next I came to his house and his mother was rattling on in her usual way about her wonderful firstborn she called him her 'little Moses'. I was puzzled by that. Later, alone with Jesus, I asked what she'd meant. He shrugged and said he didn't know – he didn't think she'd meant anything. 'You know my mother,' he said. 'She just talks.' But I suspected he did know, and didn't want to say.

Many years later, however, I was reminded of this again. It was late in the period of the discipleship, not long, in fact, before we all went together on what was meant to be his triumphal mission to Jerusalem. At that time (as I will explain later) there were beginning to be rifts among the twelve, and Jesus was, I thought, making these worse, continuing a practice (though I suppose it was unintentional – merely intuitive, like most things he did) of 'divide and rule'. He would select two or three, take them away, and tell them things which the rest of us were not to know. This created envy, jealousy, competition for favour. We were by that time, all of us in our different ways, in thrall to him; and he exerted his power over us, sometimes individually, sometimes collectively, by charm (his power to make you feel loved, and to evoke responding love, was extraordinary), logical argument, outbursts of impatience or anger, eloquence, and even threats that he would dismiss one or another from the twelve, or turn his back on us all.

I was a little less in awe of him than the others were and, even in those latter days, when he tended to flare up if he thought his authority was being challenged, I sometimes felt able to criticise him; and after an occasion when he took James and John (the brothers he sometimes called the Sons of Thunder) and Bartholomew aside, and counselled them and conferred with them alone, I told him these exercises in favouritism were having a bad effect.

Jesus listened to me, silent, serious, head bowed. When I'd finished my complaint (which rather ran out of force for lack of the expected counterblast) he looked up at me. His smile was faintly mocking. 'Is this jealousy?'

'Well, I suppose it might be,' I conceded. 'I don't mind what you call it, so long as you give it some thought.'

'Would you be complaining if you'd been one of the three?'

'Probably not. And then you wouldn't have anyone to warn you, because none of the others will say a word.'

He nodded, still amused. 'Thank you for the warning then, Judas.'

As I got up to leave he asked, 'Does it ever occur to you that you're in a sub-group of one, and that you're envied for it?'

I looked for him to explain.

'You're the only one who knew me as a child.'

I turned away.

'Judas . . .' He grabbed my wrist, punched me in the old schoolboy way on the upper arm, made me look at him. It was the smile I found hard to resist: not the intense 'We can do this together, brothers' smile he used when he addressed us as a group; nor the 'You are my rock. Never forget how much I count on you' smile that was Simon Peter's; nor the indulgent, forgiving smile he reserved for poor anxious Thomas, or the loving mentor one he lavished on Bartholomew. No. The smile reserved for me was keen-eyed, frank, conspiratorial. It signalled the meeting of amused, superior minds, as if he was saying to me, without having to say it, 'Come on Judas. You're the one with the brain in this outfit. You know how we have to play this thing if we're going to make it work.'

He flattered me with that look, charmed me with it, and, as always, won me over. When I remember such moments I deplore my own weakness; and yet at the same time I feel nostalgia for the companionship, the affection. Outside my own family (in which I include my brother-in-law) I think Jesus is the only man I've ever really loved.

So we were not to know what he'd told John, James and Bartholomew up on the hillside among the goats and goatherds. But of course Bartholomew, the youngest of our troop, had been flattered to find himself included with the two senior men, and couldn't keep it to himself. It came out first in hints, snippets, promise-you-won't-tell whispers. Then the two brothers were probed on the basis of Bart's indiscretions – all of this at times when Jesus wasn't about. And before long we all had a version of the story he'd told them, pieced together from the fragments.

It was about his birth, and I recount it now, not only from

the memory of that time, but having heard it again, more than once, from some of the evangelists who have travelled through Sidon in recent years bearing the Jesus message. It went as follows:

Although Jesus' family lived in Nazareth throughout his childhood, his father, like mine, had been born elsewhere. Joseph came from Bethlehem, a small town in Judaea, south of Jerusalem. When Mary was pregnant with her first child there had been a decree requiring every man in Judaea to return to his home town or village, taking his family with him, to pay a new tax which was required by the emperor of the day, Augustus. It was winter, and the young couple travelled the distance, he walking, she riding on an ass. Just outside Bethlehem they found themselves temporary accommodation in the lower floor of a peasant's house where the animals were kept in winter. There, in the aromatic proximity of a cow, two goats and a few sheep, Jesus was born.

But there were special signs and portents — in particular a bright new star in the east. These signs were taken by certain wise men, advisers to King Herod, to mean the birth of a new 'King of the Jews'. Herod put on a show of welcoming this news but was made uneasy by it. He hardly knew whether to believe it; but these men had been correct in their past prophecies, and this special child might represent a challenge, if not to his authority, then at least to the succession. He demanded to know where the child was to be found. The wise men conferred with others, priests and soothsayers, and decided it would have to be in Bethlehem, because there were ancient prophecies to that effect, and because the new star in the east seemed to move about in the sky leading people in that direction.

In secret Herod called together a special squad of his soldiers, ordering them to find and kill all male babies recently born in and around Bethlehem. But word of the intended massacre reached Joseph in a dream, or from an angel (or it may have been an angel in a dream), and he escaped with Mary into Egypt, only returning to Galilee, and to Nazareth, a year or two later on hearing news of Herod's death.

Well it was a good story. Forty years on it's still a good story. But it's not, and wasn't then, an easy one to believe. I was disturbed by it, by its implausibility, and by the fact that Jesus had chosen to take those three aside and tell it to them.

One day I found myself alone with him. It was another one of our trying-and-failing days, which had become rare by that time when Jesus' fame in the countryside was spreading. We were on the lower slopes of Mount Tabor, looking eastward over fertile fields towards the lake and the Jordan, and in the mood of frustration that had taken hold of me I decided to challenge him. Why, I asked, had he told that strange story about his birth?

'Why? Because it's true. What other reason would there be?' His tone was not so much truculent as commanding. It told me it was not my place to question him.

'I've never heard of a Roman tax that required you to go back to your place of birth.'

He stared at me, unwavering.

'It would be completely impractical. My father, for example, would have had to go back to Keraiyot.'

Jesus shrugged and looked away over the valley. 'Perhaps he did. Your father's usually away somewhere, isn't he?'

I let that pass. 'If there'd been a massacre of boy babies in Bethlehem, we'd all know about it.'

'You think Herod would have made a public announcement?'

I was trying hard to understand. 'Why did you tell it to those three?'

'Because they were ready for it.'

22

'Would believe it.'

'Would know it was true.'

I looked at him, appealing to him. 'Jesus, you don't believe this story.'

He said, 'When I tell a story about a servant and his master, or the keeper of a vineyard, or a shepherd guarding his sheep on a hillside, is it true or false?'

'Ah.' I thought about that. 'So it's a parable.'

His stare was meant to unsettle me, make me unsure of myself – and did. 'For you it's a parable,' he said, 'if that's what you prefer. For James and John it's history. Either way it will serve.'

But what did it serve? There were ancient prophecies that the Messiah would be born in Bethlehem. Was he beginning to believe those voices that shouted from the crowd that he was the Son of Man, the miracle worker destined to bring the Jewish people to their final destiny? That he might be entertaining such an idea, and even, subtly, promoting it, was unsettling. Its possible consequences were frightening.

I changed tack. 'If you meant this not to reach the rest of us, why did you tell Bartholomew?'

He shook his head. 'A mistake. It should only have been John and James.'

We rested in the late-afternoon light. I wanted to argue with him, at the very least try to establish clearly what claim he was now making for himself; but I said nothing more. It was one of the moments when I began to acknowledge to myself that the wheels were falling off our collective enterprise – or off my faith in it.

There was, however, another element to the story I never heard until a few years ago, told to me by one of the Jesus missionaries who pass through Sidon, and confirmed recently by a second. When Mary travelled on the ass towards Bethlehem, carrying Jesus in her womb, she was *still a virgin*. Jesus had been engendered, not by Joseph the carpenter, who fathered her later children, but by the spirit of God Himself, the Holy Ghost.

It's as well I was never asked to believe that during our time together. The challenge would have been too great.

But all that lay in the future.

Meanwhile Jesus and I had our boys' games, and our lessons with Andreas. There was also, everywhere, unavoidable, the dark presence of Israel's God. He was in our homes, in the streets, in the conversation of rich and poor alike. He was there in stories of the past, and He was today's hot news. He was in the air, on the wind, in winter storms and in the ferocity of the summer sun. There was no escape from that ubiquitous, malign force, so quick to take offence, so angry and personal in punishment, so lavish in promises of love, and so niggardly in the delivery. Sin was what our Lord disliked – sin, and disrespect. Respect we could manage, but sin, it seemed, though we never met it face to face, was always there, just out of sight, around the next corner – *our* sin, his and mine, belonging to us like our names, Jesus and Judas, and unavoidable.

We lived in baffled fear of it, and of its consequences.

> I hear jackals
> barking in the night.
> They take me back
>
> to a childhood
> when every shadow
> wore a shadow

that housed a
ghost. The desert was
alive with the dead,

fear ruled the
roost, commanding prayer
and penance, and two

small boys shook
in their beds begging
God to forgive them

for what they
were unsure, only knew
they were guilty.

CHAPTER 3

AS A BOY THERE WERE FEW THINGS I ENJOYED MORE THAN going to the house of Jesus and his family. I had no brothers and sisters of my own and, although I was shy and awkward, I liked the cosiness, the hugger-mugger of it, the way the children rolled about together, and quarrelled, and made rude jokes, and laughed when someone farted, everyone pleading not guilty and pretending to be dying of the smell. I was a cosseted only child and it must have been good for me.

They also had their times of prayer, observance and fervent worship — Mary saw to that, and Joseph played his part, silent, engaged but disengaged, as if going through the motions more to please his wife than out of any deeply held faith. There was not a proper synagogue in Nazareth at that time, but the private house of the man who served as our rabbi was where we gathered on the Sabbath. If Jesus was more seriously 'spiritual' than the rest of us, I didn't notice. But I do remember times when his cousin John was there. When there were prayers John squeezed his eyes tight shut and breathed audibly, sometimes grinding his teeth, sometimes muttering the words, nodding so determinedly that the veins and tendons stood out on his neck, his forehead sweating as if he was enduring torture. When I spoke of this to Jesus he laughed and said something I heard him say more than once later on, when both he and John had become prophets and teachers: 'Poor John – he makes hard work of everything.' As a child I found it absurd, and distasteful. It was like the time when Jesus laughed too loud at the story about Diogenes, and banged his hand on the desk – it embarrassed me and made me feel (I suppose) superior. And even as an adult, when my role as one of Jesus' followers required me to take John seriously, I found it difficult.

My mother wasn't sure Jesus was appropriate company for me. In fact I don't believe she would have permitted it at all except for the fact that he and I were studying together, and Andreas spoke so well of him. She tried to persuade me to spend more time with Thaddeus, and when that didn't succeed, she said I should bring Jesus to our house so she could get a better impression of him. He won her over completely. She said he was 'a scruffy fellow', but she found him charming, 'one of nature's little gentlemen'.

After that first visit he was welcome, and sometimes came and stayed with us. On warm nights, when the air was full of the scent of jasmine, we liked to camp out in the garden in a small red tent my father had bought for me, pitching it between the cypress and the fountain so we went to sleep to the sound of flowing water. Jesus told me that on hot nights his whole family often slept out, on stretchers and bedrolls, on the flat roof of their house, and that all the neighbours did the same, so in the dark you could hear murmuring and snoring all down the street, and even chatter back and forth from one house to the next. I would have liked to experience that, but I knew my mother wouldn't allow it. I suspect Jesus, too, knew that the little rich boy wouldn't be permitted such plebeian good fun, because he never invited me.

My household was entirely different from his. It was a spacious villa built in Roman style. The walled garden with the fountain was at the back. At the front, an open elevated area, paved with red and black mosaic tiles, looked one way over terraced hillsides with vineyards, olives and vegetable gardens, and the other over the little town in the valley, which from that angle was almost directly below. After our nights in the tent we would have breakfast on the terrace, looking down and watching the women with their jars and crocks gathering, like distant, brightly coloured birds, around the well in the square, while the labouring men, armed with their pruning hooks and hoes, moved out, spreading up into the vineyards, gardens and groves, to begin the morning's work.

Our breakfast was always the same, bread soaked in olive oil, with a stew of lentils and beans, followed by cheese and fruit. It was better food than Jesus got at home. He enjoyed it and was grateful. Unlike his cousin John, Jesus was usually a good eater, even in the days of his ministry, when he enjoyed wine as well, never made much of a fuss about fasting, and used to tell us that food was to be eaten, and that there was a very fine line between self-denial and waste.

I knew that my being an only child was a cause of sadness to my mother, who sometimes wept because there were no more children, and would be no more. I was never told why, but my parents were estranged. My father had another, larger house, in Tiberias on the shores of the lake, and ran his business from there. When he spent time with us in Nazareth he was distant, formal, rather severe, though not unkind. Once, some years later when I was fourteen or fifteen, I called on him in Tiberias without any warning, and was met at the door by a Bedouin woman who, having let me in to talk to my father, withdrew to

28

a back room. I can still see her beautiful almond eyes watching me over her veil as she withdrew and closed the door on us, so discreetly it made no sound at all.

Who was she? I wanted to know. My father said she was a servant – but I knew his servants and she was not one of them. I said she didn't have the look, or the dress, or the manner of a servant. He told me to remember that he was my father, and that I owed him respect, and that respect did not claim the right to interrogate. I'd previously wondered why he had not divorced my mother – only removed himself from her. But if the woman who had replaced her was indeed an Arab, then I suppose he would have wanted to keep it secret, and preserve the marriage as a cover. So for me as a child 'family' meant, most of the time, just myself and Mother, the servants and the gardener.

Jesus enjoyed his visits. He loved our tiled bathhouse. He loved the red tent, and those breakfasts, and the view over the village. We liked to lie on our stomachs at the edge of the terrace, looking out over the countryside and imagining a military campaign down there in which the Romans were defeated. Unsuspecting, they marched into Nazareth, a whole legion, their armour and buckles glinting in the sun, their drums and the tramp of their feet echoing off the sides of the valley. But our forces were hidden, massed in the hills on either side, and we swept down, closed off their retreat and, in a battle that came down finally to ferocious hand-to-hand fighting, destroyed them. When it was all over we put their wounded to the sword. The small number surviving as healthy captives we stripped of their weapons and armour, and even their clothes, and made them our slaves.

While we were very young our attitude to the Roman soldiers we encountered in reality was uncertain. Their presence was a fact of life, but in our region at that time it was not intrusive. After the death of Herod, who had been king of the whole of Palestine, the Romans had divided the kingdom into four, each with its own tetrarch. Our segment, Galilee, was ruled by one of Herod's sons, Herod Antipas. In my childhood I never heard anyone speak well of the Herods – not even my father, though he did say the new cities they built were handsome, modern, and matters for pride, and when invitations came to parties and celebrations at the tetrarch's palace in Tiberias, he accepted. But these so-called kings of the Jews were there only by authority of the Roman power, and were really its instruments, so they were not respected.

There was a Roman base camp just outside Nazareth on the road from Tiberias, and sometimes a legion would rest there on its way to or from Jerusalem. At other times the camp was occupied only by a small policing unit. When soldiers came through in large numbers Jesus and I used to hang about the gates. Sometimes they chased us away, sometimes ignored us, and just occasionally gave us small presents – sweets or cakes, and once a small coin each. Now and then they engaged us in conversation, asking our names, asking what the word for this or that was in Aramaic. The soldiers who had served a long time in our region were usually unpleasant, as if they'd learned to dislike the local population, whom they regarded as ungrateful, unwashed and potentially rebellious. The more recent arrivals, especially if they were young, were friendlier.

By our parents, and by Andreas, we were warned to stay clear of them and of the camp gates; but that was another of those 'rules' the child believes are made to be broken.

There were times when citizens of Nazareth were asked to billet soldiers – one or more, depending on the size of the house

– and I don't suppose it was a request that anyone dared refuse. We had two in our house on one occasion. They seemed nice enough, polite, grateful to have such comfortable quarters. I think my mother fell in love with one of them (an officer, of course), but kept it hidden, or tried to. I quite liked him, until I saw him beating a peasant who had annoyed him on the road outside the camp gates.

As Jesus and I grew older, and understood that we, though Jews, were subject to laws and edicts made in Rome by men of a race and faith different from our own, we began to resent our inferior status. But by that time we also understood the nature of Roman power, its ruthlessness, its cruelty. We feared the Romans and avoided them so we wouldn't have to demean ourselves by showing respect.

Jesus' father Joseph was the sort of hard-working man who doesn't involve himself in public matters in any way. He would never have expressed an opinion about the Romans. But I felt sure he resented them, even hated them. I knew he'd worked on the construction of the Roman camp, not for pay (there was none), or because he wanted to curry favour, but because he didn't have any choice. It had cost him time and money, Jesus told me; but when I said he must have resented it, Jesus looked wary and said nothing.

My own father was quite different. The Romans, he used to explain to me, had brought good order to our land. They'd brought modern civilisation, learning, prosperity, even (he said) morality. Above all, they had brought commerce, and made trade possible. They had cleared the sea lanes of pirates and the countryside of brigands – and these were jobs that had to go on endlessly. 'That government is good, and does well,' he liked to say, quoting someone famous (and probably Roman!), 'which guarantees a citizen safety on the highway.' Without the Romans, he assured me, our little communities would have been cut off from the larger world, and his own success as a trader would not have been possible. 'I have a caravan right now', he said to me once, with a vehemence that suggested it might be a big and risky venture, 'on the road to Amman. Do you think I would rest at night, or expect a safe return on my investment, if there were not Roman legions there to keep the road open?'

Individuals among our Roman overlords might be coarse, arrogant, bullying – he acknowledged that. But collectively I was to respect them, because they deserved respect. 'You can thank them that you're not a smelly peasant,' he told me.

I didn't feel like thanking them. I knew they didn't respect Israel or Israel's God; and I'd heard Andreas say that under Roman rule the rich Jews were getting richer and the poor poorer. But that was something I didn't repeat at home, because I knew my father would take me away from my tutor if he thought I was being taught what he would have called 'politics'.

One event in my childhood more than any other determined my feeling towards the Romans – my prejudice, if you prefer, which has persisted to this day. I suppose we knew from a very early age that the Romans executed criminals of low social status by crucifixion. It was one of those facts you know as a child and don't explore, deterred by signals the adults send out that it's not to be talked about. Now and then I thought about it. Nailing someone to a cross of wood seemed a very cruel thing to do – and my mind refused to linger on it.

I suppose Jesus and I were seven or eight when we heard that a gang of brigands that had been intercepting and robbing travellers in and out of Nazareth had been caught, some killed in a skirmish, two taken alive and condemned to die. They would be crucified in a barren field between the Roman camp and the stream, in clear sight of one of the principal roads, so the event could be seen by everyone. It would be a warning to robbers, and a signal to townspeople and travellers, that law and order would prevail.

When we asked questions about this news we were given the briefest of answers. It was a subject that clearly distressed Jesus' father; but he would say nothing except that we must stay away. My mother gave the same instruction. They were bad men and were probably getting what they deserved, but on no account were we to go near that place for the next four or five days.

There was an old wrecked house very close to the barren field, and Jesus was sure he knew a way to reach it without being seen, first along the stream-bed, which was almost dry at this time of year, and then through an abandoned shrubbery. He suggested that when we'd finished our lessons with Andreas the next day we should go and hide there and watch what was happening.

We arrived in time to see the first robber already writhing up on his cross, and the second, fighting to free himself, being held down by Roman soldiers, who beat him with their fists and kicked him while the nails were driven into his hands and feet. The one on the cross was groaning, sobbing and gasping; the other screamed and cursed, and went on howling in rage and pain as the cross was elevated and slipped into the hole that would keep it upright.

As we made our way back to the town I was sick with the horror of it. My skin and scalp prickled. I felt the slightest breath of wind as if it came in the depth of winter, and next moment the sun through my shirt seemed to be burning me alive. I had difficulty breathing. I was full of fear and disgust. But also pity.

I imagined creeping back in the night and getting them down from their crosses, killing the Romans who got in my way, ministering to the robbers' wounds, setting them free. I knew these were ridiculous fantasies, but to entertain them relieved me from the reality, its remorselessness, its cruelty; from the fact that as the minutes and hours ticked by those men were still hanging there, dying by inches.

That night I woke my mother and the servants, screaming, but when they came to my bed I pretended not to remember what the nightmare had been about.

Our plan had been that we would return the next day, but I refused. Jesus went. What he reported to me later I listened to – I couldn't stop myself – but wished I hadn't. He had seen the Roman soldiers using iron bars to break the legs of the men on the cross. This, I now know, was to speed up the dying. It meant that they could no longer 'stand' on their nailed feet, but only hang by the hands, and in that position breathing was restricted and the heart would slowly give out.

To us these men were not brigands, not villains, not bad men. They were victims. To see such suffering left no room in a normal heart for anything but pity. Whatever they'd done was as nothing compared to what was being done to them. It made us hate the power of Rome; but it also left us full of fear.

When I left Jerusalem all those years ago after the execution of Jesus I left in disgust – with the event, and with everything 'the holy city' represented, but disgust also with myself. Coming here to Sidon was meant to take me far from my past, where I could begin a new life and create a new identity – so even the burning of my few simple possessions and sentimental relics in the lightning-struck ox cart could be seen as a confirmation and a blessing. My past was behind me, and the small relics of it I had thought to bring with me had all been destroyed.

But escape from one's young self and one's past can never be total. Over the years travellers have come through with news of my homeland. I've retained my detachment, but curiosity can't be suppressed entirely, and I've taken, especially, a wry interest in the persistence of the Jesus sect, the spread of its missionaries and the growing confidence with which they now insist that Jesus was the Christ, the Messiah, that he performed miracles in life and lived again after his death.

Now and then my own name is mentioned. 'Judas of Keraiyot' I'm called in their stories – the betrayer, the evil one. At the end of their narration I always die – sometimes by my own hand, hanging myself (a barren fig tree seems to be a favoured site), or in a horrible accident in which I fall down in a field I bought with the money the betrayal of Jesus earned me. In this version I'm split open on a ploughshare and my blood and intestines spill out over the ground, which at once becomes infertile and will remain so until the end of time.

I listen, I smile, I say nothing.

> As a child
> you hold bad things
> at bay with fantasy
>
> but as a man
> you can't play fast
> and loose with the truth.
>
> Sometimes at
> night, recalling the
> dull sound of the nail

going through
flesh before striking
wood, I take refuge

reciting the old
texts — Psalms, the
Song of Solomon —

not out of
piety or faith in
God, but because

when truth is
ugly, beauty can
be a distraction.

CHAPTER 4

JESUS AND I FOUGHT — WRESTLED — AS BOYS (AND AS YOUNG animals) do, learning to fight, enjoying it, stopping before real hurt or pain was inflicted, not getting angry with one another, or not often, and usually only for a moment. My mother complained that my clothes were always dirty when I came back from playing with him. I didn't tell her how we wrestled in the barley fields for fear that she would insist it must stop.

There was just one occasion when the fight was real, serious, painful, leaving an unpleasant taste and a still vivid memory. Andreas had put on a special supper for his three scholars to mark the end of our school term, and it was already dark when Jesus and I set off to take an indirect path home, one that would allow us to go into one of the local caves in darkness. It was something frightening and challenging we both wanted, and had been forbidden, to do. Bandits, we were warned, used the caves as hiding places for stolen goods and weapons. We might stumble on some secret that could cost us our lives.

I'm no longer sure how the conversation went that led up to my mistake, but I remember that we had just reached the mouth of the cave when it happened. We were calling things into the cave, and listening to the echo come back at us, frightening ourselves, and at the same time throwing stones as hard as we could into the darkness while carrying on our usual rambling chatter. Somehow, in response to something Jesus had called into the echoing blackness, I was reminded of what I'd heard one of our servants say about him and, without forethought, I repeated it.

This woman was a day servant who came from the same street as Jesus' family and knew them well. She always greeted him, when he was visiting us, with a familiar, knowing smile, quite different from the respectful way she greeted me, and I noticed that Jesus was cool with her. What I'd heard her say to our cook was that 'that Jesus boy' was not the son of his father, Joseph. His real father was a Roman soldier. She even named the soldier – Panthera. Joseph, she went on, had loved Mary when she was a young girl and, though rejected by her, had remained so obsessed that when the Roman abandoned her and denied the child in her womb was his, Joseph had been willing to marry her and accept Jesus as his own.

I'm not sure how I came to think Jesus wouldn't be upset if I repeated this story. Perhaps I thought that if I brought it up casually, as if it was nothing special, it would seem I believed it couldn't be true. Or (more likely) it was just the carelessness, the lack of forethought, of the child. Whatever the explanation, the response was blind fury. Jesus attacked me, punched me in the face, tackled me around the waist, threw me to the ground. His anger was so instant and frightening I struggled free and stumbled away from him without having time to choose a direction, and was already a few paces inside the cave when he caught me again.

This happened two or three times, and we were soon well inside that black blank stony womb, our yells and grunts striking off the walls and coming back as if from two other boys, one terrified, one with murderous intent. I was trying to say I was sorry, that I hadn't meant to insult him, that I hadn't believed what the servant had said. He, on the other hand, was hell-bent on hurting me. At one moment, when he had me pinned to the ground, he hissed in my ear that he was going to kill me, that he would leave my body in the cave with the bats, to rot or to be eaten by jackals.

I put up no fight at all – I was too scared – or rather, I fought only to escape, to save myself. Somehow I got out of the cave but he caught me again, threw me to the ground, straddled my chest. Banging the back of my head down against the clay he told me I was an arrogant, worthless, rich boy, the son of an arrogant, worthless, rich father, and a barren mother. My father, he said, was a collaborator with the Roman occupier, a breaker of the Commandments and of the Sabbath, and he, Jesus, was going to destroy me, smash me with stones into small pieces and leave me smeared and scattered over the rocks.

By now he was playing with me, cat with mouse, and though I suppose I must have known I was going to survive, the terror continued. My limbs felt weak and I couldn't fight. I was humili-ated. I abased myself, grovelled, begged for my life. He exploited his moment of power to the full, forcing me to eat camel dung off the road and to lick his sandals. 'Eat it!' he shouted, turning me over, forcing my face down, quoting, and misquoting, one of the pieces of scripture we'd read with Andreas. 'The enemies of Israel shall be trodden into the mire of the streets. They shall lick dust like a snake, like the crawling things of the earth. All those who have ruled over Israel, and those who have profited from Israel's shame, shall die – arsehole. *Die!*'

Next day was not a school day but I went looking for Jesus and found him in the field where we most often played together. I'm not sure whether he was there to savour his triumph, or out of curiosity, not really expecting to see me. But he'd had his victory, and now it was my turn for rage. The humiliation was what hurt, more than the cuts and bruises. The fear, which in darkness had rendered me helpless, had gone with daylight. I wanted my revenge.

I attacked at once and he put up only a token resistance. I threw him to the ground, told him he was a boil on a Bedouin's arse, that he smelled like a sheep shearer's armpit, that he was a mother's boy, a teacher's pet, a pitcher of camel's piss. He put his forearms over his face as I pummelled his head and chest. I thought of trying to make him do what I'd had to do – eat dung, lick dust from the stones, kiss his feet – but I was afraid of taking revenge too far and releasing his rage again.

'I never believed that stupid woman,' I told him (though in fact I had at least half believed her story, and his rage had made me think more than ever that it was likely to be true). 'I don't ever want to see you again.'

I got up, gave him a last kick in the ribs, threw a handful of dust down into his eyes, and walked away. When I was almost out of range he threw a stone that hit me in the middle of the back. I walked on as if I hadn't felt it. Pride had been salvaged. Our friendship was over.

It was now holiday time, and I had no one to play with – or no one as interesting and satisfying as Jesus. I spent a couple of boring afternoons with Thaddeus and his sister Judith. I regretted the break with Jesus, but didn't see how it could be undone. I imagined him playing with his brothers and sisters, and with the crowd of boys and girls in the streets and on the flat roofs of the village. He didn't need me. I shed a few tears, and threw stones down into the valley where people were working on the olive trees.

My mother noticed that I was at a loose end and may have guessed that Jesus and I had fallen out. Perhaps she went looking for him. In any case, intentionally or not, she met him in the street, engaged him in conversation and invited him to come back with her. He came, and we played together as if nothing had happened. The fight, and the reason for it, were never mentioned, not then, and not later when we were Master and disciple.

But some of the things he'd said in his rage remained. I now knew that he thought of my family as collaborators with the Roman overlord, traitors to the way of the Torah, unworthy of respect. That, I'm sure, remained his and, I suppose, his parents', view of us, a view his followers would later share.

When Jesus and I were ten my father took us to Jerusalem for Passover. I seem to remember it was said that Jesus' father had managed occasionally to go there for the due observances, but that in recent years there were too many children to be left with Mary, and not enough money for him to take time away from his work. So Joseph and Mary welcomed the chance for their brilliant firstborn to see the Temple, say prayers, and offer what was called, in the fashion of those days, a Boy's Sacrifice.

I don't believe my father cared much at all about religious observances, but he knew that keeping up appearances was necessary if we were to make the most (or anything at all) of his family connections. And he thought it was time for me to meet my high-priest uncle. Taking Jesus along was a way of keeping me entertained on the journey, relieving himself of the task.

I had been to Jerusalem before, but remembered very little, so everything struck me as new and fresh and exciting. For Jesus, who had seen little of city life apart from visits to Sepphoris and, occasionally, Tiberias, it was even more of an adventure. We were both awed by the size of the Temple, its immense walls, towering columns, monumental staircases and huge interior spaces, its crowds and noise, the shouting and bustle around the money changers' tables, the blast of the trumpet announcing we didn't know what, the bleating, squealing and squawking of animals and birds taken inside for sacrifice, the smells there of animal dung, smoke, freshly spilled blood and cooking meat, the chanting of prayers, and the echoing voices of the Levites singing hymns and psalms. The further you penetrated, the darker, more mysterious, more solemn and, at the same time, more threatening became the feelings evoked by that place.

The money tables were there in the courtyard to take foreign coins – Greek drachmas, Roman denarii and sesterces, and whatever else pilgrims brought – and exchange them for the local coinage. In fact, you could spend Greek or Roman coins anywhere in the town, but not there, where the Temple tax had to be paid in the local coin. In my adult years, as a follower of Jesus, I learned that huge profits were made from this business, and that, like everything else to do with the Temple, the tables were owned and run by the priestly families. It was one of the scandals Jesus would berate and pour scorn on in his last years, as his message grew more severe; but as a boy he looked on it all, as I did, with innocent and wondering eyes.

Apart from the dark splendours of the Temple we liked especially to be turned loose in the bazaar, given a few coins to spend, and told to report back to my father at a certain hour at some prominent landmark. We discovered for ourselves the changing of the guard at the Fortress of Antonia where the Roman garrison was housed, and went back to watch it more than once. We watched the soldiers marching and saluting and shouting orders at one another on the paved square outside Herod's palace where the Roman governor, Ambibulus, was said to be living. We began to learn the geography of the city, including the names of some of the gates – the Fish Gate, the Sheep Gate, the Gate of Ephraim where criminals were executed – and how to find our way from one to another.

When it came to doing the Boy's Sacrifice my father bought us each a pigeon (grumbling at the exorbitant cost) and guided us to the marble bench where a young Levite with a knife stood looking bored and unhappy, perhaps feeling that this unhallowed ceremony was beneath his dignity. I went first, handing over my bird and saying the words we had been schooled to say. In a moment my pigeon's head was off and the bird lay twitching and bleeding on the slab.

My father's hand on Jesus' shoulder guided him forward. He stood very still, holding his bird close to his chest in both hands, his elbows stuck out on either side like wings, as if he had been the bird and the knife was ready, sharpened for him. The Levite reached forward to take it, but it was just out of his reach. 'Well, boy,' he said. 'Have you forgotten the prayer?'

My father gave a little push from behind. Jesus opened his mouth, said the first few words of the prayer, 'Lord take from these untried hands the humble offering of thy child and servant . . .' and stopped. At that moment, it seemed with deliberation, he drew his hands slowly apart, wide apart, as if performing some magic rite. The pigeon dropped, recovered, flew – wing tips clapping together, applauding – up past the Levite, who ducked to avoid it. It came to rest on a stone abutment high in the wall. We all looked up at it. It looked down, and in a moment took off again, flying away down towards the wide doors and out into the blaze of light that filled the immense courtyard.

No one spoke. I felt pleased – perhaps we all did. All three of us looked at Jesus. 'Yahweh told me to,' he said, very quietly.

'Yahweh?' the Levite repeated. 'Do you think Yahweh notices you, boy?'

I wondered why we would be making the Boy's Sacrifice if He did not. Jesus didn't answer.

'What did He say to you?'

'He said, "Let my pigeon go!"'

The Levite stared at the ten-year-old. I thought there was a ripple of amusement, even though he probably thought he should be angry. He waved us away. 'Get along,' he said. 'Other boys are waiting.'

My father said nothing. I thought he too was smiling.

That afternoon, while my father took me to meet my priestly uncle in an apartment close to the Temple, Jesus was left to amuse himself. This was the uncle who (I'd once overheard my father grumble) had been invited to my circumcision and declined to come because of 'pressure of business'. I think he had been, at that time, a member of the supreme Jewish council, the Sanhedrin, so I suppose my father's complaint was unreasonable.

The room in which we gathered that afternoon was spacious, with red walls, white pillars at one end, and a high, decorated ceiling. An enormous rug, woven in black and red geometric patterns, covered most of the floor. There were elegant couches, carved cedar boxes, low marble-topped tables, stone jars and pottery ornaments.

My uncle, looking, I thought, more like a Roman official than a Jewish priest, seemed pompous and self-important, and paid less attention to me the more my father talked about me and tried to make something significant of my modest accomplishments. I smiled, and spoke carefully when spoken to, concealing my 'agricultural consonants'. My father appeared to diminish in size and confidence in his brother's grand presence. I felt sorry for him, and decided that I disliked our relative and would never look to him for favour or advancement.

But in addition to that feeling of resentment there was another which conflicted with it. Something in me – an aspect of my character which I couldn't then identify – responded positively to the style of that apartment, to the way my uncle conducted himself, to the quiet beauty and elegance of it all. I thought of it then as Roman, but I now know (living as I do among Greeks) that it was more Hellenic than Latin; and I couldn't entirely put down the thought of how wonderful it would be to live like that, among such beautiful things.

When we got back to the place where we'd arranged to meet Jesus on the steps to the Temple, he wasn't there. We went looking for him, and found him inside the Temple talking to the young Levite who had been on duty for the Boy's Sacrifice. The Levite smiled at us and congratulated my father on having such a clever son, who could quote scripture in Hebrew like a priest of the Temple.

'If he were indeed my son,' my father replied, 'I would have taught him to be where he was supposed to be at the appointed hour.'

My faith in those days was the faith of my fathers in the God of Israel and the Word of His prophets, and it expressed itself through the prescribed forms. I have spoken of my childish fears, but as I grew older these began to fade. I suppose each of us has a God, if there is to be one at all, which is partly personal, and mine had more to do with superstition than mysticism. He, or it, was Fate, the Inevitable, the Next Thing – a force quite beyond anything I might do to control or influence. I bowed to it totally, laid my pride out before it like a washed shirt laid out on the hot stones by the stream to dry; an offering made without hope of any outcome, but in case there was any possibility that it might save me, or those I loved, from pain or accident.

As for prayers, I always said the prescribed ones just because they were prescribed, though without deep understanding or conviction. My own special prayers were never requests for personal blessings or gifts. I was, after all, a rich boy with a good heart, and seldom yearned for *things*. I prayed mostly for my mother, who was, I knew, often unhappy. I prayed that she might be cheerful, that good things might be showered on her, that she and my father might be reconciled.

I prayed for my father too, though less wholeheartedly. I prayed for my dog. I prayed for that poor shuddering brigand on the cross, that he might be given the gifts of numbness and speedy death.

About Jesus' habits of prayer and his notion of God I knew very little in those days of our childhood. I remember there was a time, in the synagogue at Sepphoris, when he turned pale, his limbs seemed to go rigid as tremors ran through them, his eyes rolled back and his eyelids flickered. It was like a person having a fit, but it passed quickly, and when I asked him about it afterwards he said it was nothing. 'I was just trying something out,' he said, with a cocky toss of the head that I knew was false.

Once I asked him how he saw God. We were lying out on one of the terraced hillsides, watching workers below us pruning the olive trees. He thought about it. 'I don't think I *see* God,' he said. 'Or hear Him. Or if I do, He's just a blinding light and a sort of rushing noise like a big wind in the desert. He's more like something that happens to me. I get bigger and bigger and bigger until I'm the whole of everything and at the same time I'm nothing.'

He sat up and threw a stone down into the dusty grey-green trees. 'It's like wanting to be sick.'

But I do remember the first time I caught a glimpse of what was to come. It was during our holiday when we'd joined a crowd gathered at the outskirts of Nazareth to listen to an itinerant preacher. The preacher held up a stone and said it was a miracle. He had a pronounced lisp. 'Thith thtone', he said, 'ith my tecktht. It containth truth. It containth God.'

We thought this very funny, and were scolded and driven away by the faithful, not amused by our giggles.

Later, alone in the shadow of the rock faces where we went to climb and explore the caves, we took turns to do mocking imitations. I found my stone and thought up a text or two to support my case that it was the living God, but I tried too hard to make it funny and soon ran out of things to say.

Now it was Jesus' turn. Normally he was hesitant in speech, with a slight stammer when afflicted with shyness or doubt, and that was how he began. But as he developed his theme it was as if he believed indeed that the stone in his hand was God. He forgot to be funny and to lisp. He became fluent, eloquent. He cited texts and recited them. His eyes shone, his brow grew pale. He looked beautiful. The words flowed like stream water in sunlight.

'You see the light which shines from within the stone?' he asked, and for a moment it seemed that I did. 'It is white. It has no colour. Take away colour and you have the mystery of no-colour, of nothing – the nothing that is more than something, more than all the somethings known to man. *That*, dear friends, is the white light of eternity. It is the holy fire. My brethren . . .'

(and here he paused, dropping his voice so that I strained to listen), 'my beloved, *it is the Lord.*'

Now I wasn't laughing, and neither was he. I was tearful. He had gone beyond mockery and I didn't know what to say.

I said, 'Amen,' and we walked home in silence.

> In the beginning
> was the word, the
> sentence, the text
>
> that made of the
> pigeon a paradigm
> of the soul
>
> and gave to
> the stone he held the
> light of the divine.
>
> He was his own
> first convert, able
> to see himself
>
> burning, bathed
> in the white fire of
> the noun and the verb.

CHAPTER 5

MY SONS ARE ARTISANS, BUT THEY ARE ALSO BUSINESSMEN.
And they are Greeks. Their mother was Greek, we live in a Greek
community and speak the language at home as well as in our
dealings with the world. I speak it fluently – even think and
dream in it – but with the accent of my native Aramaic. The
Hebrew I studied with Andreas, and those long scriptural texts
learned by heart in childhood, remain with me, and at night,
when memories, anxieties and unwanted thoughts keep me
awake, I often recite them over silently so they displace whatever is disturbing me, and let me fall asleep.

There have been times over these past four decades when
I have almost succeeded in forgetting I am a Jew. I have rejected
not only the faith of my fathers but also the primitive culture
of my childhood. That was what I wanted to achieve in coming
here to the Sidon region – to remove myself from pain, from
the death of my first wife and the loss of our unborn child,
and from the involvement with the Jesus sect that followed. I
suppose I should admit that I also wanted to turn my back
on my people because they had branded me a traitor: Judas
of Keraiyot, 'betrayer of Jesus', had become Idas of Sidon,
paterfamilias.

Since turning seventy, however, as the sense increases that a terminus to my life lies not very far ahead, I feel some of my old loyalties returning, and with them, certain nostalgias. I sometimes wish I had a friend with whom I could talk about the past; and since I have not, and now that Thea is no longer with me, I usually invite any members of the Jesus sect who pass through to dine with me – never, of course, telling them who I am, or rather, who I once was, one of the chosen twelve of Jesus of Nazareth.

The name I took when I arrived here long ago, and have kept ever since, is Idas, and my sons (I have to say it was their mother who chose their names) are Autolycus and Antigonus. I saw to it that they were taught useful crafts – boatbuilding for one, mosaic-tiling for the other. Each proved to be highly skilled at his trade, built up a local reputation and a business, employed tradesmen and subcontractors, and was soon a manager rather than a manual worker. Both have prospered, as have my sons-in-law, and I'm thankful for that.

There has been in recent years a shortage of local tradesmen, particularly in the business of mosaic-tiling, and it was this that took Antigonus ('Tig', as he's known in the family) on a visit to Jerusalem where, since the completion of Herod's castle some years back, and the laying off of the many hundreds of tradesmen who worked on it, there have been any number of unattached skilled workers willing to travel if the pay was good.

Tig found the kind of men he was looking for, and two of them are with us now. But he spent some time there – in fact was trapped in the city and couldn't leave – and consequently brought back a more detailed account of the current upheavals than we'd had before.

The city has been in a turmoil of revolt and civil war. The revolt is against the Romans; the civil war is between rich Jews and poor Jews, the rich favouring policies of compliance and caution, the poor demanding justice and even independence from Rome. But, complicating the picture further, there are warring factions even among the poor.

The first serious trouble was provoked by the Roman governor, Florus, who demanded from the Temple vaults a quantity of gold he said was owing in taxes to the emperor. The gold was at first refused, and then taken when the priests yielded to threats and force. This was a sacrilege, as well as an outrage to Jewish pride. Riots followed, people marching through the streets chanting slogans against the priests as well as the Romans. 'No Lord but God,' the ringleaders taught them to shout, rejecting both the Roman overlords and the priests who pandered to them.

Florus had his troops wade into the marchers. Many were hurt, some killed. He then called in extra troops from Caesarea and, to underscore that he and no one else was in charge, demanded Jerusalem offer this new brigade what's called 'the Grand Salute'.

The Grand Salute is an enforced ceremony (rather fine to watch so long as your pride is not affronted) in which the city honours the Roman troops, and the troops return the compliment by saluting the city. On this occasion, however, Florus ruled that, as punishment for the riots, the city would give the salute but it would not be returned.

Tig was there in the streets as the might of Rome marched by to the solemn, threatening beat of war drums. At the front of the crowd, and in elevated stands along the way, members of the priesthood and of the best Jewish families bowed, clapped and waved palm fronds as they were required to do, while the Roman soldiers remained stalwart and unresponding. Behind their leaders the people grew restless, muttering and cursing. Soon they could restrain themselves no longer. They began shouting their protests and Tig found himself joining in, chanting 'No Lord but God' along with the loudest of them. Some of the crowd had come prepared and threw rotten fruit and eggs. The shining, clattering, proud soldiery were spattered and smeared and the show spoiled.

The priests and members of the Sanhedrin up on their stands turned towards the people, begging them not to go on, warning them of the consequences, appealing for calm, for restraint. They too were pelted. The crowd laughed, hooting and jeering. Young men began to run about, tearing out fence palings, breaking branches from trees, pulling out pennant batons and tearing the side barriers off chariots, even prising up tiles and the smaller paving stones. Dignitaries and priests were pushed out of the way and missiles of every kind were hurled at the now retreating backs of the military.

To Tig (who, like all of us, feels and conceals a resentment towards the Roman power) it was an exciting moment, but he felt fear as well.

This time it was not so easy for the Romans to put down the demonstration. As they rallied at the Antonia Fortress and came storming back to inflict punishment, the crowd dispersed. It seemed at first that order had been restored, even if Roman honour had been bruised, but in fact the people were taking control of whole sections of the city. Within a week the Romans were learning they had to treat these as no-go areas, entering them only by force. One group of rebels ('terrorists' was Florus' word for them), who called themselves the Daggermen, were going about singly in crowded places with a knife hidden in the shirt, silently sticking a blade between the ribs of a soldier shopping in the bazaar, a merchant known to be taking bribes from the Romans, a citizen thought to be an informer, even a priest considered a collaborator. The crowd would move quickly away, and there was the victim, twitching and bleeding to death on the stones.

There were rumours that rich collaborators and bribed spies were being kidnapped, tried by people's courts somewhere in the maze of the lower city where the poor live, and executed, their bodies flung down into the ravines outside the wall below the Mount of Olives.

Tig left as soon as he was able, though he had to pass through more than one Roman checkpoint, and got away only by insisting on his identity as a Greek artisan with no connection to the Jewish city and no interest in its revolt. The workers he had engaged were to make their way to us separately, as and when they were able. There is one we still haven't seen. Two, each with an interesting story, got away and have been employed in our workshops. They say the revolt won't be easily suppressed, and that it won't simply fade away. But as long as the Jews are divided, rich against poor and faction against faction, how can it succeed?

Since then we've had only sporadic news. There was a story that Agrippa II, the latest of the Herods, was going to mediate between Rome and the people, but it seems nothing came of that. Next we heard that Cestius Gallus, the Roman governor of Syria, was heading for Jerusalem with a formidable force – and then that he and his troops were marching away again, with nothing changed. General Vespasian followed. It was said he had taken control of most of the towns and cities of Judaea and Galilee, and was ready to begin the assault on Jerusalem, when news came from Rome that Emperor Nero had died, and there was no certainty about who would succeed him and what the new man would want done.

Now the Senate has made Vespasian himself emperor. He has returned to Rome, but has sent his son, Titus, with a large force to bring the matter to a conclusion. Jerusalem is surrounded and besieged.

I try not to care about the outcome, but old emotions return when I allow my thoughts to dwell on it – my horror of crucifixions, my resentment of the way cruel and complacent Rome claims the right to rule the world and make us all subservient. Even something of my old loyalty to the city and the Temple comes back to me. If it were my habit to pray, the survival of Jerusalem would be high among my requests, but I long ago taught myself that even if there is a God, He is deaf to all human petitions.

Yesterday another member of the Jesus sect came through our village. He is elderly, perhaps close to my own age or a little younger, blind, and looked after by a young man. Like other recent members of the sect, he calls himself a 'Christian', the name they have taken in recent years on the grounds that Jesus was indeed the Christ. He preached in the village square to a small, interested crowd. It was the old story – that Jesus' authority and divinity were proved not only by the beauty and profundity of his teachings, but more by the miracles he performed, above all the supreme miracle of rising from the dead.

I offered this preacher and his assistant a meal and beds for the night and these were accepted – ungraciously, I thought, as if they were no more than his due, a right to the righteous. Did I behave like that, I wonder, when I went about as a disciple? I hope not; but perhaps it's in the nature of evangelism to take without thanks, since you think you are the one bringing gifts.

He asked me to call him Ptolemy, a Greek name he has taken, and he seemed reluctant to tell me much about himself. I asked him for news of Jerusalem, but he knew only that it was under siege and likely very soon to be assaulted. He didn't seem greatly concerned about the city, which, he said, the Lord might feel it right to destroy since it had condemned His Son to death. But he told me he had been deeply upset by the news that the younger brother of Jesus, James, who had been the sect's head man in Jerusalem, was recently crucified.

I was shocked at this news. My throat tightened and my eyes filled with tears. I was glad my visitor couldn't see my face. If his young helper noticed, he showed nothing. I remember James as a bright-eyed boy among that tribe of siblings, the children of Joseph and Mary. I've heard nothing of him in all these years, and didn't know he had become a follower of his brother's sect.

This morning I woke at first light and went out on to the balcony. The sea was tranquil, just becoming blue as the sun came up at my back from behind the eastern hills. There was that soothing 'hush' sound it makes in still weather, with a long gap between each flip and suck of waves. Down in the street the market people were setting up their stalls, talking in quiet voices as they do at that time of morning, knowing that most of the village is still sleeping. And then in the distance came the sound I know so well, that has come to me at intervals throughout a long life, the slap slap slap of a Roman platoon on the quick march, with just a single muffled drumbeat marking the time. The sound grew clearer and more distinct, without ever being loud, and then, sure enough, they came into view, jog marching through the village main street, heading south towards Caesarea, looking formidable as they always do, with their discipline, co-ordination and ant-like indifference to everything but the collective purpose.

At that moment there came to me, inevitably, the news about young James (I think of him as young), forgotten in sleep and then striking me again with renewed pain. That he should have suffered the same cruel death as his brother! It made me hate them down there, the controllers of our lives, the foreign enforcers. If I had not learned self-discipline over the years, or had been wanting a quick exit from the world, I might have taken a moment to lean over the rail to curse and spit on them.

> Ptolemy he
> calls himself and brings
> (he says) the Word.

> And they with their
> weapons and armour
> bring Rome's graces.

> Choose then – a short
> life of good roads, fine
> wines and cooking

> or life everlasting
> singing praises
> in the big

Upstairs. God, if
I thought you were there
I'd pray, 'Help me

escape these
greedy predators of
soul and stomach.'

CHAPTER 6

THE OTHER NIGHT I HAD A DREAM WHICH I SUSPECT WAS really no more than a vivid memory. Jesus and I, boys of sixteen or so, had just come through the monumental Gate of Tiberias with its two round towers, and were walking down the *cardo* past brightly coloured frescoes and mosaics. In the dream I felt it all, as fresh and brilliant and excitingly modern as it had seemed to me then; and at the same time I felt Jesus didn't share my enthusiasm, or was pretending not to share it, in order to make me feel guilty, a Romanophile, a colonial, a disloyal Hebrew.

As we strolled down the pavement, feeling 'grown-up', independent, rather pleased with ourselves, pleased with our new strong limbs and new deep voices, a beggar woman with a sickly child on her hip held out her hand for money. Unlike most of her kind, who were dirty and diseased, she was strikingly beautiful and I gave her a coin.

'Give her more,' Jesus said.

'You give her more,' I said.

He turned out his wallet. He had nothing.

'As usual,' I said.

'As usual because I'm not a skinflint like you. I gave my last coin to that leper outside the gate.'

He was always accusing me of meanness. I had to bite my

tongue and not tell him that what he called meanness was a husbanding of what I had; that it was easy to be profligate when you had next to nothing.

I gave the woman another coin, a bigger one, and received a smile that made me feel a momentary giddiness.

As we walked on Jesus said, 'You wanted to give her money because she was beautiful. When the leper approached us you cringed and hurried on.'

This was true but I denied it. 'I wanted her to have money because she had a sick child.'

'Liar,' he said. 'You thought it would be good if the child died and you could make her your mistress.'

This was so nearly true it made me furious. I was obsessed with thoughts about women and making love to them. Jesus seemed exempt from this, and yet he can't have been, not entirely, because he was able to penetrate my mind and ferret out my most unworthy flashes of lust.

'The thought was yours, camel dung,' I hissed at him. 'You're the one who said it.'

'The thought was yours,' he said, 'or you wouldn't get your hair in such a knot.'

He was like that; and yet not really the prig it may seem to suggest. He was full of accusations, but they came from cleverness and penetration. They were like a game. It was as if he was constantly testing his ability to read me – or equally Andreas and Thaddeus – in the same way that he could read difficult texts, taking delight in discovering hidden truths.

In those years after puberty he and I became, I suppose it's true to say, young intellectuals, though there were differences between us. We were both ashamed of Israel's submission to Rome, and we knew (by which I mean we'd been taught, and we believed it) that the God of Israel would not allow it to go on for ever. One day He would cry 'Enough!' Those who had brought shame to God's chosen people would taste shame a thousandfold. Those who had inflicted pain on us would suffer pain a thousandfold. Our enemies would be ground into the mire of the streets and made to lick dust like a serpent or a creeping thing . . . And so on.

Meanwhile, and in contradiction of this, I was learning to appreciate, and even to love, certain aspects of Roman and Greek civilisation: works of art, architecture, pottery, fine cloth; items of jewellery; and also (something new and exciting) poetry and the theatre. Tiberias, on the shores of Galilee, where my father had his preferred home and where he did most of his business, was a town the tetrarch Herod Antipas had built, and was still building, more or less along the lines (though, it was said, not quite so grand) as the city of Caesarea which his father, Herod the Great, had built on the Mediterranean. The streets ran at right angles off the main *cardo*, which was wide and straight, with granite columns on either side. Drainage ran underground rather than in open gutters. The market stalls were set up under elegant wooden shelters thatched with reeds or palm fronds, to protect sellers and buyers from the heat of the sun. The houses had whitewashed walls, red-tiled roofs, and spacious, paved court-yards. The wells were deep and their water cool and fresh and plentiful.

It was Andreas who first took us to the theatre in Tiberias, and we also went with him to see the games there – young athletes wrestling, running races in the Greek style, throwing the discus and the javelin, and jumping. Strict protocol might have forbidden our being there, because these games were dedicated to one or another of the pagan gods, but they were patronised by the tetrarch himself, and my father was relaxed about our going, only warning it was better I didn't mention it to my mother.

Jesus certainly didn't tell his parents what we did there. Joseph and Mary had a Galilean fear and distrust of the new cities, believing they were built with taxes unfairly taken from the farming countryside, and that they harboured every kind of vice. But they allowed Jesus to go because Andreas said it was part of a modern education, and Mary saw Andreas' tutoring of Jesus as something God-given, a blessing, a heavenly portent that some special greatness was intended for him.

As for the theatre, we were both instant converts. For a period of about two years we returned often, sometimes just the two of us, sometimes with Andreas, occasionally bringing Thaddeus as well. The actors wore masks and chanted their lines in huge booming voices that made the words seem more powerful than those of any rabbi – at times more intimidating, at others more beautiful. Sometimes, in comedies, the masks were animal heads; and once or twice an actor playing the part of a fertility god strutted about wearing an enormous phallus. Neither of us could understand all the words, which were in Greek, but we made sense of some, and in any case the story was always clear enough, and the end (deaths in the tragedies, marriage in the comedies) never in doubt. It wasn't surprise we looked for, but the acting out of an often familiar story, from the first error or misunderstanding, step by step to the bitter (or bitter-sweet) end.

Back in Nazareth we invented plays of our own, in our own language, and acted them. It became a part of our lessons with Andreas. We thought our version of King David's story was especially good. Even better was our dramatisation of the story of Daniel, a comedy (or we began by intending comedy, since it had a happy ending) called *Babble-on*, in which all four of us had multiple parts.

Andreas, we discovered, was a natural comedian. He made a great role of Nebuchadnezzar. Jesus was Daniel. Thaddeus and I were Shadrach and Meshach, ordered by Nebuchadnezzar to be thrown into the fiery furnace along with Abednego, played by my mother's shawl fluttering on a hook in the light of a window.

In the next act Jesus as Daniel had to interpret the writing on the wall at Belshazzar's feast. I was Belshazzar; and then I doubled as Darius, who had Daniel put into the lions' den for not obeying the order that there should be no prayers or petitions for thirty days. Thaddeus had to be a representative lion, sniffing Daniel, licking his chops and roaring as if hungry, but finding, to his surprise, that he had no appetite, and curling up with him for the night.

In the last part of the play Jesus came into his own. This was when something mysterious and important and incomprehensible was revealed to Daniel. Here we roughed out a text, but gave him freedom to invent, and each time we practised the play, the visions he proclaimed got more extravagant, darker and more beautiful. In his ringing words we saw the 'three rich kings of Persia, and a fourth, even richer'; we saw the break-up of the 'mightiest king's kingdom' and its scattering to the four winds; we saw 'the King of the North and the King of the South' go into battle, causing the deaths of tens of thousands.

Nothing could stop our Daniel. The words like the deeds, and the deeds like the words, were a torrent. When the angel appeared, and the many sleeping in the dust of the earth woke, some to eternal life, some to shame everlasting, Jesus' voice dropped and his eyes turned misty. As he played the part of the prophet looking across the river and seeing 'the man clothed in linen', and asked in a voice of hunger and heartbreak, 'How long shall it be to the end of these wonders?' it seemed to me that he himself became (in the words of the old scriptures) 'the brightness of the firmament and the righteousness of the stars'.

The end was always the same – meaning beyond any meaning his fellow actors could quite grasp, stunned silence, and then applause. Jesus, Andreas said, kissing him, had a great future in the theatre.

But despite these successes, it was our Daniel play which turned Jesus against the whole idea of poetry and acting. It happened overnight. It came to him, first in a dream, in which God spoke to him with cold severity, condemning what we'd done. We had made comedy of a holy text. We had acted out stories in which God Himself, though invisible, had a speaking part. We had written Him into a playscript! How could we believe this would not disturb and hurt the One who watched us always at work and at play?

Jesus repented. He prayed and fasted. He rejected everything associated with theatres, poetry, plays, dressing up, pretending to live and die, to kill, to engender children. Plays, he said, were untruths. The words were false. Actors and those who wrote for the theatre were professional pretenders. People who went to plays, and enjoyed what they knew was false, were hypocrites.

I was disappointed, and angry with him. We'd had such good times together, writing and acting. Who was I going to do it with if not with him?

He told me I shouldn't do it at all. I should give it up.

At first I had moments of uncertainty when I wondered whether he might be right. Had we really been giving offence to God? Would I be punished for continuing? Would there be a bolt from the blue? Would the earth open like jaws and swallow me up?

But then the words would come back to me, our own words ingeniously mixed with words taken and adapted from the sacred texts of our religion, or I would go with Andreas to see some new theatrical event, and as language exerted its power over me I would feel such rushes of pleasure I couldn't believe I was giving offence to whatever power might be out there, in charge of everything.

God for me was no longer a powerful presence. He had become a vague, flexible, inclusive Heavenly Father, tolerant, like my earthly father, not so much out of love as out of indifference. I found it hard to believe that He had much time for me, or interest in what I did or did not do, so long as it wasn't deliberately blasphemous, violent or criminal.

So I continued to attend the theatre, though there was no longer anyone with whom I could write and act plays. I think it must have been at that time I began to make poems. I would compose a poem in my head, especially when walking alone at night, and commit it to memory. I told Andreas about this in a moment of frankness when we were alone together. He persuaded me to recite one, then another, a third . . . He was very encouraging (I received a kiss!), even though I suspect he thought Greek or, at a pinch, Latin, and not Aramaic, were the proper languages for poetry.

We talked about Jesus' refusal to have anything more to do with theatre and plays. It made Andreas sad. He was anxious about his star pupil's future, and I remember he said, 'There's a shadow over our Jesus. If he doesn't find a way to escape from it, it may become a shroud.'

I have one other very clear memory of our teenage visits to Tiberias – whether before or after our difference over the theatre,

I'm uncertain. We had been to the sulphur baths (another favourite place) and were sitting outside in the late afternoon, resting after our efforts, enjoying the cool breeze that came up from the west at that time of day, waiting for someone – possibly Andreas, possibly my father – who was coming to meet us there. The baths were close to a clay-coloured building with a white dome where tribesmen gathered from time to time when passing through the town. Beyond it, the waters of the lake, in shadow at this time of day, were dark green, while the brown hills on the eastern shore were in bright sunlight. Jesus and I were back-to-back, leaning against one another. I was in a dreamy daze, watching the breeze making the palm branches wave like languid arms, when the slap of many sandals and bare feet approaching fast on the clay, and a growing babble of voices, caused us both to sit up and turn towards the street.

It was a Bedouin funeral, and it went by close enough for us to see the excited faces of the crowd, but also to see, stretched out on a board, carried shoulder-high by youths who might have been his brothers, the corpse: a young man looking, you might have thought, very healthy, with clear-cut, sun-bronzed features and long sturdy limbs outlined under the white cerements. The crowd around him, carrying him forward, moved briskly, almost at a jogtrot, like the fast-paced march of the Roman legions, and as they went they talked to one another and shouted affirmations of the greatness of God. There was no funereal drag, no wailing and gnashing of teeth, no long, weeping faces. It was like a celebration. Perhaps there was some special reason for this, but it was as if they accepted this death, not as a blow struck against them, but as the will of God and therefore not to be questioned.

At the moment when the group at the centre carrying the

corpse were closest to us, their pace was momentarily slowed by a narrowing of the road, and there, almost within touching distance, was the young face that seemed to have so little of death about it other than stillness.

When the crowd had gone Jesus and I were silent, awed by the proximity of death. I looked at him and recognised something unusually intense in his expression. His eyes shone and seemed not to be seeing what they looked at.

'I could have reached out and touched him,' he said.

'Yes,' I agreed. 'They were very close. It was strange, wasn't it?'

But he wasn't hearing me. He was speaking only to himself. 'I should have done it. I should have touched his face.'

I thought that would not have been a good idea, and said so.

He was still looking away over the lake with blind, shining eyes. 'He would have lived. I felt it – a power. Life would have been restored to him.'

I couldn't imagine what he meant. I felt uncomfortable, embarrassed, and said nothing, then or later.

> For me it was
> theatre made dead
> kings walk and prophets
>
> rise from their
> tombs. The real world
> had limits. Here and now
>
> was the singing
> of birds, vines breaking
> in leaf, and our

bodies that could
copy themselves. All,
one day, would die

and death was tongueless.
Not so for my
friend, who wanted

its silence broken,
its dark
illumined, an end to

endings, which he
knew his fingertip
touch could achieve.

CHAPTER 7

OF THE THREE OF US WHO WERE PUPILS OF ANDREAS IT WAS Thaddeus who matured first, and who proved to be the most 'normal'. I, as a young man, competitive and less than fair, would have wanted to say he was 'the most ordinary'. 'Normal' or 'ordinary', take your pick. Suddenly Thaddeus grew up – tall, handsome, athletic. He had friends, a social life, was popular, pragmatic, dependable, talkative. He was both competent and confident, but took no risks. He never said anything truly original; but nor did I ever hear him say anything stupid or malicious.

Once at that time I said to Jesus that I felt I ought to like Thaddeus more than I did. Jesus' reply was incisive. 'Thaddeus has no fanaticism. He's a foot soldier.'

He, by contrast, was developing into a brilliant, oblique, sensitive, secretive young man, aware that he was intellectually superior, but socially on the back foot. He had a sharp, defensive tongue, and people who meant him no harm were sometimes hurt by his remarks. When he felt safe, however, and trusted his companions, he was clever in a positive way – entertaining, resourceful, informative. Already he was full of concern for the suffering of the poor and the oppressed, and could be angry and combative on their behalf.

A new year was approaching and my father decided it was

time I had a more advanced kind of teaching than Andreas could offer. He found a tutor for me in Sepphoris, only two hours' walk from Nazareth, with whom I could lodge. Thaddeus and his sister Judith would also be living in Sepphoris, where Thaddeus was to take over management of one of the grain stores owned by an uncle who had suffered some kind of breakdown on the death of his wife. Judith was to serve as housekeeper and minder of the younger children.

Andreas had been willing to continue teaching Jesus, along with two new paying pupils, but Jesus told us he'd rejected the offer. 'I've already taken too much from Andreas,' he said, 'and he's had nothing by way of payment.'

We were walking home together, having said our end-of-year farewells to our tutor – tearful ones, because none of us was going back to him.

'He wouldn't have minded,' Thaddeus said. 'You saw him just now. The poor fellow dotes on you.'

'Well, that might be another reason for not going back. Time to move on.'

'Move where?' we wanted to know, and he replied grandly, but with one of his ironic, self-mocking smiles, 'To the next step on the ladder.'

'Jacob's ladder?' (That was Thaddeus.)

Jesus laughed. 'He who wants to climb Jacob's ladder must be prepared to sleep on Jacob's pillow.'

I remembered that Jacob's pillow had been a stone.

He said nothing more to explain what plan he had for the future, and next day he was gone. His way of saying goodbye was not to say it. It was slightly hurtful, but that was Jesus. You didn't look to him to be 'nice'.

So he vanished from our lives, and from Nazareth. Apart from his brief appearance at my wedding feast, I would not be with him again for a number of years.

When, during the time I spent lodging in Sepphoris, I visited my mother, I sometimes called on Joseph and Mary as well, and asked for news of Jesus. The answer was always the same. There was none.

'Nothing,' Joseph would say, shaking his head and looking anxious and sad.

But Mary's silent half-smile meant, I thought, that they knew where Jesus was, and that she, at least, approved.

One day it occurred to me to call on Andreas for news. He welcomed me with a bear hug and drew me indoors, offering a snack of figs and olives on a vine leaf, and a cup of light wine. 'Ah our brilliant Jesus,' he said. 'Our darling scholar. Didn't we love him, Judas? Don't we miss him?'

I said yes to all this, with some embarrassment.

'I have no news of him,' Andreas went on. 'I enquire of course, but that mother of his will say nothing. Just smiles her superior-camel smile. "I-know-something-that-you-don't-know." I quite like the father, but he's a sad sack – as you would be, married to such a prig.'

'She's a strange woman,' I agreed.

'But I think I know where Jesus is. I suspect he took my advice.' He hesitated. 'But you didn't know what that was? No. He wouldn't have wanted it known.'

He looked left and right in his dramatic way, as if to check there was no one listening, and leaned forward, putting a hand on my knee. 'My advice was that he should go to the Dead Sea . . . To Qumran.'

I was surprised, even shocked. Qumran was where the sect known as the Essenes had retreated. I knew only a little about them – that they were an all–male order, rebels against the Temple and the priesthood, exclusive, secretive and mystical. I'd heard my father refer to them as fanatics.

'My idea', Andreas explained, 'was that *there*, if the brotherhood would take him in, he would learn more than I – or anyone else who might take up where I left off – could ever teach him. But there's a problem. A risk.'

The question, he explained, was how long the brotherhood would go on teaching Jesus without asking him to become one of their order. That was what made him anxious – because once 'in', there was no 'out'. You were there for life.

'That would be a frightful waste,' Andreas said.

He had told Jesus if they would have him he would find it a tough regimen; but they were learned men and would appreciate his keen mind. Jesus should tell them he wasn't sure he had a vocation.

'"Stall." That's what I told him. "Stall and learn as much as you can. Use a bit of cunning."'

I said I was sure it was good advice.

'Well, I hope so, Judas. But it's a gamble. Every month that passes without word from him, I wonder whether we'll ever see him again.'

He asked about my poems and persuaded me to recite some. I quoted two or three, recently composed, and he praised them, which of course was what I wanted, and needed. There was one about a dream that caused him to raise his eyebrows. 'Nice,' he said. '*Very* nice.' He was looking at me strangely. 'Are you in love, Judas?'

'In love? No.' I didn't know what he meant. 'I don't think so.'

He nodded wisely, and said no more.

Seeing me to the door, he asked, with a slight but unmistakably hurt sniff, 'And how is your new tutor, dear boy? Is he taking you to new heights?'

'Don't ask,' I said. 'When you've had the best tutor there is, whoever follows can only be a disappointment.'

'You don't mean it,' he said, putting a hand on my shoulder.

'I do,' I said – and I suppose he could see that I did.

'Darling lad. Flattery should never be heeded, but I choose to believe you.' He wrapped me in a farewell embrace, and shed a small tear on my cheek as he kissed it.

It was quite true that my father had not done well in finding my second tutor. His name was Baruch, and his claim to be a superior scholar was either entirely false, or something that had once been true but was no longer. He not only knew less scripture, less philosophy, less history, than Andreas; I came to think he knew less than I did. Often I could outcite and outquote him. His Greek seemed to me full of grammatical mistakes; even his Hebrew was imperfect at times; and he was far from clever. His lessons, when he gave them, were full of strange pedantry. One he gave repeatedly might have been described as 'Rules for Recognising the Messiah'. The Messiah, if he were ever to come, was going to have to pass a very rigorous set of tests before my tutor would be able to give him a certificate of authenticity.

I was glad Jesus was no longer with me. He would have been impatient, outraged probably, and the whole arrangement, which, as I will explain, suited me rather well, might have collapsed.

I chose to be diplomatic. I pretended to learn, and Baruch pretended to teach. He soon left me largely to my own devices, which is what a young man wants at that age. What I had to put up with mostly was his pedantry, especially about the Sabbath, but also about washing and eating. He believed in observances in the right order, at the right time, carried out meticulously and without the slightest variation.

Baruch's wife, Ruth, mothered me, fussed about me, overfed me, but I, an only child used to that kind of attention, knew how to keep it at arm's length without giving offence. Ruth had borne seven children, she told me, five of them dead in infancy, three within a week in a terrible plague that had descended on their suburb because a neighbour had blasphemed most unspeakably against the Lord and the subsequent sacrifices and prayers had been insufficient to placate our offended and vengeful Deity. I could see those three deaths, leaving her childless until new babies were conceived and born, had created a permanent anxiety. Living in that house there was a feeling that somewhere just over the horizon there might be a terrible storm advancing to strike, or a dark legion arming to invade. You couldn't see any overt sign of what was coming, but you felt it was there, that it was bad, and that it could only be kept at bay by diligence and prayer.

Her surviving two children, both boys, were now grown to young manhood and living in Jerusalem. When I asked what they did there she explained that they worked at the Temple, sandpapering the lamps and keeping them filled and alight, swabbing the floors of the upper apartments, and keeping the seven kinds of incense resupplied and burning. 'They say the smell is so strong and sweet,' she told me, 'it makes the goats sneeze on the Mount of Olives.'

I wondered whether this was a joke, but didn't ask. She was very proud of her boys. They were only novices now, but one day they would be rabbis, she was sure of it. And they both had beautiful singing voices.

I was her son substitute. 'Your poor mother would never

73

forgive me if I let you become ill,' she told me, making me eat the special meals she prepared – lentil and bean stews, baked lamb and bitter herbs, fish soups, salads on corn-and-barley-breads she baked in her own oven. 'This will fatten you up,' she would say. 'You are too thin, Judas dear. It doesn't look right. You have nothing spare to come and go on.'

This was not a lack she or Baruch suffered from. They seemed to eat quite modestly and were portly. I ate huge meals and remained slim.

I had to assume that my father was paying handsomely for my keep as well as for my tutoring, because there were never any complaints about my appetite from Baruch, who otherwise kept a mean eye and a tight rein on everything. When I detected anxiety in him it came, I suspected, from his recognition that he was teaching me next to nothing, and that if this should be reported to my father I would be moved to another tutor, and he would lose a useful source of income.

My father's intentions for me remained unspoken. I supposed they still had to do with his ambition to re-establish a more secure place for me inside his priestly family; but as long as they remained undeclared, I could get on with my life and not worry about them.

It was during these few years that I grew increasingly attached to Thaddeus' sister, Judith. The likeness between brother and sister was noticeable, but the difference, as far as I was concerned, was that while his good looks represented health, a good diet and a strong bloodline, hers represented all that but something much less commonplace as well, an inner and unique grace.

In appearance Judith was like an Egyptian queen, a young Cleopatra, with strong features, large dark eyes, a very straight back, and a slow, rather deep speaking voice. When I talked to her she remained still, chin slightly tilted, seeming to attend closely, as if listening for some undertone, a meaning that lay beneath, or beyond, the words. There was a special charm about this, even if it was only a fluke of appearances, because it made me feel that what I said was important. Her eyes shone. Her lips were full, and her close-lipped smile was slow, warm, generous. When she spoke there was often a break in the voice, a momentary lilt, a high note among the predominantly deep ones, and often a sense that she might be on the brink of laughter.

For a long time – possibly close on two years – I had no consciousness, or no recognition, of what was happening to me. She was my friend's sister. Gradually she became the friend – more truly a friend than the brother. We talked – that was all. We talked endlessly. When I was not with her, I thought about her. Everything I did, and most things I thought, it seemed important I should tell her.

After a time I began to teach her – secretly, because neither of us knew whether it would be considered proper. She'd had no formal teaching, though she had picked up a good deal from her brothers. With me she began to learn to read Hebrew, copied proverbs, and learned many passages by heart. Since she was the housekeeper with control of the keys and the budget, she was able to arrange the household so that we found time to be alone together.

Later, looking back on those days, it is so obvious I had fallen in love with her I marvel that I didn't know. Beyond just thinking about her, and wanting always to be with her, I had soon developed all the more advanced symptoms – anxiety, difficulty sleeping, torrid dreams, moments of exaltation, plunges into gloom and despondency. But I had no word for the condition. Unlike those who grow up in the Greek culture that I have since made

75

my own, and which is full of stories of the love of man and woman, man and muse, human and demigod, we had no stories that might have put the idea into my head; or if there were such, I had not been told them. The 'love stories' I'd heard were all about man and God. One was supposed to love the Lord, and make oneself beloved of Him. That was where the word seemed to reside in the only Hebrew literature known to me. With women, one begat children and ate the meals they prepared. It was, I suppose, a gap in the education Andreas had provided.

Probably there had been more than enough in those plays I'd watched in Tiberias to teach me the nature and the madness of love. I'd been moved by them, but hadn't learned to relate them to my own life. If they had been in my own language I might have seen more quickly that they were telling me truths about myself.

Judith knew, as women do know such things, that I was in love with her. She knew (she told me later) that she was in love with me, and she was prepared to wait, if necessary for ever, for the lightning to strike.

It took some time, but not for ever. My first clear recognition of my state of mind came when we read together some passages from the Song of Songs. I don't know how we came on them, or chose them for study, but the effect was like a storm, or an earthquake. As we worked at understanding them, what seemed most surprising was that the voice, unlike that of any of the other scriptures I'd read, was a woman's. Sometimes there was a man's voice as well, but only indirectly, when the woman chose to represent what he said. They spoke their love in the most extravagant language, without shyness, without shame or apology. It was a language of love in which God had no part.

'My beloved spoke, and said to me, Rise up my beautiful one,

76

and come away. For look, the winter is past, the rain is over and gone, the flowers appear; the time of the singing of birds is come and the voice of the turtledove is heard in our land. The fig tree puts forth green fruit, and vines with their ripening grapes scent the air. Arise, my love, my fair one, and come with me.'

Soon we'd learned passages by heart and were finding, or creating, circumstances in which we could quote and, if it was more useful, misquote them.

'Let her kiss me with the kisses of her mouth; for the taste of her love is better than wine.'

'I sought him but could not find him. I went about the city late, in the backstreets and the boulevards. The watchmen on patrol challenged me, and I asked them, "Have you seen him, whom my soul loves?"'

'O my dove, in the secret places, on the stairs to the upper rooms, show me your face, let me hear your voice, let me kiss your mouth.'

With planning and secrecy, giving the impression that we were going on errands that would take us to quite different locations, we managed now and then to spend hours, and even half days, alone, far from the house and from family and friends. There was one picnic in particular when the texts we carried in our heads fitted the time and the place, and told us what we should do. 'Look at you, my love. How beautiful you are! You have dove's eyes, yes, and see, our bed is in leaf. The beams of our house are these cedars and its rafters are fir.'

After that day there could be no going back.

> Grass-soft our bed
> and a canopy
> of cedars where

spring water talked
over stones. Young love
lives longer not

put through the
wringer of the real. I was
sure-footed,

the roe among
rocks, and she
rose of Sharon, lily

among thorns. So
it was, and remains,
an insect's green

wings in amber
hoarded by an old
man, the poet

Idas of Sidon
who smiles and speaks
of it never.

CHAPTER 8

MY FATHER SENT FOR ME TO COME TO TIBERIAS. I JUMPED when the message came, as if I'd been caught out, but it was only that he wished me to accompany him while he visited an important man, a rabbi and friend of my uncle the high priest at Jerusalem. He offered no further explanation, but it suggested he might be thinking again about my future, and that gave me a twinge of anxiety. I thought, however, our being together might provide a chance for me to make known to him that Judith and I loved one another and wanted to be married.

The person we were to visit lived out of town and the journey there and back took most of a day, but there was never a moment when I felt relaxed enough to speak about so important and sensitive a subject. We ate a meal with the rabbi – his wife and daughter attending – and returned to Tiberias in the evening. Nothing of any consequence was said over the meal. The conversation was strained – we were meeting for the first time and there was little common ground.

The rabbi, a heavy-breather with plump, damp cheeks, asked about my studies and in answering his questions I failed to abide by a resolution that I would not 'show off'. The rabbi and, even more, my father should have found the glowing account I gave of my language skills distasteful, but they both seemed satisfied, even pleased with me. The hovering wife's expression suggested a person who is quietly tormented by having forgotten something – it might have been my father's name, or the reason for our being there – and who is trying to remember it without giving herself away. The daughter, a handsome young woman sitting at a distance fanning herself, had the appearance of one whose natural disposition is cheerful, but who is finding the present occasion at least boring and possibly unpleasant.

When we'd returned to Tiberias my father had a servant bring us a small supper with a jug of wine. As we sat down to it he asked whether I had liked the young woman. Wary, even alarmed, I said I hadn't seen or heard enough to like or dislike.

He asked had I not found her attractive.

I told him she appeared to be in good health, looked pleasant enough, but that she had hardly spoken a word.

'You will find silence an admirable quality in a wife,' he said.

I stared at him, angry and challenging. He broke the bread, keeping his eyes on it, avoiding mine. 'I've arranged for you to marry her.' His tone was neutral, even casual. 'I've had her priestly connections traced. They go back unbroken through six generations.'

When I didn't reply he went on, 'This will be a very great advantage for you, especially in Jerusalem. And even more to your children.'

I said, 'Father, you know you can't make me do this.'

He met my eye now. He was resolute. 'Yes. I believe I can.'

'Then you have a fight on your hands.'

He smiled wearily as he filled our cups. 'Thank you for warning me.'

I decided not to argue. A scene would do me no good. I was relieved that I'd said nothing about Judith. If I had told him even that we were friends he would have gone to work at once ensuring that we spent no more time together.

I went to bed without wishing him goodnight, resolved that I would find a way of preventing this marriage. 'May my father be attacked by bandits,' I said at the end of my prayers, and then added, fearing God might punish me for parricide, or for the wish, 'And may he escape unhurt, but chastened.'

I had one advantage. My father had long talked about travelling with one of his own caravans. If he was to do it, he said, it would have to be soon, before he was too old for the rigours of the mountains and the deserts. There were things about his business that could only be learned at first hand – what kind of people he was dealing with at a distance, whether his agents were representing prices honestly and giving him a fair percentage, what kinds of harm could come to goods sent so far, and whether there were other products of our region that might be traded.

Most of that could be accomplished on the first part of his journey, which would take him to Damascus. But he talked of going further, into Galatia, and possibly even across the Aegean to Athens. He pretended it was all 'business', but I could see there was a hunger for something more – for danger, excitement, the unknown. Previously, I'd encouraged the idea because it seemed commendable in a man of his age. Now I encouraged it because I wanted to be rid of him for as long as possible.

Everything was already arranged. He apologised for having sprung the marriage plan on me so suddenly. The 'availability' (as he called it) of such a desirable young woman had presented itself unexpectedly. He had wanted to secure the arrangement before leaving. Now that was done, the rest could wait. The time he spent on his travels would allow me to finish my studies with

Baruch and to prepare my mind for life as a married man. When he returned, the public announcements would be made, the uncle in Jerusalem informed, and the wedding would take place.

'Visit her from time to time,' he recommended. 'Think of her as the future sharer of your bed. You're young and in good health, and so is she. You won't find the prospect unattractive, I'm sure.'

I offered no further argument but behaved as I supposed I would have if there had been no Judith – reluctant (to have been suddenly acquiescent might have aroused his suspicions), but accepting that I had no right to object, and no reason to.

My father, his mind taken up with his coming adventure, worked hard at last-minute preparations and put my future out of his thoughts. He was ready to leave on time with his camel train, and I was there to say goodbye to him. Despite everything, I was fond of him, and I had never seen him so bright-eyed, young-looking, eager. His enthusiasm extended even to his plans for me.

'Study hard,' he recommended in a hearty tone. 'And as to the marriage, my dear Judas – you will grow used to the idea.' He kissed me fondly on both cheeks. 'It's something I'm certain you will have no reason to regret.'

In the weeks and months that followed I told a great many lies and half-truths. I was fortunate that my parents were even more estranged, and seldom saw one another. I told my mother that my father had no objection to my marrying – which was true, except that it left out the fact that he had someone other than Judith in mind for me. I told Judith's family that my father, informed of our plans just as he was leaving, had blessed the betrothal and expressed his regret that he would have to be absent for the wedding. He had agreed (I went on) that Andreas, as former tutor of myself and Thaddeus, should stand in for him.

My mother, of course, would attend. I even travelled to visit the important rabbi again, and told him my father's plan had been hasty and mistaken, that I was not of a mind to marry, that I wished to live a celibate life devoted to the study of spiritual perfection, and that I was thinking of joining the Essenes. This last piece of misinformation so enraged him that I had to leave in haste and knew, whatever the outcome, I had made myself safe from his daughter and she from me.

I told the truth only to Judith and to Andreas. Judith was frightened, but love made us both determined and gave us strength. We conspired, making sure we told the same lies to the same people. Andreas joined the conspiracy, alarmed and eager, anxious and enthusiastic. I worried about involving him, but when the day came he carried out his role with the ease and confidence of a natural actor.

*

Yesterday Theseus and I listened to Ptolemy, our blind Jesus evangelist, preaching in the village square. He stood on the edge of the drinking trough, steadying himself with one hand on the shoulder of Reuben, the young friend who guides him everywhere, prepares his food, washes and dresses him. Ptolemy spoke of the miracles which proved that Jesus was indeed the Messiah promised in holy scripture, the last of these being 'the miracle of miracles', his resurrection from death on the cross.

'At that moment,' Ptolemy said, 'a stone was rolled away from the tomb, and from the world, and from the mind of man. When, on that third day, the Son of God came forth from his cold cell, every one of us earned the right to come with him, to step out into the sunlight of everlasting life. I have lived long enough for my eyes to fail, but now, in my old age, I see beyond the confines of our narrow world. Beyond my personal darkness, beyond the darkness of the tomb, I see the lights of Paradise, a shining city waiting to welcome me at the end of my long road. I see because I believe. I believe because I see. We have only to believe, dear friends, and we find ourselves free of death's hideous terminus, released from its terrifying enclosure.'

I felt the powerful appeal this had for the gathered crowd. I knew so well that rhetoric and the emotion that went with it. I had experienced it often in the days of my youth. It didn't matter that there was no good reason for accepting this promise of a life after death, or for taking on trust the evangelist's stories of miracles that were meant to be its guarantors. These people, many of them poor, ill-fed and unhappy, wanted to believe, and for some of them the wanting was so intense it would be enough.

But Ptolemy was not finished yet. 'I speak of miracles,' he continued, 'culminating in the last and greatest, the Resurrection. But there had to be a beginning, a first miracle, and I would like today to tell you about it – the astonishing event which set the ball rolling, as it were, towards eternity.

'There was a marriage feast in the region of Galilee. Jesus' mother, Mary, and Mary's husband Joseph, were both present. Jesus arrived late – I'm not sure whether he had even been invited . . .'

Ptolemy told the story well, how Mary noticed that the wine jars were empty, how Jesus spoke curtly to her, silencing her when she began to panic and say the wedding would be ruined, but how, at the same time, he took charge, took the matter in hand, instructing servants to fill the jars with fresh water and to serve the tables from the contents.

'It seemed Mary would be proved right,' Ptolemy went on.

'The feast would be spoiled, the guests disappointed, the families of the bride and groom shamed. But what came from those water-filled jars? Wine, my friends. *Wine.* The finest vintage. The feast was a success; the marriage passed without incident. None of the guests was even aware there had been a crisis.

'Why, I now ask you, should Jesus have called upon his sacred powers at such a moment? One answer is simple, obvious, and true. Our Lord believed in the sacrament of marriage between a man and a woman, and wished to give it his blessing, not just at that moment, but for ever.

'But there is something more important. This was the first of his miracles, and the first, like the last, was of special significance. This is a miracle, my dear friends, he will perform for each one of you, no matter how heavy your heart, no matter what sin weighs upon your conscience. The water of your life he will turn into wine. And what will he ask in return? Only that you repent your sins and believe he died for you on the cross. Believe, and let the water of your mortal days be turned to everlasting wine.'

He ended with a prayer spoken aloud – the version of the Kaddish that Jesus had taught us to say on parting. As the people began to disperse, talking as they went, Reuben accepted small gifts while Ptolemy, kneeling in the dust beside a mule sucking noisily in the water trough, prayed, his voice silent, his lips moving, the soles of his big battered sandals turned, like his blind eyes, upward into the midday light.

It was, I conceded to Theseus, an affecting sight.

Ptolemy has taken up residence in my house for the moment and I haven't the heart, or even the wish, to send him on his way. When he came in for his evening meal I told him that Theseus and I had heard him speak. He replied that Reuben

85

had reported seeing us in the square, and that he was honoured we should have thought it worth our precious time.

'Nonsense,' I said. 'You clearly believe your message is worth the precious time of everyone in the world.'

He smiled. 'Yes, of course. But I thank you for listening.'

'It was . . .' I began, and stopped myself. I wanted to be honest with him. 'I congratulate you on your eloquence.'

He bowed his head gravely. 'The eloquence is not mine but the Lord's,' he replied, and I thought the modesty, like my compliment, was not entirely false.

As he sat down to the meal Electra had put before him, I asked about the wedding feast and its miracle. Had he been there? Had he seen it happen? Had he tasted the wine?

No, he said, it had happened before his time as a follower of Jesus, but he'd heard it described many times. The disciple John, with his brother James and their father Zebedee, had supplied fish for the feast, and so, by chance, had been there in the background among the servants.

'The story interests me,' I told him. 'What else can you tell me about it?'

He said there was little to add to what he'd told the gathering in the square, but he described the feast again, as it had been described to him by those who were present – the country setting, the guests ranged down two sides of one long table in the shade of a vine-covered trellis, the bride and groom in the centre flanked by the groom's mother on one side and the bride's father on the other. He explained that Mary and Joseph were there as friends of the groom, but that no one had expected Jesus, who had been absent a long time from his home in Nazareth. He had arrived late, dressed all in white, and had made a great impression.

'Then the jars were noticed,' Ptolemy went on. 'Delivered just that morning, and all empty.'

I asked how that could that have come about – such an oversight.

He shook his large shaggy head. 'Who knows? How do such things happen? Mistakes are made.'

'A disaster.'

'Yes,' he confirmed. 'It would have been, if Jesus hadn't been there.'

'And the families didn't even know!'

Blind Ptolemy cocked his head and frowned, as if something in my voice had begun to warn him that he didn't have an entirely credulous, or sympathetic, listener. 'A miracle, yes indeed. And only the first of many.'

I asked why it should have been Jesus' mother who noticed the jars were empty.

'Mary was a woman who noticed things.'

This was true; I didn't ask how she would have noticed from her place at the table. 'But the servants,' I pursued. 'Why would they take instructions from a stranger – a guest who, from your account, was not invited, or not expected?'

'Because, Idas of Sidon,' Ptolemy replied firmly, 'Jesus of Nazareth spoke with authority. When he preached, people believed. When he commanded, they obeyed.'

I'd been rebuked. We sat silent. Ptolemy patted the table in front of him, feeling for a piece of the bread and hummus my daughter-in-law had put there. He turned it carefully into a roll, conveyed it to his mouth and took a tidy bite. I'd resolved to say no more, but then couldn't forbear one further question.

'What was the bridegroom's name?'

Ptolemy shook his head. 'Of that I am uncertain.'

'You said a friend from his boyhood.'

'Did I? Yes, I believe so.'

I said, 'I've heard this story before.'

'It's not a *story*, Idas . . .'

'This *true* story.'

'You've heard it?'

'From another of your faith. You're not the first to bring the Jesus message to our part of the world.'

Ptolemy nodded. 'Not the first, and not the last. That's as it must be – and God will open the ears of the blessed.'

'Your colleague of a few years back – like yourself an eloquent advocate, I may say – suggested the bridegroom's name might have been Judas.'

Ptolemy tried to convert his look of distaste into one of indifference. 'It's a common enough name, but I don't think so.'

'Perhaps the Judas who became a disciple?'

He shook his head. 'I don't believe that's possible. That Judas, Judas of Keraiyot, betrayed Jesus.'

'Does that make it impossible?'

He thought a moment. 'It seems unlikely, doesn't it? I think Jesus knew right from the beginning who his betrayer would be.'

> Sleeping far from
> home beside a spring
> under date palms
>
> on a day when
> an ill-tempered camel
> had bitten

his hand, my father
dreamed a young
man in startling white

came uninvited
to a wedding by
a lake. This

he told me long
after – how he woke
to cool moonlight

and in the desert
silence begged God
not to give him

perplexing dreams
if their meanings were
to be withheld.

CHAPTER 9

JESUS CAME TO OUR WEDDING FEAST, MADE AN IMPRESSION that was remembered, talked to a few people, said his farewells, and was gone. He told Andreas and me only a little about the Essenes – that he was permitted to live in a cave on the outskirts of their community, that he worked long hours in their gardens, that he copied texts for them in their scriptorium, that he read twice a day to the brothers while they ate their early and late meals, after which he was permitted a meal himself.

'Leftovers,' Andreas suggested.

'Excellent leftovers.'

'And a cave.'

'An excellent cave. Cool in hot weather, warm when it's cold, and dry always.'

'With a bed?'

Jesus laughed. 'Yes, Tutor. I have my bedroll on a nice level area of the cave floor.'

'I hope you stay healthy,' Andreas said, squeezing his arm. 'You're very thin.'

'The Lord is my shepherd,' Jesus said.

In return for his work he received lessons from the brothers and had some hours of free access to their library.

'And they admire you?' Andreas said. 'They appreciate you?'

Jesus took his hand. 'They appreciate *you*, dear Andreas. They say I've been exceptionally well taught.'

Andreas was pleased, but shook his head and held up his free hand in a gesture of denial. 'How could our Jesus be badly taught? Your eyes are lamps and your ears are sponges. You miss nothing. You would learn from a stone.'

Jesus told us that at some point, which might come soon or late, he would be called upon by the head of the order to make the choice, either to join the Sons of Zadok (as they called themselves) or to leave. In the meantime he was living a life which he described as very hard, but full of surprises and rewards.

'What are you learning?' I asked.

He smiled. 'The depths of my ignorance.'

'Is that depressing?'

'No. It's necessary. It's the gateway.'

'To knowledge. Of course.'

'To the mystery.'

I was happy, in love, full of good food and wine and hopes for the future. I had no time for 'the mystery'. 'Spare me,' I said.

He laughed, understanding. 'Your time for the mystery may come,' he said. 'Or you may be blessed, in which case it won't need to. For the moment you are a fortunate fellow.' He gave my upper arm an affectionate punch. 'And so am I. Goodbye, both of you.'

Andreas kissed him. 'Dear boy. Come back to us very soon.'

Jesus walked away, waving over his shoulder as he went. But he'd forgotten something and came back, not to us but to Judith, standing not far from where we men had been saying our farewells. He took her by the upper arms and looked hard at her. 'Say goodbye to your brother for me. And look after my friend here, won't you. He deserves it.'

Judith blinked. She said she would try. As he walked away again she called 'Good luck.' She came over and took my hand, and the three of us watched him climb the hill. When he reached the top we looked for him to wave but he didn't pause or turn, just vanished down the farther side.

That was the last I saw of him for two years.

Those two years were lived mostly at my mother's house, in the continuing absence of my father, whose journey had taken him first to Antioch, then through Galatia to Ephesus and Smyrna, and finally, as he'd hoped it might, across the Aegean to Athens. But though he was absent he was also present, and I lived in the shadow of the knowledge that I would sooner or later have to face his reproaches. When he returned, however, and learned of my marriage, he refused to speak to me or to meet Judith. We weren't sorry. We both feared his anger and his authority. But Judith was at last pregnant, and I thought when the child was born, particularly if it was a son, we might achieve a reconciliation, or at least the beginnings of one.

Meanwhile came news of Jesus. It was Andreas who brought it. As part of a sort of apprenticeship with the Essenes Jesus had been required to live – or attempt to live – forty days in the desert, eating wild honey, locusts and the flesh and juice of certain kinds of cacti, drinking at turbid waterholes, and otherwise passing his days and nights in prayer and contemplation. He'd passed the test, lasting out the full period. This was considered a great achievement, and as a consequence he'd been invited to join the brotherhood. But the decision had had to be made at once – that was the rule. It could not be deferred. Either he joined, or he left.

In the desert Jesus had lost track of time and had spent some days – he was not sure how many – in a kind of ecstatic delirium, in which he believed he'd been tempted by the Devil and had successfully resisted, after which God had appeared telling him he must leave the order and go out into the world as a preacher. His task would be to make known the understanding that had come through study, prayer and contemplation. There was no choice about this – it was an instruction. He was to take to the poor, the oppressed, the sick and the unhappy the message that they were loved by the Lord, who wished them to know their place with Him was assured, and that every disadvantage they suffered on earth was precisely its opposite in the book of Heaven.

Jesus had given grateful thanks to the brothers for their teachings and had said fond farewells. For some months since leaving Qumran he had been back in the area of Galilee, going from one community to another, preaching his message with extraordinary power and conviction. The crowds he drew were working people – fishermen, labourers in gardens and vineyards, carpenters, stonemasons, housewives. Camel drivers and muleteers on their way through villages stopped to listen, and took the news on with them of this popular new teacher. Four or five men travelled with him as companions, returning home at intervals, but supporting him, sometimes going ahead to make it known he was coming and to secure him a billet, sometimes taking a turn to proclaim his message. The two sets of brothers who were soon to be known as disciples, the fishermen Simon Peter and Andrew, James and John, were already attached to his cause; and there were others who seemed on the brink of joining them.

All of this was of interest to me, but not in the forefront of my thoughts. I was preoccupied with the coming of our first child – excited, and then anxious, because, as the time got closer, there were signs that Judith was unwell. Her legs swelled and when she climbed the hill from the village to the house she had difficulty breathing. My mother, who tried not to frighten me, couldn't conceal an anxiety that turned to alarm as the signs got worse. When the pains began I was pushed out into the garden and the women took over – my mother, a servant and one midwife, then a second, then an apothecary, a neighbour, a soothsayer . . .

Hours passed, filled with screams, whispering, rushing feet and the sound of water being poured from pails and heated in the kitchen. Night came and seemed to stall, as if the new day, like the new life, could not find a way to be born. When at last the sun rose its light was peculiar, garish. Everything appeared shamed by it – naked and vulnerable. As the second day passed the screams became groans and sobs, then a rasping, desperate breathing, and finally silence.

There have been two unbearable episodes in my life, both involving the death of someone I loved, and a sense of such extreme helplessness I seemed to exist only in order to register the pain. Even now, so many decades later, I am not able to let my thoughts dwell long on this one. Judith, the woman I had loved to the fullest extent of my power to love, died, and with her died also our child, boy or girl – I was not to know which since he or she never found a way out into the world of light.

I was distraught. My mother did all she could for me, and perhaps kept me from taking my own life – though looking back on it from so far, and knowing myself better now, I suppose my thoughts of suicide were only another kind of helpless thrashing about.

Nothing my father said could have made anything better, but what he did say after the burial made it worse. In his bumbling, disconnected way, only half focusing on me, he said that clearly our union had not been blessed by God.

'You mean Heaven agrees with you,' I said. 'Then I curse Heaven as I curse you.'

He was not a religious man but he was deeply shocked. Even I – the rational man and sceptic of this present moment – am shocked remembering it.

It was at this time that Jesus came home to Nazareth.

He came in his role as itinerant preacher. He chose to stay with me and my mother – why not with his own family was not explained, but already the rift between him and Mary, which grew wider as he became more famous in the region, was apparent.

To me, he was a soothing balm. I had seen, often enough, his capacity for sympathy, the power he had to convey love and make a person feel its sole recipient, but I hadn't ever felt it directed exclusively at me. He sat with me long hours, holding me casually by the fingertips, while I talked about Judith, telling and retelling our story. I told him how I kept seeing her in crowds, or the back of her head in a room full of people, or her figure among women at the well – seeing her eyes, her hair, her walk, hearing her voice. The world was full of Judith. She was everywhere and nowhere. My heart was continually leaping at the sight of her, only to crash down painfully at the recognition that it was not, and would never be, Judith.

Jesus subjected himself totally to my needs, which he intuited exactly, and to my pain. If the roles had been reversed I would have done my best, but I know I would not have been capable of such patience, generosity, sensitivity.

While he was with us it was arranged that he would preach at the house, recently enlarged, that served as Nazareth's synagogue. It was on a Sabbath, and the rabbi called on him first to give a reading. The text Jesus had chosen was from Isaiah, and he read it direct from the scroll, first in Hebrew, then translated into Aramaic, the only language most of those present understood:

'The spirit of the Lord is on me
Who has appointed me to promise
Riches to the poor, happiness to the wretched
Freedom to the imprisoned
Light to all who live in darkness
And comfort to those who mourn.'

I felt that some might have thought his reading first in Hebrew and then translating was 'showing off'; but his voice, equally beautiful in either language, affected people, and I could hear them asking one another who was this young man, surely it couldn't be the son of the carpenter? Mary and Joseph were not there, and nor were his brothers; but two of his sisters were, and people whispered, pointing them out.

Jesus finished his reading, bowed to the rabbi, and sat down. The congregation were impressed – he'd won approval, but it was precarious. He needed to be modest in demeanour to confirm it, and that was not his way, or not in his mood of that moment.

The rabbi thanked him for the reading and invited him now to follow his chosen text with some moral reflections.

Jesus sat, head bowed in prayer, then got up to speak. He stared around at these townsfolk, so familiar to him, so easy for him to read. 'Here today,' he said, 'for Nazareth, this scripture is fulfilled. These things it promises, I am here to proclaim.'

The voice was still beautiful but the tone was not quite warm or friendly. He was claiming an authority. It caused restlessness in the congregation. I heard a male voice say that this idea that the Lord had called *him* was outrageous. Another suggested

Joseph should give him a hammer and put him out to do some useful work.

Jesus looked at the rabbi. 'Should I continue?'

'Please,' the rabbi said. 'Continue.'

Jesus put one forearm on the lectern and leaned forward. He stared at his challengers. 'This was not my text, but perhaps this is a moment to remind you of Elijah the prophet, who could find neither due recognition, nor shelter, nor protection in the land of his birth; who had to leave Israel and travel into the land of our enemies before he found someone to protect him, the widow whom the Lord blessed for her kindness. To remind you also that by way of punishment for the wrong they did him, the Lord bestowed on this, Elijah's homeland, three years of drought. Crops failed. Animals died. In the first year there was financial loss, in the second hunger, in the third starvation.'

He began to offer another example of a prophet not appreciated in the land of his birth, but by now no one was listening. There were interjections. Who did he think he was? The rabbi was calling for calm. Andreas, in the front seats, stood up and, facing the angry congregation, shouted, 'Please, friends, I beg you, let him speak.'

But Jesus was pushing his way through the crowd, who were telling him to go away and leave Nazareth in peace. Someone shoved him as he passed. He stumbled, recovered, and went on. I saw his sisters weeping with shame.

I followed him out into the little square, chased after him, and only caught up some streets away. He was still striding angrily. Hearing my voice he paused and turned.

I put an arm around his shoulder.

He managed a grin. 'I didn't do that well.'

It was true, but this was not the moment to say so. I gave

him an affectionate squeeze. 'You read beautifully, and you spoke the truth.'

We walked on together. We were already on the outskirts of the village. 'Home is where the hate is,' he said. 'I'll never come back to this place. Never.'

Soon we were passing the caves where we'd played so often as boys. I didn't know where we were going, and neither did he. It was a long time before he stopped again, and now he grasped me by the arm and looked into my eyes. 'Come with me,' he said.

'Where?'

'Don't ask where, Judas. Just come.'

I've heard it said that others among his disciples made up their minds in the instant of being asked; that some of them just dropped whatever they were doing and followed him. I'm not sure whether that's true, and it certainly would not have been true of me if I had not been so burdened with a grief he alone knew how to assuage. But that was how things were, and that was the outcome. In an instant the next few years of my life had been determined.

'I'll come,' I said.

He hugged me, and we walked on out of Nazareth without looking back.

Nothing cuts so deep
as the first cut
of love, of death.

She in her tomb
was the tomb of
our child and our hope.

I longed for death
but knew it would
bring her no closer.

Longed also for life
but only with her
and our child.

Pathetic my cries
as if pain were
new to the world.

Jesus was nurse
to my griefs. When he
called, I followed.

CHAPTER 10

IN THE YEAR THAT FOLLOWED, JESUS DISCOVERED HIS FULL powers as an orator, and his fame spread through the region. We were always on the move, but he made the home of Simon Peter, in Capernaum, his headquarters. A spare room had been reserved for him since his first visit there, when he'd been told that Simon Peter's mother-in-law was seriously ill, almost certainly dying, and had cured her.

Capernaum has a number of wells and fountains which appear improbably but naturally out of the rock and subsoil, and there was one, a grotto with a spring, beside Simon Peter's house. Jesus took a damp cotton cloth that Simon Peter's wife had laid over her mother's brow and went into the grotto to soak it again in cool water. The grotto is very beautiful, with water running down through maiden-hair ferns that hang over the stones into a crystal-clear pool with a floor of white pebbles. Among the pebbles there were always a few stoppered jars of Simon Peter's wine.

Jesus remained there some minutes, listening to the water running over the stones, meditating, communing with God. 'You don't have to pray in there,' he told them. 'You just have to listen. It says the prayers for you.'

He took the cool cloth and laid it again on the woman's

brow. She was very weak, restless, and having difficulty breathing. For some days she'd been unable to sleep or eat, and had spoken only a few breathless, rambling sentences. But as Jesus sat with her, holding her hand and bathing her brow, she became peaceful for the first time in more than a week. Soon she had fallen into a calm sleep. He remained with her for several hours, and when at last he left the room she still hadn't woken. Her sleep lasted on until nightfall and continued until late next morning. When she woke she was weak but refreshed, her fever gone.

The family, particularly Simon Peter's wife and the woman herself, the mother, were quite sure she had been beyond saving, that she'd had only hours to live. The mother would tell how in her wandering, fevered mind, she'd been aware of drifting on the dark smooth surface of a river, and that she was being taken to the world beyond. She could see the opposite shore, with many people dressed in white, and could hear beautiful singing. Then it was as if the boatman taking her across received a call and turned back. Jesus, they said, had called to him to return her to the shores of the living.

'I've never seen anyone go so close to death and recover,' Simon Peter used to tell anyone who would listen. 'One day we were ready to order her shroud, the next she was on her feet. It was a miracle.'

There was a lot of talk of miracles, and in those early days of his ministry it made Jesus uneasy. Someone would say to him, 'Master, last month you blessed my dying child and he recovered.'

Jesus would reply neutrally, 'I'm glad he's well again.'

Often he asked people not to repeat these stories of miraculous cures, and I used to ask myself whether he meant it, because his asking made no difference. Of course the stories were repeated! Not only repeated but enlarged upon, exaggerated beyond recognition. People came to listen to him not just because of his eloquence but because of his reputation as a healer.

If he had not been such a dazzling speaker the reputation for these other powers would not have been so universally believed; but to hear him at his best was to feel that he was capable of anything. His great strength was in words, in language. I heard him so often, and yet again and again it was as if it was the very first time. He would stand silently waiting for the spirit to move him. He might say only a couple of words – 'Dear friends' – or a simple sentence – 'The Lord has called us together in the shade of this tree' – and stand silent again. People hushed one another and strained to hear. Into the silence of the market square would come another sentence, another silence, another sentence. Slowly he would wind himself into his full range of imagery and parable.

He seldom thundered in those early sermons; often hardly raised his voice. The texts we had memorised as boys would be raided, as if randomly, and yet made to twist together, like the strands of a rope, or a flower arrangement, into a beautifully organised statement – a celebration of the power of Israel's God and a promise of what He would do for the poor, the sick, the unfortunate, the bereaved.

I, of course, was one of the bereaved. My scalp prickled. Tears filled my eyes. Thoughts of Judith overwhelmed me. The language was beautiful. It was prayer, it was prophecy, and it was poetry. More than anything it seemed to praise, to celebrate, itself. That was the miracle.

There were times (not often, but enough to add to the mystery) when Jesus seemed to look into himself, or up to heaven, or wherever the source of his power lay, and find nothing. The magic was denied him, and seemed all the more magical because he could not turn it on, or call it up, just by an act of will. He needed inspiration, a breath from beyond. And what could that have been but the breath of God?

Much later, when he felt his life was threatened, and that he should coach us, the twelve, how to carry his message on when he was gone, he would tell us, 'Don't prepare a speech. Don't be guarded. Don't think about consequences. The Holy Ghost will guide you. Have faith, and the words will come.' That was his way, right from the beginning.

He preached charity and he preached hope; but there was also an underlying message. He urged us to look forward to a time when Israel would be ruled by Israel's God. It seemed innocent enough, but it implied that Israel's God was not ruling Israel now, which in turn suggested, to anyone who thought about it, that He had been usurped by the Romans, and by those who served or were cowed by them – the Herods, the Temple and its priestly families.

We travelled around the Galilee region, from village to village, gathering followers (and flowers!) as we went. Sometimes we were not welcomed; sometimes met with hostility. And there were rare occasions, as I've said, when Jesus' powers failed him. But such things happened less and less as his fame spread. Fame, after all, feeds on itself. Jesus became, you could say, fashionable in the region – a star. People wanted to boast that they'd heard him, that he'd spoken to them personally, that they had touched his garment or been blessed by his hand.

Blessed was what we all felt during that time. It was not to last, but while it did I think we all must have experienced it (I certainly did) as a new dawn, a revolution. The sun shone and the dews (which we knew came from Mount Hermon, the holy mountain) fell, making the desert break into flower, the trees and vines, the crops and garden beds flourish. When, lying awake as an old man often does in the middle of the night, I turn my thoughts to that remarkable time, I see Jesus smiling, distributing wisdom and blessings, walking with such a light step that weariness and failure, drought and famine and disease, seem to have been banished from the earth. My grief was there, but it was held at bay. Memories of Judith could take me by surprise at any time, like a sudden acute pain; but when they did, and seemed beyond enduring, I could turn to my friend and be comforted. Even if I woke him in the night, he never complained and never failed me.

Jesus, we felt, was 'lucky', if that is not too banal a way to describe one on whom the gift of heaven had descended. That 'luck', that gift, was his own, but he was generous with it, wanting always to share it with us, to distribute it.

We were seldom far from the sight of water – Galilee, the Jordan – and if our fishermen had a bad day and complained of their catch, Jesus might come down to the waterside and say (knowing nothing of fishing himself), 'Try the other side of the boat.' Or he would suggest they row out to a patch of shadow cast on the water by a single cloud. 'It looks like a finger pointing,' he would say.

Grumbling and saying it was no use, they'd tried everything and there were no fish, they would nevertheless do what he recommended and as often as not would pull in a full net.

'A miracle,' everyone would cry, and Jesus would laugh and say, 'Nonsense. You just don't like to admit I'm a better fisherman.'

Or we might have travelled all day without food and find

ourselves, hot and tired and quarrelsome, approaching a village we hardly knew anything about, believing there would be nothing for us to eat that night; and suddenly the dusty road would be full of children running out, shouting, welcoming us, scattering flowers in our path and saying word had gone ahead of us and a picnic had been prepared for the prophet Jesus and his friends.

Why should we not have felt, as I think all of us who followed him did, that God was blessing Jesus, and through him blessing us, his team, his (as we became) disciples?

He had a special talent with the mad, which gave him a reputation for having power over evil spirits. He had no fear of them. Their raving and threats never frightened him or drove him off. He would approach slowly, quietly, talking to them as to anyone, with that calm and beautiful voice, taking a hand if he could, sometimes doing what they did – dancing (he was a graceful dancer), or singing with them in his clear tuneful voice. It never failed. He calmed them. Those of us who watched said we had seen the evil spirit driven out – and moved on with him, not looking back to see if the evil spirit returned. And then the story of the encounter went the rounds, losing nothing in the telling.

The little crowd of friends and supporters, women as well as men, who followed him whenever they could, grew in number, and Jesus decided there should be twelve who were, so to speak, 'official'. He chose twelve because it was a convenient number, manageable, not too large a group to be fed by village charity, enough for some to be absent when home or work called them back, and still some remaining for self-protection in the countryside. But he chose twelve also because it was the number of the sons of Jacob and so of the tribes of Israel of which they were the patriarchs.

I remember the day when he told us this decision. We were resting at noon under acacia trees. The colours – the green of the lake, the purple-pink of the hills on the far shore above Capernaum – were lovely, muted into pastels by the brightness of the high sun. Jesus had preached in a nearby village and we were settling to eat the food people had brought us.

There were just the twelve – no one missing, no one un-invited – something that seldom happened before our fatal Jerusalem campaign. Jesus was in high good humour and deliv-ered the news, not as a solemn pronouncement, but in a playful spirit. He wanted, he told us, to be a modern Jacob, 'a plain man living in tents' (as the scriptures have it). 'You will be my sons,' he said. 'My twelve patriarchs.'

What sprang to my mind at that moment was that Jacob was a twin, and that his brother Esau, who was a greedy good-for-nothing, had sold his half of the inheritance they shared for a plate of stew. 'Who is your Esau?' I asked.

'There's no Esau,' he said. And then, after a moment's thought: 'Unless it's the Devil who tempted me in the desert.'

Later, when the others weren't about, I told him Andreas had said his Devil in the desert was a delusion, the result of eating cactus or drinking its juice.

Jesus smiled. 'I think it had something to do with hunger.'

'Forty days on locusts and wild honey! I'm not surprised.'

'I meant hunger for the divine.'

I gave that some thought. 'Starving people see things.'

'Sometimes they see truth.'

Soon after that we made our journey to visit his cousin John. John had also become an itinerant preacher, known for his insistence on ritual washing away of sins in the waters of the Jordan. He was reputed to be grim and dark in his preaching, a moraliser, chastiser, forecaster of doom, and self-punisher.

His encampment was some distance south of Galilee, at the ford on the caravan route from Jericho to Ammon, and I think Jesus' willingness to travel so far to see and hear him in action was a matter not of rivalry, but of professional interest. If you're in the business, so to speak, you need to know who else is in it and what they're doing.

We took our time, making our way down the river mostly on foot, at times persuading someone with a boat to take us; asking people we met along the way what they'd heard of John the Baptist (he was becoming widely known and talked about); finding new friends to give food and shelter.

On the last day of the journey we camped where a spring flowed out of rocks just above the river. This was the low-lying desert region where the Jordan approaches the Dead Sea. But in places like this one, where water flows from an underground source, everything bursts into life. In a glade there were lush grasses, shrubs and flowers of every colour. 'Why doesn't he do his baptisms here?' I asked.

'Too shallow,' Jesus explained. 'It has to be total immersion.'

'But this is so beautiful.'

Jesus shook his head. 'Beautiful isn't a word in cousin John's book.'

Next morning we reached the ford. John was there, already haranguing a group in readiness for what he wanted them to understand should not be taken lightly, but which was to be the ultimate sin-shedding experience. He was up to his knees in the water, skinny arms raised above his head, facing his small flock preparing themselves on the bank. Behind him the river was broad and brown, with feathery papyrus and stalky reeds stirring in the breeze on the far bank. Beyond the green strip they made was the pale barrenness of desert sand and dry stone.

John I would not have recognised from childhood memories. He was tanned almost black, and as painfully thin as you might expect of one reputed to live only on desert fare. His beard and hair couldn't have been cut in five years and hung loose, pushed or flicked aside now and then from his eyes and out of his open mouth as he preached. He wore a loincloth and a broad strip of woven yellowish camel hair diagonally across one shoulder, pulled in at the waist by a leather thong, and spreading free at his skinny thighs. His head was bare.

I think he saw us at once, and recognised Jesus, but he continued with his preaching, perhaps even increasing the volume and the grimness of the message, which at that moment was about 'soul tourists' who came 'to see the madman John do his baptisms, and to be amused by him'. If there were any such among us today (I, at least, shifted uneasily and avoided his eye) we were vipers, not men, and could expect no benefits in heaven from the experience.

But now he moved on to larger and worse vipers: the Herods, who brought shame to Israel's people by posing as their kings; and the priests of the Temple who brought shame to Israel's God by posing as His ministers.

Could it be, he asked, that a true King of the Jews was one who sheltered under the Roman shield? Could a true King of the Jews be one who had so little sense of God's law that he would steal his brother's wife and make her his own?

These were the shames of Israel. We, however, need not partake of them. We could turn our backs on them, as he had done. And we had signalled, those of us who had come in good faith, that that was our intention.

'Repent, then,' he urged us. 'Scourge your souls. Scour your hearts. Abase yourselves before God. Destroy the sinner that lives in you, even if it leaves so small a fragment of self it will scarcely sustain a life.

'You think I speak with power,' he roared. 'I tell you I am a worm before a raging bull. I am a fly walking with delicate legs on stagnant water in the stillness of evening when a great storm is about to break. One comes, and it will be soon, whose sandal I am not fit to fasten. I can baptise you with water, but he will baptise you with fire. I can chastise you with words, but he will divide wheat from chaff and sheep from goats. He will raze the Temple, and he will destroy the world. He will bring us to the end of time.

'Who am I?' he went on. 'I am a prophet only. I am a voice crying in the wilderness. But I am a warning and I speak true. Heed me, repent, be baptised, and be saved!'

There were amens and hallelujahs, and we all surged forward, following John as he turned and pushed out into deeper water – up to our thighs or waists – where one by one we submitted to the prophet's bellowed call to the Lord to forgive and cleanse and bless us, followed by the push down, head and shoulders, everything under, held there longer, I thought, than necessary, this being after all a symbolic ablution not a scrub down.

I can't say I came up feeling anything but wet and breathless. Jesus submitted to it along with the rest, and was not acknowledged as anyone known to the prophet until the whole process was complete and the day's crowd was dispersing.

The cousins were fond of one another – there was no doubt of that – but there was also rivalry, mixed with disapproval on either side, which had been there since they were boys. Jesus, I'm sure, thought John heavy-handed, unsubtle, a blunderer in the thickets of theology. John probably thought Jesus lightweight, too ready in those days to forgive, too full of clever parables, riddles and indirections. But they kissed now, pleased to be meeting, and sat together talking.

The half-dozen of us who had come with Jesus sat apart under the trees, wondering how and where we would eat a proper meal (there had been no breakfast), and whether it would mean sharing John's raw locusts, since he was known always to refuse cooked food of any kind, including even bread. We'd asked about this along the way, and Jesus had given his usual answer, that we shouldn't give too much thought to eating and drinking. God would provide.

'*John* will provide,' I corrected. 'That's what's worrying us.'

Jesus had smiled. 'I can tell you from my days in the desert, there's nothing nicer than crunching up a mouthful of locusts when you've worked up an appetite.'

Now, since the immersion, we'd been given a jug of goat's milk to pass around, and some figs and wild honey on a vine leaf, so some of the anxiety, though not all of the hunger, had abated.

I found myself beside Bartholomew. The youngest of the disciples, Bart in those days was always in a state of excitement, exaggerating everything, misreading every sign, always out of his depth, swept along by the beauty and power of Jesus.

We were all loyal to Jesus. We were a team, he was our captain and we were proud of his fame, some of which rubbed off on us. We might quarrel among ourselves, but against the world we presented a united front. But Bart was more than loyal. He was blind. He was in love. Jesus could do no wrong. Jesus was the greatest.

'Did you notice what John said about Jesus?' Bart asked me. 'He acknowledged Jesus was his Master.'

I shook my head, irritated by this naive lad's excesses. 'I don't think he said anything at all about Jesus.'

'Didn't you listen? He said that one will come whose sandal –'

'He won't be fit to fasten. Yes,' I acknowledged. 'He did say that. He meant the Messiah.'

In a kind of triumphant whisper Bartholomew hissed at me, 'Fool! *He meant Jesus.*'

> Ptolemy, our
> visiting evangelist,
> relates
>
> how Jesus drove
> devils out of a
> madman. They fled
>
> into a herd of
> swine which in turn
> panicked and ran
>
> into the sea. I
> recall it differently
> of course –
>
> how we were blamed
> for the pig stampede
> and asked to leave;
>
> how the farmer
> cursed us, weeping
> at his loss, raving

close to madness;
and what guilt we
felt. Truly it seemed

if these were God's
ways, they were
darkly mysterious.

CHAPTER 11

THERE WERE OFTEN WOMEN IN OUR GROUP. SOME WERE DISCIPLES' wives, although I noticed that most of those stayed at home, and two or three disapproved strongly of their husband's attachment to Jesus. Some were wives or widows who believed they owed Jesus a debt for having cured a family member, usually a child, of an illness. Others hoped for a cure themselves. Some, I thought, were in love with him, dazed by his good looks, his rich voice, his charm and virtue; and there was always one or another bringing him a special dish, or waiting for a chance to wash his feet, or wanting permission to anoint his head with an expensive oil. But Jesus looked at them, and looked at us all, with such an equal, benevolent, undifferentiating – even unfocused – gaze, I thought there was no chance that anything inconvenient or disruptive would come of it.

They came and went. Their number waxed and waned, increasing whenever a story of a miracle went about, and then declining until there was another. We were a ragged bunch. There were some lovely people among the followers, some strange and unwholesome people, and some who were stupid, thick as bricks, crazed, or stark mad. I was forever noticing differences, evaluating, criticising, awarding pluses and minuses. That was my way, my temperament. Once it had been his, too; now these distinctions seemed to pass Jesus by. Gone was the clever intolerant lad of our childhood and youth. With the Essenes, it seemed, he had learned the secret of tolerance. As long as they accepted him on his terms, and as their leader, all were welcome; all were God's creatures and loved by a Father whose arms would always be open to receive them.

This openness to everything was admirable in its way and yet I not only couldn't rise to it, copy it, make it my example, I couldn't even (though intellectually I thought I probably should) admire it. My sense of order was affronted by it. A part of me – quite a strong part – thought it was sloppy.

'How can you stand that creature near you?' I would ask.

Jesus might smile and say nothing; or he might say, 'So long as she can stand to be near me, there's no problem.'

Or if I made my complaint too emphatic, too explicit, he would kiss me mockingly on the cheek and say, 'Judas, darling, at heart you're a Pharisee.'

When I worried about where the next meal was coming from (I was often extremely hungry) he would chide me for fussing. He would urge me to look at the ravens, which didn't sow or reap, but which the Lord made sure didn't go unfed.

I wanted to tell him this 'don't fuss, God will provide' attitude was easy for him because he'd learned with the Essenes to live on scraps, but I had not; also that if he would take time to observe the ravens instead of just rhapsodising about them, he would notice that in their own way (which did not, of course, involve sowing and reaping) they worked very hard.

But by now he had a degree of authority over me. He was no longer just my boyhood friend. I needed him, acknowledged him as my leader, sometimes rebelled inwardly, but remained silent.

And then, too, just when I might be reaching the end of my patience, working myself up to complain that one of our supporters was a layabout or a thief and that we needed more order and discipline, he would say something striking in conversation, or in one of his sermons, something so beautiful I would be lost in wonder at it and feel ashamed of myself. 'Look at the lilies of the field. They don't labour, they can't spin, and yet Solomon in all his glory couldn't match their beauty.'

He often spoke of the 'pure in heart', and in him, at that time, I saw what it meant. He made sense of the phrase by exemplifying it. That was his character, or the part of his character that had developed at Qumran with the brotherhood. But it was a quality I knew, or thought I knew, couldn't survive, unchallenged and untarnished, in the real world.

He never enquired how his followers lived their lives. There were irregular relationships among them, 'sinful' unions, but he seemed not to know, or to want to know. The message was what mattered, and after our visit to John at the ford the message became more than ever one of love, charity, harmony, forgiveness and peace. It was as if the darkness and rolling thunder of John's preaching, its threats, its lack of charm and gentleness, had helped Jesus define the different path his own teaching should take. There was from him at that time no talk of vipers.

We were not to judge others. If someone deserved to be condemned and punished, that was God's business, not ours. Ours was sympathy, understanding and forgiveness. We were not only to love our neighbours but to love those who hated us, and wished us ill, and conspired against us. If someone struck us a blow on the face we were to offer the other cheek so the angry one could strike again if he felt he needed to. If we were asked to give a coin, or a coat, we were to give two coins, two coats;

if we were asked to do something, we should do it twice over.

The meek were blessed and would inherit the earth. The merciful would themselves receive mercy. The hungry, the ill, the poor and depressed would be fed, made well and made happy. The pure in heart would see God.

These were his promises, which he offered with such a clear-eyed innocence one felt they came with a warrant, sealed and stamped in heaven. And if as a consequence of following this way of life we found ourselves hated and reviled in our own communities, we should, he told us, take heart and be glad, because that had been the case also with Israel's prophets. We would be with the prophets in heaven.

He kept us on the move and we liked that, especially those of us who had no ties, no dependent family, no sense that there was work or business being neglected at home. He favoured villages and rural communities, avoiding, for the most part, the larger towns. He also stayed clear of barracks and garrison towns. Sometimes we would see a few Roman soldiers listening at the back of the crowd when he was preaching, but there was no sign their interest was official or threatening.

On the other hand some among the disciples recognised, in the crowds, men they knew to belong to one of the residences of Herod Antipas. We thought these had probably been posted as spies, and Jesus took care not to give them cause to report back. There was an element of rebellion in his message but it was always hidden, oblique, unspecific. Asked by a spy whether people should pay their taxes, he said one should give to Caesar whatever was due to Caesar, and to God whatever was due to God. It seemed a compliant answer, but the more you turned it over in your mind, the more ambiguous it became.

He also avoided Nazareth. Once, when the most direct route

to our next stop would have taken us through our home village, he insisted on an alternative. I asked about his family, and suggested we should surely call on them, but his face set hard, he shook his head and turned away.

'What about Andreas?' I persisted.

He kept his back to me. 'I've given my instructions,' he said.

I bridled. 'I have a mother in Nazareth.'

He turned on me, his eyes blazing. 'And I have a Father in heaven.'

I was astonished. What did he mean? 'Well you go to heaven,' I said. 'I'm going to Nazareth.'

And I went. I stayed two nights with my mother, spent a lot of time in the bathhouse, and had her cook me some very large meals. I called on Andreas, who cooked me another, not so large, but wonderfully rich in ingredients and (as he would say) 'beautifully presented'.

I told him he shouldn't take offence at not seeing Jesus. 'He hasn't forgiven Nazareth. He says he's shaken the dust of his hometown off his feet and he won't be back.'

'I'm not surprised,' Andreas said. 'We treated him very badly.'

He told me he'd heard one of Jesus' brothers say he was insane and needed to be locked up. 'I hear stories about his preaching,' Andreas said. 'And healing.' His tone didn't make it seem he was altogether pleased.

I said it was a pity he hadn't heard him at his best.

'It's said there are . . .' Andreas hesitated, and then brought it out. 'Miracles?'

'Cures. Yes, it seems so.'

He asked had I seen these things myself and I said I thought I had.

'Blindness cured? The lame made to walk?'

I explained that we often used those phrases as metaphors. They weren't always meant to be taken literally.

'But they are.'

I shrugged. There were bound to be misunderstandings, exaggerations.

He persisted. 'So there have been no miracles.'

'People say there have.'

'But you haven't seen them.'

I said I'd seen people cured of illnesses. And I'd seen a madman, one who seemed quite out of control, mysteriously calmed by Jesus. I acknowledged that I hadn't seen anything that could be called a miracle. Not unequivocally. Not yet. 'The time will come,' I said.

He sighed and patted me on the arm. 'Yes, I suppose it will.'

When I returned to Capernaum I found my fellow disciples in a state of excitement. Something had happened – 'a miracle' (or 'another miracle') – but each new account I heard was different from the one before. A man in the village, one of the fishing community, had been suddenly attacked by a palsy. One day he was strong and well, the next his hands shook violently, he was weak, his whole body trembled when he tried to hold himself up.

It was Zebedee, the father of James and John, who first said aloud what others must have been thinking: 'Jesus will fix him.' The disciples were uncertain, knowing that Jesus reacted angrily to the idea that he could be counted on to cure anyone at any time. 'I'm not a repairman,' he would say. But soon a crowd had gathered outside Simon Peter's house, carrying the man with the palsy.

I heard different accounts of how Jesus had behaved. One told me he'd 'taken it in his stride'. Another insisted he'd tried to escape, but that he'd been unable to get away because the street and the courtyard were full of people calling for him to 'come out and do his stuff'. He was in the room he always occupied, up under the roof, refusing to move. There was an outside stone stairway from the courtyard up on to the roofs, and some of the crowd got up there. Soon they had torn away some of the tiles and were lowering the man into Jesus' room. Others got in by forcing the front door.

The man, supported by his friends, was pushed at Jesus. He couldn't speak, just shivered and gibbered. He tried to put his hands together in supplication but they remained apart, wavering and shaking in the air like the hands of one who couldn't swim, sinking into the sea.

Jesus looked at him without his usual kindness or warmth and said, 'Your sins are forgiven.'

There was a rabbi in the crowd who had lately complained of Jesus, and in fact of all of us, saying we neglected the Sabbath, were careless about observances, and committed many kinds of sacrilege. He was hanging in through the broken roof, not able to let himself down but unwilling to miss the drama. 'What do you mean his sins are forgiven?' he demanded. 'Only the Lord can forgive his sins. Are you putting yourself in His place? This is sacrilege.'

Jesus looked up at him and then looked at the fisherman, still trembling and shaking. Jesus took him by both wrists, very tight, and spoke to him, close up and so quietly no one was quite sure what he'd said.

What happened next depended on who was telling the story. Some said the cure was instantaneous, others that it didn't happen until next day. But no one seemed in any doubt that the palsy was now gone, that Jesus was responsible, and that it was a miracle.

The man was back at work, out on the boats, casting nets as before, and Jesus' reputation in all of Galilee, if it had ever been in doubt, was secure. People were saying they rated him ahead of John the Baptist. John, after all, for all the power of his preaching and the thoroughness of his baptisms, was not known to be capable of miracles.

Jesus made no mention of this to me when I returned, though I'm sure he knew I would have heard about it. He didn't speak of my defection either. I wasn't reproached, but I didn't feel I was forgiven. There was a chill between us. He'd grown closer to the fishermen, or wanted me to feel that he had. They were simpler and, as I suppose he saw it, more loyal, less questioning, more trustworthy. They, of course, had never trusted me, seeing me as a spoilt rich boy, a snob, sceptical, over-educated, clumsy as a net caster and no use at all at mending. When they told me of the cure of the palsied man I felt they were putting me in my place.

It was only a short time later that Jesus' family turned up at the lake and wanted to talk to him. Word of the miracle had reached them and I suppose they'd begun to think he might be worth reclaiming. They came like a delegation, led by Mary, but with Joseph there too, looking embarrassed and reluctant, and some of the brothers and sisters.

Jesus had taken to preaching every second evening from one of Zebedee's fishing boats anchored a few yards out. People assembled on the shore to listen. Quite a crowd had gathered, and Jesus was just going into his preparatory mode – a state of deep prayer that always preceded his sermons – when James called to me and pointed out that the family had arrived. 'You know them, Judas. You'd better deal with them.'

Mary greeted me in her usual effusive, slightly mad way. 'Judas dear, how healthy you're looking. This life must suit you. I think you must be a Bedouin, are you? You look sunburned enough, for heaven's sake. A regular heathen in those colours. But you're very thin, aren't you? Are you getting enough to eat? I'm told you've all become beggars, I hope it's not true. But why *is* that naughty boy of mine keeping you away from your poor mother?'

I forced a smile and said it was nice to see her, and to see them all.

'Well of course we're here to see Jesus,' she said. 'Will you tell him please?'

'Now?'

'Yes please, dear, if you wouldn't mind.'

I said he was just about to begin.

'Well I'm sure he can spare me a moment, Judas. I am his mother, after all.'

I told her I thought she might have to wait until he'd finished, but I would take the message.

I pushed my way through to where Jesus was about to wade out to the boat. It wasn't easy to reach him. People were jostling for places near the front and didn't want to let me through.

I grasped his arm and told him his mother had come. 'In fact your whole family. She wants to speak to you.'

His face flushed with anger. 'My family?'

He turned away from me, but I still had my hand on his arm. 'What do I tell her?'

'Tell her these are my family.' He waved a hand over the crowd. 'Tell her to go away.'

'I can't give her that message.'

He looked at me with what I thought of as his stone face. 'Tell her.'

I started to protest. Why should I be the one? But he'd shaken me off and was wading out to where James was holding the boat.

I was angry now, caught between this weird woman and her powerful son. Should I care if he hurt her feelings? I pushed my way back through the crowd. 'He won't speak to you,' I told her. 'He says these people are his family.'

Mary's face set hard. It was the same face Jesus had just turned on me – the stone face. Joseph was squirming. The lachrymose sisters began to weep. The brothers were muttering 'We told you so' kinds of things.

Mary's eyes glittered. 'He stabs me to the heart, that boy. Of course my pain doesn't concern him, it never has. He was always indifferent to my suffering. Come,' she said to her flock. 'I won't stay to listen to such an ungrateful child.'

'Now that we're here . . .' Joseph began.

'Never,' Mary said. 'I won't give him that satisfaction.'

Jesus was already speaking, beginning with a prayer, and must have seen and heard his mother leaving, making as much noise and disturbance as she could. It affected his preaching. At first he seemed to find no coherence, no clear direction. Then, gradually, after she'd gone and the crowd had settled down, it came to him. It was something new, something I hadn't heard from him before. He bristled with threat and anger. He had not come into the world to bring peace, but a sword. He had come to set brother against brother, child against parent, to divide families and people in the name of the Lord. Only thus would the Lord's purpose be fulfilled. It was important to be resolute, not to be weak.

The message was powerful and, in its uncompromising way, exciting; but I was astonished, and disconcerted. Where was the Jesus who had said the peacemakers were blessed and would see God?

When he was finished and the crowd had gone we gathered, as we did most evenings, around a fire on the lakeshore. There was an awkward silence until Simon Peter said what a powerful sermon it had been. There were murmurs of agreement. 'Wonderful.' 'Remarkable.' This was the reassurance Jesus needed and looked for. I felt contempt for them. Surely this wasn't what they really thought.

I asked, 'Is it enough for us to feel the power? I thought we were supposed to understand the message.'

Jesus turned to me, slowly. I felt his anger again. 'There's something you didn't understand, Judas?'

I said, 'You've preached forgiveness and harmony and peace, and now, suddenly, you tell us you've come to create dissension and war.'

His eyes blazed. 'Why did you go to Nazareth?'

It was no response to what I'd said, and so surprised me I could find no answer.

'And if my mother comes again,' (he was addressing us all now), 'keep her away from me.'

He turned from us and walked up the beach towards Simon Peter's house.

'You've upset him,' James said, and I saw they were all looking at me reproachfully.

Why was I never
there when the palsied
limbs were touched

out of tremor, when
the eyes of the dead
were opened

and met smile with
smile? In my dream
the wood fire still burns

by the lake, your
hand on my shoulder
is forgiving.

'The sceptic is
blind,' you tell me
and I answer, 'Yes,

blind to what never
happened.' You turn
away from me

and I wake
remembering my role:
'The Betrayer'.

CHAPTER 12

THE ANGER ABATED, I WAS FORGIVEN, AND THE EVEN-
tempered Jesus, the advocate of peace and harmony, the defender
of the poor, the downtrodden and unfortunate, returned. I'd had
a glimpse of another Jesus, but some time would pass before I
saw it again.

There were at that time two influences on him from outside
the chosen twelve, both women, both called Mary. One was
known as Mary Magdalene because her family came from
Magdala on the shores of Galilee. The other was the Mary who
lived at Bethany with her sister Martha and her brother Lazarus.
They were as different one from the other as both were from
his first Mary, the mother he couldn't abide.

Jesus had first befriended Mary Magdalene, and had very probably saved her life, while I was still a married man waiting for
the birth of my child. He had a way of striking up conversa-
tions with strangers in public squares and at wells and fountains,
even sometimes with women if they would listen – a practice
that was found scandalous by some of his more conservative
followers. He had met Mary Magdalene in this way and found
her straight-talking and responsive to his message. Later, in entirely
different circumstances, he encountered her again.

She was this time accused of having been unfaithful to her

husband, and Jesus had come on the scene (that chance itself a miracle, Mary would later say) in a little town square outside the synagogue where he had preached only the night before, urging the forgiveness of sins. Mary was standing, head bowed, her accusers, husband and brother-in-law, on either side, grasping her by the arms. While the rabbis hearing the case were discussing what the punishment should be, the senior of the three noticed the 'would-be prophet' of the night before who had argued that God had more reason to give His love to a sinner than to a virtuous person, because the virtuous person was already saved.

It's possible they were having difficulty arriving at a decision. There were witnesses to the crime, but uncertainty whether they were honest, or merely bribed by a husband who wanted to be rid of an inconvenient wife. In any case an amusing idea occurred to the senior rabbi, who liked to set traps for itinerant preachers. He would trick this one into either contradicting himself, or contradicting the prophet Moses.

'Jesus of Nazareth,' he called. 'There are witnesses to this woman's sin. The law of Moses decrees the punishment, that she be stoned to death. Must the law be applied?'

Jesus was standing in the shade of some trees at the edge of the square and, instead of replying, he crouched and wrote something in the dust with his finger. The three rabbis crowded around him, craning to see what he had written, but it seemed to be in a foreign script, one they couldn't read.

There was a moment of hesitation and confusion before the senior rabbi put the question again. 'Well then, do you have an answer, prophet of Nazareth? Should the law of Moses be applied?'

Jesus looked at him and said, 'You are the judicial authority here?'

The rabbi replied that he was.

Jesus asked, 'And what is the Lord's part in the process?'

The rabbi pulled an impatient face, as if the question was meaningless, or impertinent, or the answer obvious. 'We must interpret the Lord's will.'

Once again Jesus crouched down and wrote with his finger in the dust, and once again, although this time they knew it would be unintelligible, the rabbis couldn't resist craning to look.

Still crouching, Jesus said to them, as if interpreting the mysterious script, 'You must decide the sentence. But if this woman is to be stoned to death, the Lord would want the first stone to be cast by one who has never sinned.' He stood again, looking at the little crowd. Speaking now as if authorised by the rabbis, he asked that such a person, 'a man without sin', step forward.

Jesus had a penetrating gaze and an air of authority. It was possible at times to believe God was looking at you through those eyes. 'A man without sin,' he repeated in his very clear voice that echoed off the stones. They all looked away, up into the air or down at their feet. After a moment they began, first one, then two and three at a time, to shrug and turn away, as if the matter was of no interest, or none of their business, or they had more important things to think about. Soon there were only the rabbis (now arguing among themselves on the point of law Jesus had raised) and the two accusers, who looked less confident and had released their hold on Mary's arms.

'Let her come with me,' Jesus said. 'You will be rid of her, and she will be saved.'

He led her away, leaving silence and uncertainty. The junior rabbis were angry with their senior for confusing the process by engaging the upstart from Nazareth. The senior regretted it too, but saved face by assuring the complainants it was an excellent outcome.

Jesus and Mary travelled together, and kept on going through the night in case there should be a change of mind behind them. Late the next day, tired, hungry and dusty, they came to a village where Jesus knew he had followers. He found one of these who kept a lodging house, and asked him to take the woman in. The man said he would. He provided them with a meal.

When they'd eaten, Jesus said his farewells. 'You're free,' he told Mary Magdalene.

'I'm a divorced woman,' she said. 'How will I live?'

Jesus assured her that God would provide. He gave her the example of the ravens, kissed her, and departed.

Two years later (by which time I was part of the team) Jesus was back in the same region with five of us. We were invited to supper with a man called Simon who believed his skin condition had been cured by a laying on of hands and a blessing bestowed during the earlier visit. While Simon's servants were preparing the meal the door opened and a woman, whom Jesus recognised as the same Mary Magdalene, came in carrying a small alabaster box. Simon stood up, apologising. 'I'm sorry. This is not a virtuous woman, but she has been very insistent. There's something she wants to thank you for.'

To Mary he said, 'Please say what you have to say and leave.'

She knelt in front of Jesus and asked for a bowl of water. It was brought and she washed his feet, dabbing them dry with her long hair, and kissing them. She opened the white box, elegantly carved with the shapes of palm trees. A scent of spikenard filled the room. Jesus' feet were cracked and sore from walking. She massaged the ointment into them.

When it was done she stood up, took his hands and kissed them. 'That is my debt to you,' she said. 'You saved me. I thank you for giving me my life.'

Jesus' expression was uncertain. 'Did I save you? This man says you are a sinner.'

'You told me God provides for the ravens,' she said. 'I am not a raven, so I have to provide for myself. I sell my body to live.'

Jesus hesitated only a moment. I could see that he liked her – probably remembered liking her at their earlier encounter. 'Come with us,' he said, 'and I'll show you how the ravens keep house – without sin.'

Simon Peter, James and Andrew, and even young Bartholomew, were shocked. So was Simon our host. They didn't spare her feelings, pointing out it was a kind of ointment, and a kind of box, that would have cost a great deal. Where had the money come from, if not from sin? If this was an act of repentance, wouldn't it have been better spent on the poor? And did Jesus really want a woman of doubtful virtue kissing his feet and hands, and tagging along with us?

Jesus shook his head at them. 'I welcome this woman, as I welcomed you, my friends. It's the same welcome.' He raised his cup and drank. 'As to the poor, you will have them till the end of time. Me – I might be gone tomorrow.' And he laughed.

Mary Magdalene became one of his most dependable followers. There could be no doubt he loved her, trusted her, forgave her trespasses, enjoyed her robust personality, and I'm sure would have made her one of the disciples if she'd been a man. When he was in his dark moods and harangued us for our failings, he often accused one, or all twelve, of lack of faith. He told us we were weak, untrustworthy, vacillating, irresolute. In those moods he would compare us unfavourably with Mary, telling us she never wavered, and would never doubt, deny or betray him.

Simon Peter complained once that he loved her more than he loved the rest of us. And it was sometimes rumoured, especially among people on the fringes of our movement, that she was his secret lover. I don't believe this was so. Jesus was capable of self-contradiction (you could say, in fact, that he was a specialist), but not of secret hypocrisy. If he had wanted Mary Magdalene in his bed that's where she would have been, but he was not like ordinary men. I sometimes lay awake at night, missing Judith, weeping for my loss, aware that the lithe body of Mary Magdalene was lying not far from mine and that I might find comfort there, but knowing that, though she might do me that favour, she didn't want my body, wanted only the body of Jesus, who didn't want hers.

Jesus loved us, his followers, some more than others, but all of us, I think, only as representatives of humankind. Likewise he loved humankind, but only as representative of the Creator. It was a love so unspecific, so vast and generalised, I look back on it now and can no longer understand it – and perhaps could not understand it then.

The other Mary, the one from Bethany, was the sister of Martha and Lazarus. All three loved Jesus and he them – but they were very different from those of us who travelled with him. Puritanical and proper, I can't imagine any of them would have been able to put up with the uncertainties, the restrictions on possessions, the 'making do', the erratic meals, the casualness about observances, and the begging that were our lot on the road – not to mention the rigours of dealing with adoring crowds, which became, as time went by, as bad as the rigours of rejection we'd suffered during our earliest days together. Then there was the tribe of the diseased, the leprous, the crippled, the insane, who pushed themselves at us, or were pushed by their families and friends, clamouring for cures, breathing in our faces, stinking. Lazarus and his sisters would have been upset, too, by the quarrels, the competition for the Master's attention, which were becoming a part of our daily life. Like a number of Jesus' better-off supporters (Joseph of Arimathea was another) they were not cut out for life on the road.

Of the three siblings it was Mary Jesus especially loved. Was there something about the name – that he'd failed to love his mother Mary and so had to love anyone else of that name who crossed his path? Martha loved him too, quite as much as her sister did, and even complained to him, when he visited, that she had to cook and serve while Mary sat at his feet and engaged him in conversation. He told her Mary had chosen that role for herself and should be allowed to keep it, which seemed a less direct but hardly less brutal way of telling Martha to get on with being the servant and stop complaining.

Lazarus was the darkly brooding one of the three. When Jesus first knew them the brother had been deeply unhappy, not about anything in particular, but from some profound inner gloom, some dark hand (as he described it) that closed upon his heart and squeezed tighter week by week, keeping him in bed for days on end, unable to work, to eat, to wash, or even to pray. The sisters had heard of the powers of the new preacher from Nazareth, and had gone to him asking whether he could help their brother. Jesus had warmed to these two plain, unmarried sisters, and agreed to come to their house, where their brother was in bed, close to death.

He stayed with them for some days, talking to Lazarus about Israel's history and Israel's God, and about the scriptures, retelling the ancient stories of the prophets and prophecies, quoting long passages, reminding him of what futures were predicted for the Jewish race, and attempting to interpret those prophecies in modern terms.

Lazarus was inspired. For the first time in many months he began to wash and to eat the meals that were prepared for him. He got up, worked at their little garden plot, fixed things that had been broken, smiled and sometimes laughed – a laugh, his sister said, that was like the sound of last season's rusty, unoiled shears.

Lazarus had been so emaciated, spiritless and close to death, the sisters referred to Jesus' first visit as the time of their brother's resurrection. Jesus, they said, had raised Lazarus from the dead. Thereafter his life had focus, purpose, direction. He was totally committed, the first person I heard say boldly and without embarrassment that Jesus was the Messiah. At the time I took this (I was a slow learner!) as a symptom of his return to health, not as an idea anyone would entertain seriously. But I was later to wonder to what extent Jesus himself had been responsible for planting it during those long sessions they'd had together in the bedroom, when the scriptures and the prophecies were discussed with such intensity.

We were now on the road more than ever, always moving on, never all twelve together, but anything from six to ten of us, depending who might be ill, or called home by family or work. Sometimes we stood in support of Jesus while he preached; sometimes we went ahead to announce his approach; sometimes (as he required) we presented the message ourselves. My own talents as a preacher were only as large as my convictions, which were always shaky, but I was not alone among the twelve in this failing. Jesus urged faith on us constantly. Faith would move mountains. If we believed, we could do anything, could live without food, could walk on water. That was something he told us often, and I was not the only one to have a nightmare in which Jesus, walking on the lake, called to me to come to him from Zebedee's boat. I set off towards him and, after a few safe steps, began to sink, and woke thrashing about in my blanket, gasping for air and calling him to come and rescue me. Simon Peter had the same dream, and we used to joke about it and tell one another, 'I've had the walking-on-water nightmare.'

Belief was what he required of us, and it was where we all, at one time or another, failed him. We did our best, some much better than others. Temperamentally sceptical, I was clearly first among the non-achievers.

This inconsistency of faith even in a team so bound to him and to the way of life he'd created probably explains his secret revelation (if that's the right way to describe it) to Simon Peter, James and John – the three whose faith in him was strongest, simplest and least wavering. We were travelling along the Jordan Valley after visiting Lazarus and the sisters at Bethany. The intention had been to go on to Jerusalem – a prospect that excited us, provincials as we were. And then, so close to our goal, Jesus told us the plan was cancelled. It was as if he'd received instructions from above, or suffered a sudden lapse of confidence. We were not to go there, he said, until all thirteen could go together, and then it would be for the festival of Passover.

So we were back on the road to Galilee. Jesus had been moody and reflective, perhaps disappointed not to be making for the holy city. He'd declined his share of generous baskets of food given by a family who believed he'd cured their baby of an illness – and he remained silent through the afternoon.

Our road was taking us around the base of one of the mountains of that region when he came abruptly out of his trance and announced a further change of plan. We would make camp where we were, and spend the night in one of the caves in the hillside. The chosen three were to come with him up the mountainside. We remaining four should prepare a supper from food left over in the baskets; if they were not back by sundown, we should eat our share without waiting for them.

We ate our meal, and when it was time to retire there was still no sign of them. Next morning we were arguing whether we should sit tight or go in search when we saw them in the distance coming down out of the fawn- and mauve-coloured upper hillside and entering the green of the lower, cultivated slopes. In single file they waded through fields of grain, Simon Peter in the lead, waving to us, then James and John, Jesus bringing up the rear.

We gave them what was left of last night's meal. They ate hungrily. Nothing was said about where they'd been and what they'd done. The three who had accompanied Jesus looked solemn and (I thought) smug – self-important. It was one of those times when Jesus created dissension by favouring one or several of us over the rest.

I took him aside and demanded to know what had happened. He shook his head. 'When it's time for you to know, you'll hear.'

I asked what was wrong with the present.

He said, 'You're not ready.'

'And those three are?'

He inclined his head. 'Your faith is not secure, Judas.'

'You mean I'm not gullible.'

'I mean you're not innocent.'

'Are you pleased to be believed by three very stupid men?'

He patted my arm. 'Be patient. Your time will come.'

I thought for a moment, and then said – it was an impulse,

not the first nor the last of its kind – 'I think I've had enough of this.'

It came out like that, sadly. He looked into my eyes and held me by the wrist. 'Are you going to leave me?' His eyes filled with tears.

I didn't answer, but I was surprised, and already I was wavering. What did I have to go back to? My mother's house with all its reminders of my beloved Judith; my father's, full of his coldness, displeasure and disappointment. Here I had companionship, and it seemed I had love.

He asked, 'Who will I have to talk to if you go?'

I replied, 'The three you took up the mountain.' But he could see I was relenting.

He put an arm around my shoulder. 'Trust me,' he said. 'Everything will make sense in the end.'

So I was told nothing. But inevitably the hints and rumours about what had happened on the mountaintop began at once, and the stories grew more astonishing, without ever being relayed in anything more than whispers and asides. Jesus had led the three up there and had asked them to wait and keep watch while he prayed. He had knelt a very long time in the wind that always seems to race vertically up those steep slopes. This much was common to all versions of the story. Also common was that each of the three crouching, and finally lying, in the shelter of thorn bushes, fighting hunger and exhaustion as darkness came down, had fallen asleep, but had woken later, sure that something remarkable was happening – some kind of revelation, a divine presence.

In the most particular account Simon Peter was said to have seen Jesus' torn, travel-stained burnous transformed, as he knelt in prayer, into a garment of perfect whiteness, the whiteness of fresh snow shining in the dark. At that moment two mighty persons appeared above his head. Simon Peter knew them to be Moses and Elijah, though he didn't know how he knew. They talked to Jesus and Jesus answered.

James had seen nothing at all, but had heard a big voice speaking out of the darkness, saying, 'This is my Son. Worship him.'

John had slept a tormented sleep from which he remembered nothing but a sense of magnitude and terror unlike anything he'd experienced before. Hearing what Simon Peter had seen and James had heard, he too was convinced that Jesus had brought them into the divine presence.

Three of our number, it could be said, now knew, or believed they knew, that we had been engaged in the service of the Messiah.

> In an Arab tale
> the hero comes armed
> with a sword
>
> to defeat the stiff–
> backed fathers and
> bears her away
>
> on a white
> stallion. Jesus came
> on foot armed only
>
> with argument
> and a finger
> to trace in the dust.

Was he remembering
our play, and the
power of words

that only One
could read? Was his
secret text in Greek

or as Mary
believed, in the
language of Heaven?

CHAPTER 13

TWO DAYS AGO WE HAD FRESH NEWS FROM JERUSALEM. THREE OF the Jesus sect, two men and a woman, came looking for Ptolemy, and I heard the news as they relayed it to him. But something else became clear to me. I've sometimes wondered why Ptolemy seems so familiar – partly his appearance, but more his voice. These visitors treated him with such respect I took one of them aside, the older of the two men, called Ezra, and asked was my guest very senior in their movement?

I was told he was 'one of the most important persons alive'. I must have looked disbelieving.

'Ptolemy has authority because . . .' Ezra fixed me with the look (how often I have seen it!) of one bound to secrecy but longing to tell. 'But I am not permitted to say.'

'Because he is one who saw Jesus?' That was a thought that had crossed my mind once or twice when I'd heard him say things it seemed only someone who had been there could have known.

Ezra bowed his head, a solemn affirmation. Clearly the thought of having been in the divine presence was overwhelming to him.

'But you mean something more?'

Again he bowed in the affirmative, even while repeating, 'I am not permitted to say.'

He didn't need to. It had come to me. 'He was one of the twelve,' I whispered, and the man's face screwed up tight, squeezing against the tears that flooded his eyes.

'The secret's safe,' I assured him. 'I'll say nothing, and I won't ask his name.'

But I knew. Ptolemy. Bartholomew. It was his blindness, in addition to the depredations of forty years, that had concealed his identity from me. And of course the same blindness meant he could not recognise me. I was protected by that – and even more (since blind men develop excellent ears for voices) by his 'knowledge' that I, Judas of Keraiyot, was dead, hanged from a fig tree, or impaled on a ploughshare in a field bought with the money my betrayal of Jesus had earned me.

'He was not always blind?' I asked.

'After he had seen the crucifixion,' Ezra explained, 'God wished him to see no more.'

I tried to make sense of that, and couldn't. Bartholomew had been one of those who ran away when Jesus was arrested, and so had not seen it.

I asked why secrecy was necessary.

'We have enemies.' He frowned. 'Perhaps there's no longer the need there once was. But we protect Ptolemy – along with the two other surviving disciples.'

'There are just two?' I wanted to ask who they were but I could see he was beginning to feel he'd said too much.

'Just two,' he confirmed, and turned away from me.

But the news from Jerusalem: it seems the Roman noose has now closed tight on the city, but while there were still, now and then, people escaping, and a few given permission to pass through the Roman lines, the picture emerging from within was one of revolution and a reign of terror. The people – the plebs – are in control, though even among themselves they're divided into competing groups, each led by a rebel chief. There are now no Romans left alive inside the city; but neither are there wealthy Jews. They, together with most of the middle class and the Temple priests, have either escaped, or have been tried before people's courts and executed. A few have survived by convincing these courts that they are, and have always been, passionately opposed to Rome, to the Herods, and to the priesthood. Some have been allowed to become officers in the militia the city raises against the Romans, and have led heroic attacks outside the walls. These, however, always end in defeat.

Food is running out. All kinds of animals, from camels to cats, and not excluding donkeys, birds, rats and snakes, have been butchered, cooked and eaten. Stored grain that might have kept the siege at bay for years has been burned in the course of warring between the different insurgent groups. The population is starving.

There are stories of men marching into battle over the bodies of their dead comrades killed in the battle before, and the one before that, advancing against the massed Roman shields on roads so slippery with blood no one can easily keep a foothold; and of daily crucifixions of captured militia and escaping civilians, as many as five hundred every day. With supplies of wooden posts for crosses running low, victims are sometimes nailed to wooden doors or walls, arranged at different angles, sideways, upside down, limbs interlocking and overlapping – however they can be made to fit into the space. So a vertical surface is turned into a writhing groaning weeping shrieking mass of nailed and dying men and women.

Sometimes, as the battle goes on, the Roman soldiers grow weary of killing, complaining of pulled muscles, strained backs, tired arms, and ask to be allowed to stop and rest. But inside the city another troop of doomed defenders is formed, and another, and another, every man terrified of the people's courts and willing to take his chance outside the walls in the hope that he will be able to make a show of fighting and then escape into the countryside – which a few succeed in doing.

Ezra tells us a story of a group of Jewish merchants who, while the Romans were still allowing some of the wealthy to escape, bribed their way out through the siege lines, having first swallowed enough gold coins each to begin life and business again in some faraway place. Past the Romans, however, they were stopped by a tribe of Bedouin who, suspecting they must have wealth hidden somewhere, tortured them for information. When one admitted where their gold was, all were disembowelled, robbed, and left to die in the late-afternoon sun, while the jackals slunk closer and the vultures went to work on their entrails even before the last breath had been taken.

As these stories are told of a turmoil that has spread right through Judaea and into Galilee, I find myself grieving for the holy city, for my region and my people. I wonder how friends and family have fared, consoling myself that most of those once near to me are dead, but still feeling distressed at the knowledge that everything that framed the society of my childhood is being smashed and swept away. I thank God, or my stars, or Fortune – anyone listening – for the blessings of a new identity, a new home and culture, a wife and children and grandchildren, and for the blessings of peace.

Ptolemy (I watch him more closely than ever now I know he is Bartholomew) puts on the stern face of a judge as we consider the news. 'This destruction', he pronounces, 'was foretold. The

Lord sent His son to rule over Israel, and our people gave him to the Romans to be crucified. How could it be expected that, after such a betrayal, Heaven would protect us, and protect our Temple?'

Though he says this coldly, even with a certain satisfaction, and though I'm sure he means it, I think there's also shock – a twinge of sadness too.

This afternoon we all, including Theseus and Autolycus, went to the little square where Ptolemy now has a regular following, some of them ready to declare themselves 'Christian', and even to submit to an informal baptism at the trough, the broad rim of which he uses as his speaking platform. Ezra asked permission to preach, and Ptolemy yielded to him, perhaps reluctantly, but with good grace.

Ezra told his ragged congregation a story about Jesus having performed yet another miracle, proving again that he was the Son of God, sent with special powers to redeem mankind. A large crowd ('at least five thousand', Ezra said) had followed Jesus into a remote place not far from the lake, where he preached to them, assuring them that though they were poor they would be rich in heaven; and that on the other hand the rich would, most of them, be debarred from entering. A wealthy man, if he'd led an exceptionally virtuous life and given generously to those in need, might just get in, but only after the last of the poor had been housed in the heavenly mansions.

These teachings, Ezra went on, were cheered by the Galilean crowd, which Jesus then led in prayer.

But now the disciples pointed out that there was no food, and suggested the people should be sent on their way quickly, in time to get to their homes, or to the nearest villages, for supper.

Jesus asked what food there was and was shown five loaves and two fishes. He ordered that the crowd should arrange itself into groups of twenty or thirty, and that each should send one or two representatives to a table the disciples had set up, on which these inadequate supplies were laid out.

Jesus then broke and blessed the bread, and soon the five loaves became fifty, became five hundred, and so on . . . Likewise the two fishes, which became twenty, then two hundred . . . The table was brimming with food which was replaced as soon as it was taken by the group representatives, who were instructed to form lines. Within the hour, the five thousand were all eating happily in the late-afternoon sun.

Ezra struggled as he told this story, as if he could scarcely believe it himself. The details seemed to defeat him. I felt the sort of embarrassment one does feel when a public speaker falters, and I could imagine what was going through his mind. Was the fish served raw? Was there nothing to drink? When the meal was eaten there were supposed to be twelve baskets of leftovers, but where had the baskets come from? Who had brought them and for what purpose? I thought he'd added the table to the story, as a practical measure, but where had it come from in that (as he'd described it) 'remote place'? And in any case it wasn't sufficient. The food, as it multiplied in his imagination, was spilling everywhere, falling into the dirt trampled by the five thousand.

His listeners were restless. Some frowned, struggling to believe, or to understand. Some turned away. I heard one say, 'I liked that Ptolemy – the old blind guy. This one's not so good.'

Ptolemy himself looked anxious.

'These things are hard to understand,' Ezra said, rocking slightly up on the water trough and reaching out to the branch of a tree to steady himself. 'But that is the test the Lord God has given us through His blessed Son our saviour Jesus. Believe, my friends, and you will be saved. And now, let us pray . . .'

In the evening I went for a walk with Ptolemy, taking his arm, relieving Reuben, whom I urged to go and find entertainment in a café or tavern. We walked along, listening to the calm sea's regular breathing, enjoying its salty breath in our nostrils. I described the scene he couldn't see: the silky black water, with light from the mirror lamps on the south Sidon pier wavering across its surface; the nets spread along their racks to dry; the fishing boats moored just offshore, looking trim and ready for the predawn run; and now and then a night watchman's brazier. We stopped to listen to a group in a tavern yard playing on stringed instruments and singing Greek ballads to forlorn and lovely melodies.

We came to a part of the shore where there were no houses and no fishing boats. My mind returned to the news from Jerusalem. I felt a surge of anger at all the Jesus talk of what might be waiting for us beyond the grave – empty promises and threats that divert attention from the horror of what men do to one another in the real world.

I asked, 'Do you ever wonder why the God of Israel so favours the Romans?'

He didn't answer, but after a moment he said, 'A very long time ago I knew someone who used to ask just that kind of question in just that tone of voice.'

'A healthy sceptic no doubt.' I said it in a deeper voice, clearing my throat to excuse the altered pitch.

He was silent for a few more paces. 'Do I know you?' he asked.

'I'm your host, Idas.'

'Of course. But in the past . . . No?'

'No,' I lied. 'I'm afraid not.'

I asked whether he'd been impressed by Ezra's preaching.

'He's new to it,' Ptolemy said. 'He has to learn what's essential in a story and not let himself be distracted by details.'

I said, 'A table in a remote place – that strained credulity.' When he didn't respond I asked, 'Was there really such a miracle?'

I was testing him. I knew there had been no crowd of five thousand, and no magic multiplication of loaves and fishes into a banquet for a multitude. Ptolemy must have known it too.

'There was a miracle,' he said.

I felt pleased to have caught him out, but then he added, 'It was the miracle of *sharing*.'

'You were there?'

'People had been told to bring food but many of them were very poor and it seemed there was only a little – not anything like sufficient for a crowd of three or four dozen.'

I interrupted. 'Three or four dozen? Ezra said five thousand.'

He was unconcerned, or pretended to be. 'These stories lose nothing in the telling. And numbers don't matter.'

'Credibility matters.'

'A miracle is a miracle. There will always be doubters and disbelievers. Fifty or five thousand – the point is not in the number.'

'The point?' I was irritable. 'There's a *point*?'

'What Jesus showed us that day was that if people who have more than they need will only give to those who have less, or nothing – then there will always be enough to go around.'

'That's politics,' I said. 'Nothing to do with miracles.'

'My friend,' Ptolemy said, 'when you persuade people to share their possessions, that's more than politics. That's a miracle.'

Stories of food, of
eating, stories of
starvation —

baked rat, dried
snake behind the walls
of Jerusalem

besieged; and on
a lakeshore five
loaves and two fishes

multiplied, a
lesson in the
arithmetic of

taste. It's said eyes
are windows of the
soul, but the gut

it seems is its
door. How we wash,
what we say, before

eating concerns
the Lord, and it was
Jesus offered

his good self as
supper, bread and
wine, body and blood.

CHAPTER 14

AFTER THE MOUNTAINTOP REVELATION WE RETURNED FOR A time to the old stamping ground of Galilee. One regular route took us around the lake – Bethsaida Julias, Gergesa, Hippos, Beth-yerah, Ammathus, Tiberias, Magdala, Gennesaret, and home again to Capernaum. These were the towns and villages; but there were smaller, often unnamed, clusters of homes and farmlets, and some-times it was there that Jesus got his best hearing. Sometimes we went west to Sepphoris and the villages round about (by-passing Nazareth, however); and once, all the way to Tyre and Sidon in Phoenicia, giving me my first sight of the sea and the city which, for the past forty years, I have looked out on every day.

Capernaum remained home base. Jesus had his room in the house of Simon Peter, and the rest of us had either home and family there, or a regular billet. Mine was with Zebedee, the fisherman father of James and John, who had homes of their own. Zebedee was a crusty old gentleman who had at first been angered and upset by the two sons' neglect (as he saw it) of the family business. But since his wife's death he had found comfort in the teachings of Jesus. 'He has a way with words, no ques-tion,' Zebedee acknowledged. 'Takes a force ten to bring tears to these old eyes, but that son-of-a-bitch can do it in five minutes.'

Jesus' preaching at this time had returned to the themes of peace and harmony, with promises to the poor, the maimed, the sick and the enslaved that their burdens would be lifted in heaven. But he also drew attention to scriptural prophecies that spoke of a new dispensation, soon to arrive, when the divine power would rule in the land of Israel, and when justice would prevail on earth as in heaven, something he taught us to pray for every day: 'May your Kingdom come, your will be done on earth as it is in heaven.' Perhaps, after all, the poor would not have to wait until they died before blessings were visited upon them.

The more thoughtful people of the region listened for seditious meanings hidden in his teachings, and believed they found them. Most were pleased. They saw Jesus as their own prophet, and even (some dared to say it) as the Messiah who would liberate Israel. As this idea got more currency some of the disciples began to echo and endorse it, citing in undertones and innuendos the mountaintop revelation to Simon Peter, James and John as confirmation. It was supposed to be a secret but, like every secret about Jesus, it was soon one that everybody shared.

From time to time among the crowds who came to hear him I would see men who came in pairs, were not 'local', and had an official look, a sinister alertness, pointing things out to one another, commenting out of the corner of the mouth, or behind their hands. These, I was sure, were Herod's spies. I tried to warn Jesus: this talk of him as a liberator, and of displacement of the civil powers, could get him into serious trouble. He smiled. 'I make no such claims for myself,' he said. 'I can't help it if others make them for me.'

I decided to be more frank. 'Haven't you noticed that some of the twelve believe you're the Messiah?'

We were sitting on a jetty beside one of Zebedee's moored boats. Jesus looked down through the spaces between the planking into the clear, gently lapping water. 'I've noticed', he said at last, 'that some of you don't.'

This was a shock. Was he beginning to believe it himself? 'Should we?' I asked. And then, 'Do you?'

When he didn't answer I repeated what James claimed to have heard up on the mountain. '"This is my Son. Worship him." You want that? You want us to worship you?'

He frowned, and took my hand. For a moment he was not Jesus of Nazareth, orator, leader of our small band, hope of the downtrodden and threat to the established order, but my old schoolfriend, uncertain what he should do or say. 'I have these . . . *powers*,' he said.

'You have powers of oratory.'

'To *heal* . . .'

'Some of the sick get better, yes. Is that your doing?'

'No. It's God's doing.' He looked at me, frowning hard. 'God's doing,' he repeated. 'But *through me!*'

I think this was the first time I felt real fear for him – fear for the balance of his mind perhaps, but more for his safety, and I suppose for ours, his followers. I wanted to tell him he was putting us all in danger, but it seemed unworthy. What would danger mean if you believed you might be the Messiah?

He said, 'When I feel that force go through me, when my own voice speaks sentences I couldn't myself have invented – words that are not my own but God's . . .'

He stopped there, and I could find nothing to say. They were not his words perhaps, but they were his variations on those wonderful texts we'd committed to memory as boys. Those were the foundation of his eloquence. His genius was to reshape them spontaneously, but he seemed not to recognise it as coming from himself. He felt that some external force was speaking through him, using him as its conduit.

So we sat in the sun, two friends, one, it seemed, beginning to believe he might be the Son of God. I wanted to say to him, 'You began with a message. Now you think you *are* the message,' but that seemed too harsh.

'Look,' he said, pointing down between the gaps. An eel, silver-grey, was lingering in the shade of the jetty, catching the light that came through in fine shafts, idly turning this way and that but scarcely moving.

I watched it, thinking about the Pentateuch's account of the Creation, and wondering in what frame of mind you could even begin to write yourself, or see yourself written, into the story. 'Son of God the Creator.' It was absurd. It was embarrassing.

And then, my mind wandering by association, or with complete irrelevance, I thought of the story of the Flood, and that Noah would not have had to take eels, or fish, or any swimming creatures aboard. It seemed to make a troubling anomaly.

Jesus stood up. His movements were decisive, as if something had been resolved in his mind, or perhaps set aside. He said, 'We have to wait for the unfolding of events. We have to be patient. Don't let fear spoil what we're achieving. We have to believe in ourselves. Believe, and be happy.'

'Be happy' was one of his themes at that time. He could still radiate some of that innocent optimism and promise of earlier days, when it seemed as if the trees and bushes broke into flower and the birds sang as he passed by. In that upbeat mode he was the shepherd who would bring his flock to good pasture; he was the dove on the waters, the light shining in darkness, the Word made flesh.

He had his critics, of course, even among his own people. The Pharisees said that he allowed his followers to eat and drink to excess; that he demanded faith and little else; that he healed the sick on the Sabbath, allowed lepers to touch him, talked to women met by chance. They said he neglected the purity rituals, and made friends of prostitutes and tax gatherers.

Once, returning home to Capernaum on the Sabbath, we took a short cut through cultivated land. We hadn't had breakfast and some of us broke off ripe ears of corn and ate as we went along. On the far side of the field we ran into a group of Pharisees, walking in single file, making their way to the synagogue. They recognised Jesus waiting for us in the pathway as we straggled out of the field in twos and threes munching on the corn, and their leader reproached him for our behaviour. We were stealing, we were breaking the Sabbath, and I've forgotten what else.

Jesus replied, citing precedents (he enjoyed scriptural debate, and usually won). David, he said, had taken his friends into the temple and encouraged them to eat from the twelve sacred loaves.

'And are you David?' the indignant Pharisee demanded. 'Is this the temple?'

Jesus' smile at that moment was the cheerfully challenging one. 'I can be a David, old man, if that's what's required to make eating a few ears of corn lawful. And this', he waved at the blue sky, 'is certainly God's temple.'

Sometimes we were rowdy in the night and were accused of drunkenness and licence. Sometimes the accusations were not unfounded, and it was Mary Magdalene rather than Jesus who called us to order. On the road she was a kind of overseer, not puritanical, but concerned for our reputation and for keeping the peace.

When I felt the power and the beauty of Jesus' preaching, I didn't care about literal truth. My scepticism was alive. It belonged to my brain, to my intelligence, and I would not have wanted to be without it. But it could be set aside, rested, while I enjoyed the spectacle: his warmth, grace, intelligence and eloquence; above all the hope he gave to the unfortunate. Even if it was false hope, it was better than the despair it replaced. 'Jesus of Nazareth' was a story. Day by day he was telling it by living it, and I couldn't put it down. What did belief matter?

But it mattered to him – and that was the difficulty. He demanded it constantly – of us, his disciples, and of the crowds, his followers. He could do without food. He could cross the desert without water. He seemed not to need the love of a woman. He could trudge endlessly on blistered feet. But he couldn't live without believers. We had to have faith in him, that was what he required of us, and then, he assured us, every good thing would follow. I resented this challenge to my own common sense, because it threatened my enjoyment of 'the story'. No 'real' god, I used to tell myself, no 'Son of God', would demand faith as he demanded it, or need belief as he needed it. The problem was that he himself had difficulty believing the story, even as he told it, even as he acted it out.

And then began the darkening of his message, and of his personality. I don't suppose it can be attributed to any one cause, but if there was a trigger it was the news of the arrest of John the Baptist. I didn't notice the effect straight away. But slowly it became obvious, such a change of tone and manner and content, you couldn't miss it. It was as if he acquired some of John's foreboding and threatening tone, not by imitation, but because his view of the world we lived in had been darkened by the turn events had taken.

We heard the news of the arrest from a camel driver. Herod Antipas had been visiting his fortress at Machaeros on the Dead Sea and had sent out spies to listen to John preaching not far away at his usual place, the Jordan ford. They came back with reports of his lack of respect for authority; but worse, his condemnation of what he called, baldly, Herod's seduction of his half-brother's wife, Herodias, and his marriage to her after they had each achieved a divorce.

This was a scandal in the land, spoken about by everyone, but only in whispers. John didn't whisper. He growled and brayed and thundered his outrage. It was an offence against the God of Israel. This 'King of the Jews', Herod Antipas, was not even a king, only a tetrarch, a 'quarter of a king'. He was not even a Jew. He was an Idumaean, and a Roman stooge. He should be dragged from his throne. He should be made a slave and put to serve in the galleys. He should be stoned . . . And so it went on.

Herod didn't hesitate. He sent a troop of armed men to the ford. John was found asleep in a nearby cave. He was dragged out, wrested from followers who fought to protect him, and taken away in chains to the fortress, where he was thrown into the deepest dungeon.

The Machaeros Fortress was a formidable place, on the crest of a hill, with massive walls looking west over the Dead Sea to the desert of Judaea, and eastward to the barren hills of the Nabataean kingdom. The thought of John locked up in there was upsetting to us all, but especially to Jesus, and his next sermon, given from Zebedee's boat on the evening of the day the news came, was full of indignation.

'When our rulers hear there is a prophet in the land, a voice crying in the wilderness, and they send out their spies to report, what do they expect to hear? That he is timid, speaks no ill of sinners, is a mere reed shaken by the wind? That he is wearing fine silk and eating off silver platters? Silk and silver and weasel words are *their* style, not a prophet's. And my cousin John is a prophet, a man of virtue and truth, honoured in heaven.

'If the Lord sends us a guide to show us the path of salvation, and to warn of wrong turnings and snares along the way, is that guide likely to come on tiptoe, speaking in whispers? No, he will thunder as John thundered. He will be the lightning that splits the stubborn oak.

'This arrest is a violence against the Kingdom of Heaven.'

Jesus seemed to feed off his own anger, even railing against his own people, against the towns and villages of Galilee, which, he said, would probably accept the fact of John's arrest without a murmur of protest.

But had it occurred to us (he went on) that we might avoid the wrath of Rome and incur instead the greater wrath of God? A terrible and deserved vengeance might be brought down on us, one that would make the fire and brimstone poured on Sodom seem a shower of rain. None would be spared, not even Capernaum.

'It will come,' he shouted. 'It will happen. You think you're safe, Capernaum? Exempt? *Don't count on it!*'

His eyes flashed. Holding on to a rope from the mast with one hand, he leaned out from the fishing boat over the little crowd sitting along the shore blinking and wincing in puzzlement and alarm. The frogs had fallen silent at that last shout. The hills held their breath. The jackals stopped their barking. There was only the faint lapping of water.

He closed his eyes and seemed to pray into the silence. When he began again his tone had changed. His voice was low, husky, a projected whisper. 'What I say to you I say in the name of

Heaven. I am as the son who speaks for the Father. If you have cares that weigh you down, bring them to me. That is the Father's wish. I will bear the burden. I will wear the yoke. At the heart of my message there is love, and it is the love of my Father.'

I don't suppose I was alone in feeling alarmed and confused. A rain of fire and brimstone on his beloved Capernaum! A punishment worse than God had visited on Sodom! And then the about-face, as if that voice he alone could hear, murmuring instructions into his ear out of the silence his threats created, had reminded him that he was Jesus the Good Shepherd, not John the Scourge of Sinners.

But as it happened there was something more immediate to distract me. As the crowd was departing James came to tell me that a man waiting in the shadows was a servant who brought a message for me. I went to him at once and he told me he'd come from my father.

'He sends you his blessing, Master, and asks you to visit him. He instructed me to be quite sure you understood he has something of the utmost importance to tell you, and that he urges you to come at once.'

It was no great distance to Tiberias and I was keen to go, but uncertain what I should say to Jesus. He'd become inconsistent and unpredictable about our absences, at one moment relaxed that one of our number went home to do urgent work, but then taking offence because another was (as he saw it) putting family ahead of our collective ministry. Recently, when Thomas had received news that his father had died, Jesus had told him he should not travel to the funeral. 'Isn't this where you belong? You have a Father in heaven. Let the dead bury the dead.'

I asked Mary Magdalene what I should do. 'Don't worry him with it now,' was her advice. 'Just go, and come back as soon as you can. I'll tell him you didn't want to trouble him while he was worrying about John.'

I slept fitfully and had Zebedee wake me before first light as he rose to go to his boats. By noon next day I was in my father's house. We embraced silently, not finding words for the emotion we both felt. A meal for two had been prepared.

'What I have to tell you', he said, as we sat down, 'concerns your way of life. Don't be alarmed, it has nothing to do with approval or disapproval. It has to do with safety.'

Lying by the lake
once, on a summer's
night I heard

Andrew recount
how, at the baptism
of Jesus

a dove appeared
in a beam of light
and a Voice said

'This is my beloved
Son in whom
I am well pleased.'

Did I believe
this? No. I'd been there
at the ford and

seen no dove, heard
no voice. Yet it's true
I was perplexed

not that God's grammar
should be perfect
but that it seemed

beyond the
reach of fisherman
Andrew to invent.

CHAPTER 15

MY FATHER, IT SEEMED, WAS CONTINUING TO PROSPER. THERE had been great gains made in his business as a result of the part of his journey that had taken him through Galatia, and he was, from time to time, when Herod Antipas was in residence in Tiberias, invited to official celebrations at the palace. He considered Antipas (he told me this in a lowered voice when the servants were out of the room) a man of some ability, but wilful and self-indulgent. His taking his brother's wife was only the most conspicuous example; and now he was very much under her thumb, afraid of losing her, and willing to do foolish things to please her.

Herodias, my father said, was beautiful, with a certain charm. She was capable of generous acts, but also of meanness and cruelty. What made her dangerous was vanity. She took offence easily, noticed every slight, even where none was intended, and used her influence with her new husband to take revenge. She'd received a message from Machaeros that Herod would be bringing her a special gift, and she was overjoyed when it turned out to be the prophet who had slandered her, dragged in chains and thrown in the dust at her feet.

John had been transported from Machaeros in a cage so small that, even in a sitting position, he'd had to bend his head forward. When he complained of this he'd been dragged out and made to walk barefoot, pulled along behind a mounted soldier, a chain attached to a metal collar around his neck, and wearing shackles that prevented him from taking large strides. Sometimes he fell and was dragged through dust and over stones. He arrived at Tiberias filthy, half dead, covered in cuts and bruises, and was paraded naked for Herodias before being thrown into his cell.

Herodias had wanted him executed, but Herod, fearing that it might provoke unrest among the people, refused. By that refusal he lost the gain with his wife he had made by the capture. For a few days she continued to weep and sulk, berating him with hysterics and rhetorical questions. What sort of a man was he, what sort of a *king*, who could have in his hands the rebel who had so maligned and slandered his *queen*, and allow the scoundrel to go on living?

But then, in a characteristic turnaround (part of her fascination, my father assured me) she'd announced a party for her husband's birthday, at which, as a present, her sixteen-year-old daughter, Salome, newly returned from Rome, would perform for him the dance of the veils.

It was a Roman-style party and my father was one of the guests. A great deal of excellent food was eaten, and many carafes of fine wine were drunk. The cooks and servants and slaves were hard at work, and as the night wore on there was much use of the vomitories. Some time after midnight Herod, drunk and obsessed, as his wife meant him to be, with his step-daughter's beauty, asked that she dance the veils again. When she refused, kissing him and stroking his thigh, he offered her more or less anything she asked for if she would only do it again.

'Hear me when I make this promise,' he shouted to his guests, 'and condemn me if I fail to deliver.'

Clearly it hadn't occurred to Antipas that Salome might ask something not for herself but for her mother. 'Please, honoured stepfather,' she said in a clear, audible, sixteen-year-old voice, 'give me the head of John the Baptist.'

The dance had been wonderful – full of charm and grace, but also full of adolescent belly and buttock and breast. Herod was drunk, a man of power, used to having his way. Everyone could see he was disconcerted by the request, but he swallowed another cup of wine and shouted at his guests, 'Shall I give her what she wants?'

'Yes,' they shouted. 'Give her what she wants.'

'The head of the prophet?' Herod asked.

'The head of the prophet,' they shouted, banging palms and fists on the tabletops.

My father, not quite sober, was not so inebriated that he didn't feel horror and shame at what he was seeing. Herod was showing off his power and ruthlessness to people he knew considered him weak and vacillating. The girl wanted the prophet's head? Very well, he was tetrarch and she would have it!

The executioner was sent for and given whispered instructions. This was Mannais, who had been executioner to Herod the Great. He was an old man, but still strong and healthy, an artist of unrivalled skill. He'd dispatched a number of the senior Herod's troublesome relatives – including even one of his sons, Antipas' half-brother – strangling one, drowning another, burning a third alive, and beheading the rest.

A fearful hush settled over the party. Surely this wasn't going to happen. Herodias appeared more anxious than pleased. Herod had become pale and tense, downing another cup, shutting his eyes tight and then opening them wide, giving his head little sideways jerks. The musicians struck up to fill the silence. No one danced or sang, and the music faded away.

When the executioner returned the whole banqueting hall, with its chandeliers said to hold more than ten thousand candles, was silent. Everyone was apprehensive. Many were ready for it to prove an elaborate joke.

The executioner had stopped off at the kitchens for a large silver meat dish. On it, arranged with a few herbs and sprigs of parsley, was the head of the prophet, his hair matted with gore. Blood slopped from the dish on to the floor and over the executioner's hands and forearms and shining naked torso.

This trophy was held out first to the sixteen-year-old dancer, who cringed and turned away, gagging. Herodias, quick enough to be alarmed at what she'd achieved, was the first to regain composure. She waved the executioner and his prize away, took up a position in front of the now slumped and bewildered tetrarch, hiding him as best she could from the guests, and made a pretty little speech.

The party, she suggested, was another milestone ('Millstone,' my father murmured, but only to himself) and, sadly, was nearing an end. She thanked the guests for coming, and for their generous birthday wishes and gifts to the tetrarch. She mentioned especially 'our Roman friends', indicating the prefect of Galilee and his companion, a visiting representative of Pontius Pilate, and expressed her own and the tetrarch's continuing respect for, and gratitude to, the divine Tiberius, whose name their city honoured. She hoped everyone present would remember only what was worth remembering of their evening together, and that what was unimportant would be quickly forgotten, as it deserved to be. The tetrarch would consider foolish chatter unhelpful.

'I took that as a warning to us all,' my father said, 'so I tell you this at some risk to myself, but out of concern for your safety. I heard talk of your man Jesus at that party, and I've heard more since. He's talked about everywhere, and you need to understand that Herod is having him watched.'

I said we'd guessed that was happening.

'Herod's dangerous,' he went on. 'He's unpredictable, especially with that woman in his bed. He could wipe you all out on a whim, and the Romans would just shrug and turn away. It wouldn't affect them. They wouldn't care.'

My father was adopting a tone of reason, man to man, warning me, being careful not to seem to interfere in my life or give orders. I knew how difficult this must be for him, how distasteful he must find Jesus and his crew, and how much he must dislike my association with them. There could be no professional opening for me now through the good offices of the lofty uncle in Jerusalem. My father must have accepted that, and wanted, nonetheless, to regain the love of his only son. Though none of this was said, I felt it, and was touched by it.

'I had to warn you,' he said.

I thanked him, and we clasped hands. I asked him to forgive me for the disappointments I'd caused. He said, 'Of course, of course' (embarrassed), and gave me his blessing.

No one seeing that low-key moment, hearing our unraised voices, could have imagined how much emotion it contained.

I was back in Capernaum that evening, and found Jesus sitting on a bench outside the fountain grotto, whittling a reed pipe of the kind his father used to play after supper outside their door in Nazareth. I guessed he wasn't pleased with me – I'd gone without his permission – and that pitched me more quickly into my story.

I tried to break the news gently that John was dead. He listened. His hands held the reed and the knife, but they didn't move. He shed no tears, but sat quite still, saying nothing, his expression remote, inward, dreaming. 'I need to think about this,' he said at last. 'It will come to me what we should do.'

He spent a good part of the night in prayer. By morning he'd decided we should remove ourselves for the time being from the jurisdiction of Herod Antipas. That same day we crossed the lake, all thirteen of us, with Mary Magdalene and some wives and supporters, ferried by Zebedee and three of his men in their fishing boats.

We came ashore where a river runs out into the lake, not far from Hippos. Jesus had followers there, and with their help we made a camp and were given food. It was a lovely place, with olive trees for shade growing on flat, partly tilled fields, and fig trees and mulberry bushes growing among rocks. Higher up the slope that rose from the lake there were clusters of yellow vine flowers. I can still call up in memory the lemony scents of that place in the early morning, when the lake was grey turning to green, and the clouds over the eastern hills were rose-coloured.

We spent five days doing very little. Just once Jesus was prevailed upon to preach to a small crowd that came, having heard we were within walking distance of their village. This was when 'next-to-no-food' was transformed, by goodwill and the principle of sharing, into 'enough-to-go-around', the occasion which, in Ezra's recent retelling, became the miraculous feeding of five thousand.

For the rest we waited on Jesus while Jesus waited on God. No word came from the Father, so there was none from the Son. He and I played the word games we'd played as boys. We competed to remember passages of scripture. We exchanged memories of Andreas and talked about the history he'd taught us, and the philosophy. I reminded him of the story of Diogenes and Alexander the Great, and told him how his loud reaction to it had embarrassed me.

He laughed. 'I knew you thought you were superior.'

'It didn't last,' I told him. 'You were so clever and so pretty . . .'

He was amused by that too. 'Was I pretty?'

I assured him he was.

'I didn't know,' he said. 'We never had a mirror at home.'

We sat on the lakeshore watching the two sets of brothers, James and John, Simon Peter and Andrew, competing at throwing their nets while catching fish for our supper. With a sling and stones we tried (unsuccessfully, though one or two direct hits were claimed) to knock out foxes among the grapevines. We made friends with a tethered goat, and moved his peg to let him reach the best grass. I named him Scapegoat, but assured him it was a joke and that he would not take the punishment for my sins. Not yet full-grown, he liked to practise butting and pushing. One of us would rest the palm of one hand against his brow and he would try to outpush his human competitor.

We fished in the river, and swam there. Once, walking under olive trees in the evening, Jesus and I, joking and pushing one another, found ourselves wrestling as we'd done when we were boys. I was surprised how familiar it seemed and how peculiarly comfortable to be locked in one of the 'holds', feeling pain and yet enjoying the closeness, the warm clean smell of his body.

We sang, separately and together, Bartholomew doing a sort of falsetto descant. One evening Jesus had us all dancing around our open fire. It was a dance he'd learned while with the Essenes.

He taught us some of the basic steps and then accompanied us on the reed pipe – and there we were, all twelve on the lakeshore with Mary Magdalene and three or four others, some of us graceful, some clumsy, twirling and reversing, waving arms and tossing heads to the kind of melodies we used to pick up in the villages, which sounded as though they might have come from the time of the ancient prophets.

We were happy during those days, and I found myself hoping Jesus would take the warning of John's murder and go back to the safe teachings he'd begun with after his time with the Essenes. What I craved was a return to the simple, anonymous life of the dog philosophers, led by our own Diogenes, advocating, by word and by example, plain living and basic morals – a life in which at some times and in some places we'd been welcomed, fed and housed, at others ordered to 'clear off' and sent on our way with a volley of small boys' stones.

If he had not been such a powerful orator it might have been possible. But as long as that power persuaded people to think he might be the saviour Israel craved and had been promised by the prophets of old, he couldn't hope to preach inconspicuously, nor live a simple life. He was condemned by talent to fame and its consequences.

On the morning of the sixth day he emerged from his tent with a look of renewed purpose. His eyes were bloodshot and there was something of the frowning, passionate, effortful – even manic – personality I associated with his strongest preaching. 'How many weeks are there until Passover?' he demanded.

It took us a few minutes and some disagreements before we'd worked it out. 'We must be there in good time,' he said.

I asked where, knowing what the answer would be, but hoping it might be somewhere else.

'Jerusalem,' he said. 'But there's a lot to be done first.'
'All of us?'
'All of us.'

Even as a child
I hated the
ceremony

that chose a goat
to wear on its horns
as tags the sins

our village
confessed to – then stoned
it and drove it out

bleeding to take
its chances alone
in the wastelands.

I wanted to make
it my friend, but they
said, 'Those are

our sins we are
rid of for another
year. Leave them.'

Jesus, I see
it now, wanted to be
the scapegoat,

to take on
himself the sins of
our village, our world.

CHAPTER 16

ONE CONSEQUENCE OF REACHING SEVENTY IS THAT MANY OF the people you dream about are dead. I suppose you could say it's a way of keeping in touch. My dreams are very often about Thea, during our first years together, and when the children were young; but they take me back further, to Judith, and sometimes all the way to my own childhood. I have days or weeks when the only dreams I'm able to remember are about my father. Then there'll be a switch and my mother takes over. And of course Jesus is there – Jesus the boy, Jesus the living evangelist, Jesus 'King of the Jews', mocked and scourged and nailed to the cross.

Last night I dreamed that there was a man lying dead in the room I occupied as a child and I asked my mother what I should do. Then I noticed Jesus was also in the room, dressed in white as he had been at my marriage to Judith. He offered to 'do a miracle'. His tone was not grand or Son-of-Man-ish. It was practical and helpful – the tone in which a handyman neighbour might offer to patch a cracked cistern or repair a broken shutter. My mother thanked him and he went to work. Like a tradesman he grunted, swore occasionally, and his eyes screwed up with the effort. At last the dead man began to breathe. His face twitched, his eyes flicked open, and he groaned pitifully as if it was painful being brought back from the dead and he would rather not have been disturbed. I looked across the bed on which he was lying and saw myself in a mirror. Then I recognised that Jesus was the man on the bed.

After the death of John, and in the period of our slow journey to Jerusalem, there was a lot of talk of raising the dead. Mostly it was the usual metaphorical stuff – Jesus was making the blind see, the deaf hear, the lame walk, the dead come to life. These were things done to, rather than for, the afflicted. They had been blind, or deaf, to Jesus, unable to walk with him, dead to his message. Now all that was reversed.

But I recognised these claims were becoming ambiguous, and perhaps for some always had been. Hints became suggestions, suggestions became claims that were to be understood literally – or might be in certain instances. Jesus could say to a crowd, 'Have I not made the blind see truth, and the deaf hear the word of the Lord?' and the rhetorical question would raise shouts of affirmation, and hallelujahs, as it would if he asked, 'Have I not made the dead walk among you?' But what was the crowd's understanding at those moments? What did he mean them to understand? And what, in his own private thoughts, did he believe?

Once, when he was making his way to the front of a gathering in a market square, a blind man at the back began to shout, 'Jesus, Son of David, help me.'

Jesus took no notice, and people tried to silence the man, but he kept repeating, 'Jesus, Son of David, help me.'

Jesus stopped and asked Matthew to bring the man to him. I was quite close and could hear what was said. 'What is it you want?' Jesus asked.

'I want to see you,' the man said, reaching ahead with searching fingers and taking hold of Jesus' sleeve.

'You know who I am,' Jesus said, stroking the man's cheek and touching his empty eye sockets. 'You've heard my voice and shown faith in me, and that faith will make you whole. Be content.'

That touch to cheek and eyelids, and the soothing words, silenced the blind man; but later I heard it said, more than once, that Jesus had restored his sight.

It was during these weeks that I began to face up to just how far I had separated from the other disciples, and from Jesus; or, more accurately, how far they had separated from me. I was where we'd begun. They had changed. There had always been a gap. Now it was a chasm. As Jesus claimed greater powers for himself, I became correspondingly more sceptical. I felt he was still my friend, but there was a tension that hadn't been there before. He, I think, liked me less, or cared less about me – and how could it be otherwise? He saw himself now as fulfilling a commission from God. He didn't have time to be concerned with one who had been – mistakenly, he probably thought – brought into the enterprise on the less than adequate grounds of schoolboy association, and who was showing unmistakable signs of lack of faith.

There was no noisy quarrel or open rift, but there didn't need to be. My silences were enough to tell him where I stood, and also to make it clear to the other disciples, who were constantly demanding to know why I would not affirm this or that about the Master's powers and his greatness. (Referring to him as the Master was a recent development – one I found distasteful but which he didn't discourage.) What had gone wrong? I was asked. Why had I become so unhelpful and mean-spirited and silent?

Not that everything in our group was otherwise sweetness and light. We were like a little court in which vying for the prince's favour was constant, at times bitter and ugly. But in that period I replaced Matthew, the tax gatherer who, to begin with, had been the one we all disliked, the one it was always acceptable to speak of disparagingly. There were even times when I shared their feelings and disliked myself. Our faith, which was always shaky, needed the confirmation of unity. We were the jury on the divinity of Jesus, and our verdict was supposed to be unanimous.

This was the nature of my 'betrayal', not (as Ptolemy and the other Jesus evangelists who come through Sidon tell their congregations) that I took a bribe of thirty pieces of silver 'for information on his whereabouts'. My 'betrayal' was in my refusal to affirm what I couldn't believe. I think of it now as a parable of the Jesus message: Believe, or go to hell! I couldn't believe and didn't pretend, and, ever since, his followers in their narratives have been sending me to hell.

Contrary to what I heard them say about me, I didn't like to be odd man out. I felt guilty. I reminded myself during those weeks that it was my old schoolfriend I'd undertaken to accompany, not the Son of God, but I was increasingly uneasy, often lonely, and occasionally fearful.

Jesus' preaching grew more confident, sometimes in the old gentle manner, with incomparable charm and sweetness, but more often defiant, bold, masterful and extreme. I admired and even enjoyed it, sharing the loyal pride it produced in the disciples, and the fervour of the crowds. But I was nagged at by anxieties. As the crowds grew larger there was an increasing triumphalism in his manner, and in the way we began to stage-manage his appearances. Jesus the lamb was becoming Jesus the lion. And the cautious Jesus, who had given a circumspect answer when asked whether taxes should be paid, was becoming careless, even, at times, reckless. My anxiety was for us as a group, but it was especially for him. John, after all, had been wrested from his supporters, isolated, and 'dealt with'. Why should the same not happen to Jesus?

And this was something he now seemed to invite, even to welcome. He began to predict his own death, but with hints that he would not be dead for long. Soon afterwards would come that fiery chariot, followed by the Selection, dividing those with heavenly passes from those destined for infernal slavery and an eternity of torment. This was the part of his message that unsettled the disciples most and caused disputes. Sometimes, I could see, the thought of life without him shook them to the core. At others they grew argumentative about their places in the chariot, and in heaven, and who would sit closest to his throne.

On that last morning in our camp, where the little river hurried out into the lake, he gathered us together to receive instruction. I sat at the edge of the group in the early sun, watching the clear stream where fish – some kind of trout – kept their heads pointing into the flow, swimming just hard enough to stay in one place, peeling off sometimes, turning side-on to the current to be carried back towards the lake, and then swimming hard to return to the same spot. Now and then a light breeze would shake small green beetles from overhanging branches into the water. A beetle floundered a few moments on the surface of the current, and then disappeared in a flash of silver. It was all so beautiful, so natural and effortless, it seemed not to need a Son of God, or even (though I would not have said it then) a God. It was self-sufficient and could do without us.

Jesus' talk that morning also had its moments of beauty. He spoke of children and how they must be protected. The idea that anyone might hurt a child caused him anguish that turned easily to rage.

Then he changed direction, asking us each to close our eyes and think of him, and think what he might best be compared to. It was a game he'd played with us before, and he probably knew how much I disliked it. As he explained it, it was a training exercise, a preparation for the time when we would have to preach without him, would have to tell our listeners about him and make them believe what we believed. That was its logic, but it was so focused on himself I thought he should find it embarrassing, and since he didn't, I felt the embarrassment myself. I felt it *for* him.

My fellow disciples seemed untroubled by any such concern. Some, as always, were shy, others inarticulate, but none lacked an answer. For Simon Peter Jesus was like a messenger – an *angelic* messenger. For Matthew he was a wise philosopher. For Andrew he was like a fisherman; for John a fig tree.

So it went on while I, not wanting any part of it, averted my eyes. Bartholomew, who had been under a cloud since our last visit to a town, where he'd spent his evenings in the taverns with pretty young men, kept waving a hand at the Master, signalling that he had an idea, but was ignored.

I was looking into the stream, listening to its rushed whisper. A silence drew my eyes back to Jesus. It had to come. He was looking at me, waiting to catch my attention.

'Judas.' He said my name in a way that made it ring like something hollow. Could I, he asked, tear my eyes away from the wildlife for a moment? Did I have a contribution?

I shook my head, trying to look as if it was beyond me.

'A likeness?' Jesus coaxed. 'It doesn't have to be flattering.'

He should have left me in peace. I knew even as I spoke that silence would have been better. 'Right at this moment,' I said, 'you're like a blind man asking for a mirror.'

He gave me his full hard stare and turned away to the rest with a tight smile. 'And Judas is my mirror,' he said. 'He's the little bit of Nazareth I carry about to prevent me from thinking too well of myself.'

He took a few paces up and down, and began again. It was time, he said, to prepare ourselves for the road – a different road, a harder one. On the journey to Jerusalem we would often be obstructed by the authorities, and sometimes reviled by the people, but we should remember we were bearers of truths that had been concealed and which must now be thrown open to the light. We should be fearless, because we and our cause were known in heaven, and what harm could mere men do to those who are in the care of the Lord?

'If you meet resistance,' he told us, 'don't listen and don't argue. Go. Don't give what is holy to dogs. Don't waste pearls on swine. And don't put yourselves at the mercy of clever men's logic, which can be cruel as a knife-blade, and equally unhelpful to the human heart.'

But when we had eager listeners whose eyes shone with the recognition of truth, then we were to speak our message clearly and boldly. 'Remember that words can be like fire and set the world alight. They can be like gold, and enrich it. And they can be like dung, and pollute it.'

We would travel as before, sometimes together, sometimes in groups or pairs, dividing responsibility for the smaller villages, but moving always by pre-arrangement, and making our way towards Bethany, where whichever group arrived first would wait for the remainder at the home of Lazarus and his sisters. From there we would go on, all together and with whatever supporters had chosen to come with us, into the holy city for Passover.

In each new town we were to enquire who was a worthy man, and lodge there if he would have us. If he would not, and if the villagers or townspeople refused to welcome us, we should continue on our road without complaint, taking away the blessing our visit would have bestowed, and knowing that on the Day of Judgement those who had rejected us would suffer.

'How will they suffer, Master?' Matthew asked.

Jesus frowned, his eyes narrowed, his face hardened. It would be terrible for them, he said. Women with child would wish they were not. There would be torment, tears, cries of pain and remorse . . .

It was the same fire-and-brimstone stuff he'd threatened at Capernaum. I got up and walked away. It happened without thought. I couldn't sit and say nothing, but knew I shouldn't speak. As I went I was remembering a parable he'd told a few weeks previously about a king who sent servants out to bring people to his son's wedding. One who came, among these more or less conscripted guests, was not correctly dressed for it. On the king's orders he was bound hand and foot, taken away, cast into a cell with no light at all, and left with no prospect of ever being released.

It had seemed such a cruel story, such a harsh and undeserved punishment, I'd asked him what it meant and he'd said (stone-faced, as now) it meant 'many would be called, but few would be chosen'. Was this the new message we were being asked to preach to the towns and villages – that God's punishments would be not only cruel, but arbitrary?

Upstream I found Mary Magdalene making a little fire of our rubbish. 'Does it ever strike you', I asked her, 'that our leader suffers moments of insanity?'

She looked at me with her level, totally sane stare. 'No,' she replied. 'Never.'

In my dream the
water won't support
my walking feet.

It closes over
my head and becomes
a furnace.

I drown, I
burn, I choke, hanging
from the black fig tree

while ravens
peck out my eyes, and
a voice from heaven

cries, 'This is
the blind betrayer of
Jesus, my Son.'

CHAPTER 17

WE WENT BACK TO CAPERNAUM FIRST WHERE THERE WAS, AS
we had all foreseen, a good deal of low-level domestic wrangl-
ing, some weeping from wives who would have to remain looking
after children, and some shouting from old fathers and younger
brothers who would have to work harder while the chosen ones
followed their Master to the holy city. Not that Jesus lacked
support in the town. He was a hero there. Many believed he
was indeed the Messiah, destined to bring all manner of good
things to Israel and its people, including even, by some divine
power yet to be revealed, a lifting of the Roman yoke. But that
was in the long term; that was the larger picture. In the same
minds, capable of imagining the Son of God, the End of the
World, the Chariot of Fire, there was usually also a down-to-
earth practical person who asked how, in the meantime, children
were to be fed, crops harvested, bills and taxes paid.

So they were difficult days. There were negotiations in which
Jesus himself became involved, and I took the opportunity to go
on ahead, detouring through Nazareth and making my own
peace with my mother and with Andreas. There must have been
in my mind some sense of an ending, because I said goodbye as
if for a very long time. I found my mother tranquil and seem-
ingly content to be locked into a very tight daily and weekly

routine of insignificant duties and minute observances, at the end of which the Sabbath came as a welcome rest. For the first time she seemed to me 'elderly', and none the worse for it. 'The years go around so quickly,' she explained. 'It's all I can do to keep up.'

She was concerned at my still being a follower of Jesus. She'd accepted it at first because of her pity for me at the loss of Judith – welcomed it, as she would have welcomed anything that seemed to distract me from my pain. But she hadn't expected it to last so long.

'He was such a lovely little boy,' she said. 'But you know, Judas . . .'

I wasn't sure what I was supposed to know, so I remained silent.

She asked was it true he raised the dead and 'mixed with lepers'? I told her he was a very remarkable man. 'He inspires loyalty,' I told her.

'But does he inspire faith?'

'In his followers – yes, of course.'

'And in you, Judas?'

It was a good question, and I evaded it. 'He demands it,' I said.

She told me she'd talked to a woman in the market whose cousin's best friend had gone to one of his rallies. 'She'd had a swelling on her knee for six weeks. She could hardly walk. Next day it was gone.'

'Well there you are then,' I said, and I kissed her cheek.

My clothes were faded and dirty and she insisted on going with me to the bazaar where she bought me a new burnous – a rich dark red colour with gold trimmings – and strong new sandals. I felt very clean and spruce, and only slightly guilty at the pleasure I was taking in comfort and an improved appearance. When it came time to leave she said, 'Don't neglect your poor old mother so long. And next time you're in the area, bring Jesus.'

I didn't like to tell her that he'd turned his back on Nazareth and bore it a grudge.

'Bring him to lunch,' she said.

Andreas also looked older, but venerable and wise. He'd kept abreast of all the news and rumours about Jesus, much of it (I was able to assure him) exaggerated, some entirely untrue. He was still fond of his former star pupil, but now had a new favourite, which meant his concern for Jesus was more relaxed, less possessive.

'Must he go to Jerusalem?' he asked. 'And if he must, Judas, should you be going too?' He told me I should think about the risks. 'I don't mean you should be disloyal, or deceive him. But given the turn his teachings have taken . . .' He tailed off. 'Well,' he said, 'you're big boys now. But do be careful.' And he hugged me.

My father too repeated his warnings. 'These are dangerous times,' he said. But when were they not?

On my last day there I visited Joseph and Mary. Joseph was as warm and kind as ever. Mary, I think, now suspected I was part of a conspiracy that had turned her favourite child against her. Jesus, she told me, had been led astray. His great talent, which came from God in a special way (she smiled her 'secrets' smile and didn't explain), had been manipulated by men who didn't understand its true worth. But he would break free and would return to his roots. She was convinced of that.

I said I was sure she was right, and said goodbye. I never saw either of them again.

During those weeks of our progress towards Jerusalem and Passover, Jesus kept to the plan he'd outlined by the lake. It meant that, more than ever before, each of us had to do a share of preaching. I think it's fair to say that, apart from Jesus, only three, or at most four, of our company had any real talent for it. Of the rest, some managed passably and some very badly.

Confidence didn't necessarily go with style. Simon Peter was capable of eloquence, but he was shy, so his performance was spasmodic. Sometimes he forgot himself and his sincerity shone through; at others, something upset him or distracted him from his train of thought, self-consciousness took over, and he became inarticulate and inaudible. His brother Andrew was consistently dignified, serious, with a deep, sonorous voice. He was a man of few words, but they were well chosen and people were usually interested and impressed.

Bartholomew was theatrical. He liked long showy sentences and elaborate analogies, but couldn't keep himself out of the picture, so his preaching consisted mainly of stories in which he and his friend 'Jesus of Nazareth' (it was always 'Jesus of Nazareth') did something important together.

Matthew sounded like a bureaucrat insisting rules must be obeyed. He demanded faith be demonstrated, as he must once have demanded taxes be paid – instantly and in full. The only time I saw Thomas called to preach he was struck dumb at the sight of a crowd of faces staring at him, and had to be pulled down and replaced by Philip.

The brothers James and John liked to operate together, usually in taverns and with small crowds of working men, with whom they would 'yarn' about Jesus – James doing most of the talking, John backing him up with 'That's right,' and 'It's true.' Now and then they would get into fights with listeners who not only weren't persuaded but chose to argue. They were not supposed to fight, and they knew it. Jesus had warned them to leave it to the Lord to punish those who didn't welcome his message. But wine flowed freely, the brothers had quick fists, and sometimes words weren't enough to convey the strength of their loyalty to Jesus and their conviction that they were now in the service of the Son of Man.

I once overheard them in a tavern saying they alone had been allowed to watch when Jesus raised a little girl from the dead. I'd come to tell them we were moving on from this village, but I hung back to hear what was being said.

'She'd had a knock on the noggin,' John was explaining.

'Dead as a doornail one minute,' said James. 'Sitting up and smiling at us the next.'

'It's true,' John said, and drained his cup.

'What else?' their companions asked.

'That's right, keep up the camel shit,' said a doubter at the back. Fortunately neither of the brothers heard, and a moment later James was telling of the time when Jesus had taken them, together with Simon Peter, up the mountain.

'When I woke up,' he said, 'Jesus was all in white. Lit up like a torch, he was. I could hardly look at him, he was so bright. He was talking to Moses and another one . . .' He hesitated, uncertain.

'Who? You don't mean . . .'

James looked at John. 'Who did he say? Elijah, wasn't it?'

John nodded slowly, looking deeply serious. 'Elijah.'

There was a lot of head shaking and amazement. Someone asked what they were saying.

'I couldn't hear the words,' James said, 'but the two of them said things to Jesus, and when he said things back, they listened.'

More head shaking. 'They listened, did they?'

'They did.'

'I suppose he was telling them about you fellows.'

'They were having a pretty serious talk,' James said.

As we made our way south, the talk of miracles continued. Whenever one of the disciples was called on to speak and found himself at a loss, out would come a miracle. Jesus had driven out devils; he had restored sanity to the madman, sight to the blind, hearing to the deaf, clear skin to the leper, mobility to the cripple, and even life to a corpse. I didn't like this. I thought it cheap and unconvincing and untrue, but they were offering what people wanted to hear. When Jesus preached, the crowds asked for miracles and were disappointed that he refused. When he wasn't there, his disciples were asked to tell about him 'doing' one.

'Give us a miracle,' was a shout that accompanied us everywhere.

Once, when we'd crossed into Judaea and were heading in the direction of Samaria, our next meeting point, I was in a village with Philip and Barthlomew. A small crowd, which seemed to know very little about us except that our leader was a prophet who performed 'wonders', brought us a baby that was obviously going to die if it wasn't dead already. They asked us to cure it. I said there was nothing we could do except pray for the child, and that they should probably take it indoors out of the noonday sun. The mother kept pleading for help, and Philip decided we should try.

I walked away. The weeping, distraught mother, the desiccated child with its distended stomach, lolling head and rolled back eyes, the hopeful faces of the little crowd of people, all of them in rags, the willingness of my fellow disciples to 'try for a miracle' – it was too much for me. I left them attempting to pray and pummel the child back to life and health.

When we were all together again on the outskirts of the town, Philip asked Jesus why he was able to perform miracles and the rest of us were not. Jesus told him our faith was insufficient. If we had true faith, he said, we could move mountains.

As for my own preaching, I had none of the spontaneous eloquence of Jesus, none of his ability to draw and project emotion from deep within himself. I stuck to his message as I'd first heard it, the part I believed in, or at least could think of as worthy and in some way consoling and helpful; and this had its modest effect. People didn't yawn, or laugh, or walk away. 'He's sincere,' they said. 'He means it.'

But they were hardly swept off their feet. You don't, after all, make 'converts' to common sense and charity. People believe they believe in those things already – and they do, at least in principle. Those just happen to be the hardest principles to live by.

I had no talent for parables of the kind Jesus used, and in fact I had little patience with them. They made the message less clear – which I could see was part of their appeal. Obscurity was mysterious. It allowed people to make sense of the story in their own different ways, and to argue about it afterwards. Often the disciples had to ask Jesus what he meant by a parable and he would explain it with another. My own preference – a reflection of my own temperament – was for clarity. I liked where possible to be understood.

So I spoke of the encouragement I'd seen Jesus give to the poor, the ailing and downtrodden – the hope he gave them that their suffering would have an end. And if I couldn't quite believe it *would* end, at least I believed it *should*, and that the power of their oppressors must one day (even if the day was far distant) be broken.

Then there were the questions of crime and punishment,

revenge and forgiveness, war and peace. 'An eye for an eye and a tooth for a tooth' was the old way, I told them. The new way was the way of Jesus, who said if a man strikes you, turn the other cheek so he can strike you again. Was that too difficult? I acknowledged it wasn't easy, but it was something to be striven towards – an ideal that would curb our aggressions and make for peace and harmony.

I told them they should try not to judge others. Judgement belonged to the individual conscience, and to God. We should treat others exactly as we would want them to treat us, with compassion and understanding. The brother who wronged us should be forgiven, not seven times, but seventy times seven. Forgiveness should have no limit.

We should love family and friends; but we should try to love humankind at large, even our enemies, recognising everyone, near and far, foreign and familiar, as brothers and sisters, or at the very least as cousins, members of the human family. This would not be easy, but again it was something to strive for.

Jesus' message, I told them, was one of hope and trust. We should not ask where tomorrow's meal was coming from, but should have faith that God would provide. 'Ask and it will be given, knock and it will be opened, seek and you will find' – that was what he had taught us, his disciples, to say and to believe. As I tried to explain it to my listeners, and saw their deprived faces screwed up with the effort of understanding, I remembered the clear, open, believing faces of a crowd hearing Jesus offer these same assurances. I tried to explain my way past the knowledge that some who asked would *not* receive, that some who sought would *not* find. But that was where I failed. The 'truth' was in the saying, never in the explaining. If you had to explain, where was the faith?

I never came away feeling elated, or that I had been a great success. That was partly because I was not a natural orator. But it was also (I now recognise, forty years on) because the message I had to present was his, not my own. I had not at that time worked out a philosophy that was an expression of my own individual soul. I used what I'd first been drawn to in his preaching, and could still propose in good faith. It was the simple, heartfelt Jesus of Nazareth I offered them, my fellow dog philosopher, my good companion in the barley fields and on the roads of Galilee, not the scourge of sinners now raging towards Jerusalem to call down God's wrath on the murderers of his cousin.

As we moved towards the holy city we were gathering people wanting to be there for Passover. Some had already been making plans to go; others were inspired by Jesus' preaching to decide that the time had come.

In Samaria a rabbi came to hear the man everyone was talking about, and to invite him for a meal. Jesus was preaching in the town square, accompanied at the time by the four fishermen, Simon Peter and Andrew, James and John. I was there as master of ceremonies and keeper of the purse, the roles that had progressively fallen on me. The rabbi told us his name was Levi, and that he'd heard many stories about 'the new prophet'. 'I hope you will accept my invitation,' he said. 'I see it as my job to learn about you at first hand rather than by rumour and gossip.'

That was commendable, and Jesus accepted with good grace, but he didn't suppose he was about to make a convert. In fact the rabbi's manner of speaking to us was subtly superior. He was polite, but there was a smile playing around the edges of his mouth and the corners of his clever eyes — not ill-humoured, but ready to mock. I was sure those stories he'd heard about Jesus would have included accounts of miracle cures and divine interventions.

Arriving at the appointed hour, we were shown to a table laid in a small courtyard surrounded by an ancient wall. Two of the rabbi's friends, a scribe and a lawyer, were already seated. A fig tree curved out and up from a crack in the wall and hung above the table, a natural awning. A spring fanned down rocks green with algae into a pool, creating quiet water-talk in the stone enclosure. Three or four oil lamps burned in iron brackets fixed in the wall, but there was still some light in the evening sky as nine of us, all men, assembled around the table. Servants waited on us, and three women, who might have been the rabbi's wife and daughters, brought in the principal dishes.

I noticed bowls of water with towels set out on a trestle table in the shadows at the edge of the enclosure, but since Jesus either failed to see them, or ignored them, I followed his example and took my place.

The conversation was general at first, and remained so through two courses. There were subjects raised, including some matters of law, that might have been meant as traps — who could say? — but if they were, Jesus steered his way past them effortlessly. At times I felt the mood swing a little in his favour, but mostly I was aware of the three well-bred gentlemen, our host and his friends, on one side, and on the other the four ungroomed fishermen with their thick fingers and Galilean accents. Between these two sets was the old firm of Jesus and Judas, Galileans also but educated, groomed by Andreas, and consequently aware, as the fishermen were not, of the subtly patronising tone adopted towards us. Oh what smart and witty things these three were going to say about us when we were gone!

It was when the meal had reached its final course, a cooling mix of fruits and curds, that our host, glancing at his two friends with a smile, told Jesus he'd heard 'stories from all over' about his eloquence, confirmed by what he'd heard in the marketplace this afternoon. But he understood (he went on) that Jesus had other, even greater powers.

'The power is not mine,' Jesus said. 'The power is in the word.'

'A power sufficient to perform wonders,' Levi said.

Jesus didn't respond.

'Miracles.'

Jesus remained silent.

'Can you demonstrate that power to us?' the host asked. 'I and my friends would be honoured . . .'

Jesus was wincing with distaste. 'Don't we worship the same Lord? If you have need of Him, call on Him, and if He hears your prayer, and sees the need, and knows you are deserving, then surely He will help you.'

'Perhaps I'm not deserving,' Levi said, smiling.

Jesus stared at his hands.

But the rabbi didn't give up. 'I lack the power people say you have. Will you not demonstrate it so we too can believe as,' he waved a hand at the four fishermen, 'as these good fellows clearly do.'

Jesus' face was flushed. He was very angry, only holding on to himself with an effort. 'I am not a performer.' He ground the words out slowly. 'I am a prophet.'

'A prophet who neglects to wash before eating?'

We were all shocked. Levi was playing to his own little gallery, but perhaps, at that moment, took himself by surprise. Jesus stood up so suddenly his chair clattered to the parterre behind him. He stared down at them, his face hard, his eyes burning. 'You think I didn't see your stupid bowls and towels? You think this was some kind of oversight?'

'I'm sorry,' Levi said. 'I spoke incorrectly.'

But Jesus didn't stop. 'You Pharisees are so obsessed with the form of things. Form rather than essence. And yet you believe, as I do, in the eternal life. You think you can wash and eat your way into heaven? You think the Lord will prefer your clean hands to these' – pointing to James's and John's fists, twin pairs clenched in anger side by side on the table – 'hands grimed and gnarled with hard work? You think well-washed cups and pots will rate ahead of clean hearts and minds? Are you hypocrites, or merely fools?'

He turned his back on them, moving towards the door that led through to the street entrance. Levi and his friends were silent, wide-eyed. I signalled to my four companions that we should follow, and shepherded them out, but at the last moment John turned back, shrugging past me. With a sweep of his hand he knocked the basins off their trestle table. They crashed to the slate-tiled floor, shooting water across it.

Why did I go
on that final
fatal adventure?

Was it to see
the story played out
to an ending?

Or because
I'd developed a taste
for the limelight?

From him we
borrowed a radiance
each lacked alone.

How nice to be
cheered and admired
by beautiful girls!

How risky to
play guardian to
the Son of God!

CHAPTER 18

LAZARUS, MARY AND MARTHA WERE EXPECTING US AT Bethany. So were many others, made aware of our approach by the work of Lazarus, who, 'raised from the dead' as people told one another (some believing it, some tongue-in-cheek), now preached the Jesus message. The sisters too, each in her quiet way, had gone about the villages of the surrounding region making it known that the prophet of Nazareth would soon come through on his way to Jerusalem for Passover.

We ourselves brought with us, or in our train, an ever-growing crowd of ragged enthusiasts whose belief in him gave courage and strength to Jesus and, I think, to all but one of his disciples. Thomas didn't doubt – not then. Neither did Simon Peter deny. And if Judas betrayed it was only, as I've said, in failing to share the unmixed excitement of the fellows and followers, their confidence that our leader would be triumphant in the holy city and that, as a consequence, a new dawn would break for Israel. We were like a circus come to town – the circus of the Son of Man.

That evening there was a feast for about two dozen people: Jesus and the twelve; Mary Magdalene and the three or four women who had become regular close attenders; and Lazarus, Mary and Martha with a few who were their closest friends and fellow workers for the cause in Bethany and Bethphage. It was held in a large tent, but in the field outside many more were camped, eating around cooking fires, singing, talking, praying, dancing. I said nothing of my fears and doubts, and tried hard (with some success – helped by the wine) to overcome them and to achieve faith. Jesus was as happy as I had seen him since his beginnings as prophet and preacher, and the happiness came off him like a bright light, casting a glow over us all. It was as if the quantum of belief in him, that medicine he was in constant need of, was, for this brief moment, sufficient.

He was full of confidence, and I no longer doubted that, despite his vagueness or evasiveness at times, he now saw himself as the promised Messiah come to save the chosen people from oppression, poverty and sin, and finally, most importantly, from death itself. How long had this been clear in his preaching? How long had I blinded myself to it? Or was it not so much that I had blinded myself as that he had tailored his claims for himself according to what he thought each of us was capable of accepting? These are questions I ask myself now, and find no certain answers. In my memory I'm sure I have pushed together things that were spread over time. I know there were moments when, carried along by the excitement of it all, I achieved something close to belief. But what grew alongside the excitement, and those flickering moments of faith, was fear: fear for myself, yes, but much more for Jesus. Cold, efficient and brutal, the Roman power was seldom far away; even when out of sight it was not, for me, out of mind.

Jesus had taught us to pray, beginning 'Our Father in heaven . . .' Now in his preaching '*our* Father' had become '*my* Father'. 'My Father's house is infinite. There is room there for all of you who wish for the peace and harmony and joy of the life after death. But there is *only one way to it* and that is *through me.'*

That had become his message. 'I am the truth and the way and the light.' I heard it clearly now, was alarmed by it, and asked myself whether he had gone mad, a madness fed by the adulation of crowds who seemed to believe as he had wanted us, his disciples, to believe – fervently, unconditionally, unreasonably.

As his confidence grew, so did his anger, as if the certainty that he was indeed the Messiah justified the rage and frustration he felt at those who looked into themselves and found only doubt or incredulity. The anger was no longer repressed and restrained. It was a guard dog let off its leash. To his listeners he pictured these unbelievers burning in hell, crying out too late, begging the Lord to forgive them.

He was in a state of exaltation. Through him, he assured us, the old order would be destroyed, sinners would be punished, and the righteous taken up to live for ever in the light of the divine presence. I have spoken of some of my fears, but there was another, which lurked in the shadows of myself and nagged at me in the night. Supposing all that he said, all that he now claimed for himself, should be true: would I, with my equivocations, my anxieties and failures of faith, have earned a small corner in heaven? Or was I the one among twelve destined to spend eternity crying out in pain and grinding my teeth at the recognition of my own folly?

On the morning of our second day in Bethany Jesus sent Philip and Andrew to bring in an ass that had been promised. Word went out that he would today be making his entry into Jerusalem, and soon there were crowds – our own people from Galilee, people from Bethany and Bethphage, and finally, as we neared Jerusalem itself, city people who had heard of him and came out to watch. The feeling of excitement grew. There was an undercurrent of rebellion that could rise in a Jewish crowd at any time – rebellion against the Roman power that oppressed us, and against the Jewish power, royal and religious, that served the Roman one. None of this was openly declared. It didn't have to be. We all knew it and felt it – I no less than all the rest. Jesus was daring to enact a prophecy that said the one destined to be our liberator would come not on a noble mount but on a humble ass.

People cheered, waved from balconies, laid palm branches, and even beautiful garments, on the street, and the young ass, not full-grown, walked over them, breaking now and then into a trot, as if it knew this was the Messiah it carried into the holy city. Little boys ran alongside, shouting and waving. Stallholders offered us gifts of fruit and flowers. I heard a woman calling out that Jesus was the king of Israel come to claim his throne, and though another, close by, shouted back, 'Yes, and I'm the queen of Sheba,' it was good-humoured, the voice of someone enjoying herself. Some believed and some did not, but either way a visit from Galilee's now famous prophet and miracle-maker was welcome.

And then, as we rounded the Mount of Olives by the cypress-lined hill road and came down, past Gethsemane Gardens, into the valley of Kidron, there was the city I hadn't seen since childhood, its massive, pale, orange-pink walls giving it that look, half fortress, half palace, with dome and towers, great gates and battlements. It was a moment of triumph and I still recall it with a shiver of the old excitement. My fears were gone for a day. What did it matter whether he was the Son of God or the son of Joseph the carpenter? He was Jesus of Nazareth promising a *new* Jerusalem, and the people were rallying to him.

Inside the walls of the city, beyond the eastern gate, the ass was left with a lad in charge to wait for our return, and we climbed a great stairway into a courtyard where we were greeted with a certain frosty politeness by a delegation of Temple high priests and scribes. They affected a respect I'm sure they didn't feel, careful not to give offence to one who arrived with such a display of popular support. The people, there as anywhere, were powerful when they acted together. It was best not to confront them head-on unless you were sure of Roman support, and since the Romans tended to be indifferent when quarrels among Jews came to blows, the Temple authorities couldn't count on protection.

So we had parables from Jesus and challenges from the Pharisees, a kind of preliminary skirmishing while each side tested the ground of their differences. When one of the high priests, backed up by his confrères, asked Jesus to silence his followers, whose noise was making debate difficult, Jesus refused. 'If my friends fell silent,' he said, 'the stones would cry out.'

At that moment a group of Bethany children, coached by Lazarus, who was in charge of them, began cheering and chanting that Jesus was the Son of David. 'Jesus, Son of David,' they chanted. 'Jesus, King of the Jews.' Lazarus beat time for them. 'Jesus, *Son-of-David*. Jesus, *King-of-the-Jews*.'

The high priest was shocked. This was blasphemy. He protested again to Jesus. 'Don't you hear what they're saying?'

Jesus smiled. Yes, he heard. And had the priest not read the scripture that said for perfect praise one must listen to the cry of a baby and the chatter of small children?

People close enough to hear turned around to call to those further back what Jesus had said. It was an answer that brought a ripple of applause from the crowd.

The high priest frowned. 'But are you then what these people claim for you? Do you claim it for yourself?'

Jesus didn't answer the question but parried with one of his own. 'When my murdered cousin, John, baptised his followers in the waters of the Jordan, did the blessing come from God?'

It was a cunning question. To say that John's blessing was not from God might anger this volatile crowd. On the other hand, to confirm that it was indeed divine might seem to acknowledge that these self-appointed prophets had powers equal to, or even beyond, those of the priesthood and the Temple. The high priest's answer matched cunning with evasion. 'That is a question only the Lord can answer.'

'Then likewise,' Jesus said, 'only the Lord can answer by what authority I preach my message to the world.'

The priests would have liked to debate further but Jesus turned away from them, raised his voice, and spoke to his followers. He told a story about a landowner who planted a vineyard and left husbandmen in charge. The husbandmen stole the harvest for themselves. When servants were sent to collect the owner's share of the profit, they were beaten and sent away. When the owner sent his son to claim what was owed, the son was murdered.

As so often happened when Jesus spoke in parables, there was uncertainty about what he meant. Slowly, however, it became clear, at least to some of us, that the landowner was God, the thieving husbandmen were the priests, and the good servants were Israel's prophets. But who was the murdered son? Who else but Jesus himself? Once again he seemed to be predicting his own death. I'd noticed this in recent days and weeks. The more he believed in his own divinely ordained role, the more readily he accepted – even welcomed – that it must end in his murder or execution. It was an acceptance that came out of him at moments of public euphoria, and seemed to leave him, afterwards, puzzled and depressed.

That evening, as we were returning to Bethany, I felt his mood had changed. The excitement with which the day began had increased to a high point as the crowds flocked with him into the city. Now his face was dark. He was still exalted, but his joy had turned to anger.

On the edge of the village the ass was returned to its owner and we continued on foot across the field still occupied by supporters intending to spend another night or two awaiting Passover. Jesus, in the lead, marched like a general through his camp, so preoccupied with thoughts of tomorrow's battle he failed to notice his foot soldiers. In the garden at the back of the house there was a fig tree. Seeing it, Jesus declared he was hungry and wanted fruit.

It was spring, not the time of year for figs or any other fruit, but I supposed he must be exhausted and confused. He stared up into the branches, finding only leaves. I expected the recognition of his mistake to strike him, and that he would laugh at himself, but not at all – he seethed with rage. The tree had denied him. It would be punished. He cursed it. Let it never bear fruit again! *Let it die!*

I looked at my fellow disciples. They were avoiding one another's eyes. No one spoke. Jesus set off again, still black with rage, and we followed, an unhappy band at the end of what should have been a day of triumph.

Back at the house he couldn't settle, couldn't rest. Martha had cooked a meal for us all, with a special dish for him, but he ate very little and didn't thank her. Mary sat at his feet waiting for wisdom, but none came and he ignored her. Lazarus mentioned the children's contingent, expecting commendation for the way he had organised it, but he got none from Jesus. I took him aside and told him how much his work, both today and in advance of our arrival, was appreciated.

Lazarus gave me his gaunt, red-eyed, gloomy smile. 'I'm happy if the Master is satisfied,' he said in a voice that seemed to echo up from the sepulchre of himself. I could see why people believed he had indeed been raised from the dead.

I worried what we should do with Jesus. I'd watched him closely over recent weeks and I guessed that what he needed at this moment, what he craved, was not the love of individual friends, but of the crowd. He needed the reassurance of numbers, the chance to display his power to himself by displaying it to them. The multitude had become his mirror. I was afraid to make a direct suggestion, which I thought he would reject; but at last, seeming to receive it by the silent transference of ideas we'd practised as boys, he leapt to his feet, answering as if I'd spoken, telling me to go out and set up lights in the field and call the flock to gather around.

He called to Mary Magdalene too, half tripping over the other Mary as he went, not noticing her adoring eyes and her look of hurt. 'Go with Judas. Get things organised out there. There are things that need to be said.'

That night, with oil flares burning and smoking, and the faithful wide-eyed with exaltation and terror, Jesus preached a sermon of extraordinary ferocity. It began with an attack on the priests and scribes – especially those among them who were of the Pharisee sect. They were fools, hypocrites, iniquitous dissemblers, parasites. They and their kind were the murderers of Israel's prophets. They were serpents and vipers that would not escape the fires of hell. The Temple was the Lord's house on earth, but, sullied by the corruption of the priesthood and abandoned by the Holy Spirit, it was no more than a heap of stones. Stones that could be torn down. The day was not far off when that would happen. Not one stone would be left standing upon another.

That was the terrible day (he went on) which would presage the end of time. Nation would rise up against nation, kingdom against kingdom. Within nations and kingdoms there would be dissension, rebellion, civil war. Brother would betray brother, father would betray son, children would rise up against their parents and have them put to death. There would be famine and earthquake. There would be that *abomination of desolation* spoken of by the prophet Daniel.

'*Be warned.*' His voiced echoed out over the stony field and seemed to shake the cypress points so that bats flew out in a silent black shower and flickered over our heads. 'Be warned, my friends. When that day comes, and it will be within the life of this generation, let the man who finds himself on the roof not go down into the house and discover the horror that is there. Let the man in the field not return home to his family. Let him take flight at once, let him escape into the hills of Judaea – and pray it be not the winter season, because it will be a winter like no other that ever was.'

He glared at us in silence. The torches behind him flared in the breeze so that it seemed for a moment as if his body was burning with a golden flame. The light faded, then flared again. 'I tell you the truth when I say, she that is with child on that day, and she that suckles her newborn infant, will wish they had been barren. The sun will give faint light and the moon none at all. The stars will fall like hot rain, the heavens will be shaken, and then, my friends, oh then . . .'

Knuckles white, pressed against hips, chest expanded, face half-turned away, jaw jutting, he seemed to grow in size, looming over us. The crowd was full of fear, and for that moment I was one of the crowd. I held my breath.

'Then, my friends, if you live, you will see the Son of Man coming through the clouds in all his glory, accompanied by his angels who will gather the elect about them. Imagine there are two of you working in a field. The angels come and one is taken, one left behind. Two women are grinding corn at the mill and the angels come. One is taken, one is left.

'Heaven and earth as they have been will be gone, but my words, which are the truth, will remain. Be prepared, my friends. Expect it — *soon*. Watch and wait, remembering what I have told you. There is only one way to the Father in heaven. *I am the way.*'

> Believe in me
> and book your seat
> for Heaven's Glory —
>
> refuse and die
> to everything
> but endless torment —
>
> the old infallible
> carrot and stick,
> he used it
>
> like a master —
> Jesus, my brilliant
> friend, who held us
>
> fearful, yielding,
> as men do, to the
> lash of language.

But power
comes at a cost and
he had yet to pay.

CHAPTER 19

WE WERE ALL RESTLESS THAT NIGHT. JESUS PACED UP AND down, still wound up and tense from the effects of his own oratory. Some time after midnight Martha offered to cook him something, or prepare some fruit and milk, and when he waved her away saying the thought of food revolted him, Mary suggested 'a little walk in the moonlight'. That was greeted with a frown of incomprehension, as if he'd been spoken to in a foreign language, and the two sisters retired to the room they shared, disappointed, and probably offended as well. Lazarus, sitting in a chair, leaning forward, elbows on knees and hands anxiously clasped, watched Jesus in his pacing, staring at him like a faithful dog but unable to suggest anything, afraid to speak. By now, from one of the two rooms in which we disciples were to sleep on the floor, came the snoring of the two brothers Jesus called the Sons of Thunder.

In the early hours of the morning I was woken from a shallow sleep by the voice of Mary Magdalene, speaking to Jesus in soothing tones and singing, very softly, one of the songs of the Galilee region that he and I had both known as boys. I got up and went out into the garden. Coming back I glanced in on them. He was lying face down and in the dim light I could see her massaging his shoulders while she sang. I don't know whether the singing worked for him but it did for me and I sank at last into a really deep sleep.

I was shaken awake by James. It was morning and everything was in motion around me – people passing to and fro through the house, shouts and action coming from the garden and the field beyond. We would be heading back into the city, I was told, all together, gathering supporters as we went. Jesus had received some kind of visionary instruction, James thought, telling him he must return and make his mark on the holy city. 'Yesterday was all talk,' James said, repeating what he'd been told. 'Today calls for action.'

I wanted to know what 'action' meant. 'We'll find out, won't we,' he said in the special, dumb-argumentative voice he'd reserved for me since I had fallen from favour. It wouldn't have surprised me if he'd said, 'Ask no questions and you'll be told no lies.'

Out in the garden some of my fellow disciples were staring at the fig tree, trying to decide whether it was dying. They were agreed its leaves were drooping and that it needed water, but was that new, or had it been so yesterday? Simon Peter, John and Bartholomew were sure it was already failing under the weight of Jesus' curse. Thomas said he couldn't be sure. Matthew thought perhaps there was no change – 'as of *now*,' he added, not wanting to be accused of lack of faith.

That morning Jesus broke bread for us, blessed it, reciting the prayer of thanksgiving, and handed to each of us a share. It was a moment of stillness, in which his mysterious power over me, over each of us, reasserted itself – and I felt it all the more keenly because before and after there was such urgency. We ate in silence, passed around a jug of goat's milk, and prayed together: 'Our Father in heaven, your name is blessed . . .' The prayer was routine, but it seemed full of unspoken meanings that were particular to us and to the moment.

What I remember next is the crowd straggling out of the field and along the dusty road, those in front turning to urge the ones lagging behind to keep up; the feeling, so different from the day before, that time was important, that we didn't have a moment to lose. Yesterday had been a triumphal entry and welcome to the city; today was more like an assault. In his sermon the previous night Jesus had spoken of tearing down the Temple, and it was as if we were about to begin. Local people came out to stare again, but there was no longer a carnival atmosphere. Now the looks were anxious. Children who had raced along beside us, shouting and cheering, today were silent, held back by their mothers. And at the front was Jesus, frowning, formidable – the self-proclaimed prophet come from the provinces to tell the city folk what they needed to know.

We made our way in by the same road, around the Mount of Olives and through the same eastern gate; but this time, following Jesus (who might indeed have been under divine instruction, his path was so unhesitating), we climbed steep stairs into that vast courtyard of the Temple I remembered from our childhood visit.

It was unchanged, redolent of woodsmoke, spilt blood, defecation, and the seared meat of never-ending sacrifices. There was the same lowing, bleating, chirping and bellowing of doomed animals, the same shouting of the money changers making their rates known, the same stallholders' chatter, and, coming from somewhere directly above, the solemn chanting of a choir of Levites.

We must have seemed, to those whose day we were about to disturb, no more than a rabble led by a ragged preacher. The scene in that courtyard was neither solemn nor beautiful, but it had its own system and order. This was the place where divine and human met and traded, man acknowledging sin and offering propitiatory gifts, God accepting the sacrifice and granting absolution. This was the Temple practice Jesus had condemned in his teaching, and he was now intent on disrupting it.

He was full of energy, his confidence at that moment unwavering. I lumbered along in his wake with no confidence at all, alarmed at the prospect of violence, worried about the consequences.

The first objects of his wrath were the stalls and tables of the money changers. Not wasting words, he took the corner of the first table he came to and heaved it off its trestles, sending it clattering to the floor. His followers cheered, throwing stools about, pushing pedlars and traders to left and right, kicking aside anything that came in their path. Coins of every kind, Judaean shekels, Greek drachmas and leptons, Roman denarii and quadrans, rattled down on to the stones and ran away in all directions. Pieces of paper recording transactions were scattered, blown across the court and trodden underfoot. There were shouts of outrage. People rushed about, bent double, some on hands and knees, trying to rescue their money or help themselves to coins that belonged to someone else. Fights broke out. 'That was mine.' 'No, mine.' Jesus hurried on to another table and another, turning them over, throwing them to the ground.

'My Father's house was a house of prayer,' he shouted, 'and you have made it a den of thieves.'

'Den of thieves,' shouted his followers. '*Den of thieves. DEN OF THIEVES.*'

There was a line of stalls selling doves and small animals for sacrifice, and with help from the fishermen these, too, were overturned. Doves, released from their cages, clapped away up through the smoky air. Lambs and kids, untethered, ran bleating and bewildered, lost in the crowd.

I took no part in creating this uproar. All my thoughts during those minutes were focused on how to get Jesus out of there and save him from arrest. I could see three or four Temple guards trying to fight their way through to us, held back by the crowd we'd brought in our train. There was also a group of young Levites halfway down a stone stairway, watching from above, pointing, talking urgently to one another. One ran back up the stairs, another down towards the main entrance to get help. We'd been told the Temple authorities would never invite the Roman soldiery in, but they might think the disorder serious enough to bring in some of Herod's militia who were housed only a short distance away.

I grabbed Jesus by the arm. He was panting, so out of breath he had to lean on me, recovering. 'The job's done,' I shouted, trying to look as if I was excited and pleased. 'Now we have to get out of here before they bring in troops to arrest you.'

He frowned, uncertain.

'To arrest us all,' I said.

He nodded, gulping for breath.

I didn't wait for him to change his mind. I grabbed Simon Peter, and then Andrew. 'Jesus says it's time to get out. Before the militia arrive. Head for the gates.'

We came together, the thirteen of us forming a group as we retreated. Our supporters, those who weren't already running away, followed, scattering into the warren of streets south of the Temple. By the time we'd reached the Gethsemane Gardens there were only a few of them still with us. The rest had hightailed it for safety, knowing the priests would be unforgiving and that Herod Antipas was tough on public disorder.

Back at Bethany Jesus was subdued. He looked to Mary Magdalene for comfort. She sat with him in the garden, in the shade of a vine-covered trellis, and held his hand. I joined them there. 'We should go back to our own region,' I told him. 'You're not safe here. The city people were interested in you, but that was yesterday. It won't last.'

'We've come for Passover,' he said.

I looked at Mary. Her face was calm, reasonable, trustworthy. 'Tell him,' I said.

She smiled and seemed amused. 'Tell him? What should I tell Jesus? You think there's something you and I know that he doesn't?'

I persisted. 'If we set off now we could be in Jericho some time tonight.'

He shook his head and turned away.

I went indoors looking for someone to support me. 'Let Jesus decide,' Philip said, and the rest agreed, taking my eagerness to get away as just another sign of my lack of faith.

Jesus came in from the garden. 'How much is left in the bag?'

I brought it from under my bedroll and tipped it out on the floor. Jesus stared at the silver coins. We all stared, counting. There were thirty. 'Take it all,' he told me.

I was to book an upstairs room in a tavern and order a generous meal, fit for the time of Passover; also beds for the night, which would be expensive because the town was filling up with visitors for the festival. The supper was to be just for Jesus and the twelve. If there was going to be trouble, arrests, punishments, he wanted no one else caught up in it – not Mary Magdalene, not Lazarus and his sisters, not the helpers from Bethany.

'Go now,' he said. I hesitated and he looked hard at me, reading my thoughts. 'If you'd prefer to cut and run . . .'

That was what I wanted, but I knew I couldn't do it. 'Only if we all go together.'

He shook his head. 'The work here has to be finished.'

That evening we sat down in one of the better taverns in Jerusalem for the meal that Ptolemy, and other members of the Jesus cult who come through Sidon, often describe in their preaching as 'the Last Supper'. There was certainly an atmosphere of doom about it, though none of us, except perhaps Jesus, would have known it was to be our last together. In fact I remember, before we sat down and the mood became serious, there was joking and laughter of the kind that had gone on in happier times. The fishermen brothers boasted of damage they'd done in the Temple, and the pleasure they'd taken in 'knocking city heads together'. Matthew told one of his off-colour jokes from the time when he'd been on the road as a tax collector. Thomas objected, saying it was inappropriate at the season of Passover. Everyone looked to Jesus to rule on that, and he pretended, with a sly smile, not to have understood it. Bartholomew, who had been missing since we left the Temple, arrived late and out of breath wearing a brooch we hadn't seen before, and we teased him about his newest friend, a young jeweller from Bethphage.

But he had news for us that put an end to jokes. Looking for us, he'd gone back to the home of Lazarus and the sisters. Herodian militia and Temple guards had been there already, demanding to see Jesus. They'd searched the house, breaking locks, throwing things about. Lazarus had assured them that Jesus and the disciples were on their way back to Galilee, but he wasn't sure he'd been believed.

I looked – I suppose we all looked – to Jesus for some response to this. There was none, or only acceptance. Everything was going to God's plan.

The meal was of lamb with the prescribed herbs. But first Jesus broke the unleavened bread for us, blessed it, and gave us a cup of wine from which each was to take a sip, passing it on. He stood at the head of the table, speaking in a tone of sadness that compelled attention. When he was gone from us, he said, we were to do what we were doing now. We were to take bread and wine as a holy sacrament. The bread would be his body, the wine his blood.

I looked around the table for some sign of the alarm I felt at this. There was none. His beautiful voice, so unwavering, so exalted, held them, possessed them, and I could see I was the only one not believing that we were in the presence of the divine. In the past there had been doubts and uncertainties, but at this moment it seemed there were none. Eyes squeezed tight shut, or cast upward, or shedding tears, or simply staring (as Bart's were) full of love and trust at our leader – all, in their different ways, were telling the same story. A jury of his peers was returning a majority verdict, eleven to one in his favour. Jesus of Nazareth, they were affirming, was the Son of God.

Forty years on, what Jesus said to us that evening is as deeply marked in my memory as it would have been if I had been one of the believers. All the dark fire had gone from his eloquence, replaced by the charm and gentleness that had persuaded me to leave Nazareth and travel the roads with him. His thoughts now, as in those early days, were for the poor, the unhappy, the enslaved, the weak. Their time, he assured us, was at hand. The anger and rage, the promises of terrible events and individual punishment, the flames of hell, the separating of wheat from chaff, sheep from goats, the weeping and wailing and grinding of teeth – all that had dissolved into a message of hope and reassurance. He was one of us, he told us, our equal not our chief. Or, if there must always be masters and servants, he would prefer we saw him as our servant. He was going from us, but only to the Father, to prepare a place for us, and for all who believed in him. We should not be distressed by what happened to him in the coming days, but accept that it was for the best, that the dead rose to eternal life, and that what was troubling and obscure would in time become clear. We would lose him, but in a little while we would see him again, alive and well and walking with bright steps upon the earth. There would be sorrow, but it would turn to happiness and celebration. The pain would be the pain of a birth, and the joy would be the joy of a new life. The Father loved us because we had loved the Son, and because of that love our prayers would be answered and we would have our reward. We would have our moments of weakness, when faith might waver. One of us might deny that he was ever a disciple; another might betray the trust that existed among us. Such things, if they happened, should not shake our faith. We were, each of us, human, and therefore capable of mistakes and failures; but we believed in him, and that was what mattered. Belief was the key to the Kingdom, and by being here this night, each one of us proved that we possessed the key.

Jesus was wrong in that. I felt the old fondness for him as my friend, and admiration for his oratory, but as a disciple I failed. I failed to believe he was the divine Messiah. If he was determined, as he seemed to be, not to make an escape, determined, even, to die, I knew I would never see him again, not as a man, and not as the Son of Man.

I would not betray him; but I lacked what he chose to call the key.

Imagine your
friend insists you
must eat his body

and drink his
blood because he's
on his way to heaven —

and yet his
other friends seem to
accept what he says

without question —
and there's a feeling of
reverence, a

stillness, as if
the stars themselves are
holding their breath —

and you know
somewhere the cross and
nails must be waiting . . .

You will understand
how it lives with me
like a dark

dream, an exalted
nightmare, never to be
expunged.

CHAPTER 20

THE STORIES I HEAR FROM PTOLEMY AND HIS FRIENDS ABOUT that 'Last Supper' and what followed are always detailed and strange, part true, part invention. Jesus predicts that I, Judas of Keraiyot, will betray him, and that Simon Peter, the rock on which his church was to be built, will deny him three times before the cock crows. He predicts his own death. He predicts his resurrection on the third day. So Judas duly betrays him to the authorities, and Simon Peter denies him three times before the cock crows. Jesus dies. Jesus rises from the dead. The stories are self-fulfilling. Jesus knows how they end, and the stages by which the end will be reached. His divinity is confirmed by his foreknowledge.

I was there and I recall very little of this – certainly no accusations of denial and betrayal except (as I've reported them) in the most general terms. Of course Ptolemy (Bartholomew as he was then) would make the same claim: he was there, one of the twelve. He sat at the same table, was witness to the same events. Has his memory been shaped to confirm the faith he lives to propagate? Or did my lack of faith blind me to what was going on? To put it more simply: am I wrong, or is he? Only God can answer that question, if there is a God; and if there is, He's silent and has remained so throughout these forty years when, Jesus assured us, we would see the fiery chariot, the divine wrath, the choosing of the elect, and the end of time. 'Where are you Jesus?' I sometimes ask the night sky. It's a joke, of course, not a solemn prayer; not even a serious question. The man is dead, and if ever an answer came to me out of the darkness, I think I might die of surprise rather than fright.

This morning came news from Jerusalem, no less terrible for having been expected these many months. The Roman legions have at last broken the siege. The city has been burned, smashed, reduced to ruins. Very few of its inhabitants survive. The story, brought first by drivers of a camel train, and confirmed later by a Jewish family from Bethphage, is that citizen defenders set fire to a Roman siege engine somewhere near the Damascus Gate. Flames were blown back on to wooden fortifications, and soon fire was raging through the city, where wells were low and there was almost no water to fight it. The fire brought down a wall, making an easy entry for the Romans, who swept in finally from the Hill of Scopus where they were massed, killing all in their path. The citizens put up the best fight they could but, weakened by starvation, disease and despair, were soon overcome. While the battle continued no one, man, woman or child, was spared. We were told that Titus, the Roman general, son of the new emperor, wept at the destruction wrought by his troops. Ptolemy and I wept at the news. For a moment we were brothers as we had been long ago. I wanted to tell him who I was, but couldn't speak for grief, and the moment passed.

'What will become of us?' I ask myself, thinking like a Jew, forgetting for a moment my new identity in this Greek community. I imagine myself as one of the survivors, a little Hebrew band, hounded, destined to wander again in search of a home. I thank my luck it isn't so. I thank my scepticism, my unbelief, my observing eyes and open mind, for the life I have been allowed to live. I thank my late wife Thea, my Greek children and grandchildren. I thank the cloak of a new language and a different culture. But I grieve for Jerusalem and for its inhabitants, and hope that in the provinces the Jewish people will recover and be spared to live and make new beginnings.

It was Theseus who first brought me the news. He'd been in a little crowd that gathered in the square, plying the dusty camel drivers with drinks and food and listening to their story. After Theseus had gone I took a walk down to the waterfront. I found Autolycus in his workshop and told him what I'd just heard. He looked hard at me, trying, I thought, to gauge my feelings.

'Well at least it's not your home region,' he said.

And that was true. Galilee, though not unscarred, would have been spared the worst of the Roman wrath. But Jerusalem stood for something. I surprised myself by saying, 'You know, don't you, that my name was Judas before I came here.'

He looked puzzled. Not surprised – my children have always known that I was named Judas by my parents. But Autolycus didn't think of it as a different name. 'Isn't Judas just the Jewish form of Idas?'

I said I supposed so, although I didn't think it was – not really. But my son showed by that question that he was a Greek; I, by the way I thought of it, that I was still a Jew.

I said, 'I'd better not interrupt your work.' He put an arm around my shoulder, awkwardly, as if he wasn't sure whether it would be appropriate to comfort me, or excessive.

I walked on along the shore to a place overgrown with tamarisk and oleander, where I keep a little skiff. I pulled it free of the undergrowth, waded out and jumped in, sculling in small pushes over the still clear water, watching a school of sprats that moved precisely together, rolling slowly left, then right, like a single sea creature made up of many units.

Suddenly the single creature became many, panicking, escaping, scattering in all directions. I didn't see the larger fish that was after them, or no more than a flash of it. The water was no longer clear. Scores of sprats sprinted along the surface, trying to escape into the alien element – the mirror of men diving into the sea to escape capture or death.

And then all was calm again – still, silent, beautiful. The sea around my skiff settled, became transparent. The predator, satisfied, was gone, and the tiny survivors re-formed into their indifference, a silver, undulating, underwater cloud.

I sat a while, not thinking of anything, just feeling it all, self and scene, present and past, as if I and it, or I and they, were not separate at all but were one body; and then they came back to me, out of a long-lost corner of my brain, some lines of a psalm whose 'rough justice', as he called it, had troubled our gentle tutor, but had excited his star pupil:

> By Babylon's waterways we remembered Zion, and wept.
> Our captors demanded music. They mocked us. 'Give us the songs of your homeland.'
> But we hung our instruments in the branches of the poplars.
> How could we sing the Lord's song to alien ears?
> Jerusalem, if I forget you, may my right hand freeze on the strings.
> May my tongue fall silent if I fail to exalt you above all the places of my heart.
> Punish, Lord, the Edomite betrayers, who cried, 'Raze Jerusalem! Tear it down!'

And you, Babylon, its destroyer — there will be joy for
those who pay you back in kind.
Destruction for destruction, death for death, child for
dead child,
Smashed on the stones.

Those lines are grim, and I felt their power again, though without
believing, as I perhaps once did, that the wrongs done to Israel
(or any other) will be righted by some ultimate balancing out
of brutalities.

But Jerusalem will rise again. There will be survivors. Our
race is resilient. As for myself, I am Idas of Sidon, a Jew but not
a Jew, father of a Greek family and therefore, by election if not
by birth and upbringing, a Greek.

When our supper was over Jesus led us out into the street. We
had two or three rooms booked in the tavern, enough beds for
all of us, but it wasn't late and we followed him without question. He led us down into the Kidron Valley, across the stream,
and uphill into the Gethsemane Gardens. He'd remarked on them
each time we passed on our way into the city. Now he wanted
to pray there. It was a fine clear night and we walked in twos
and threes behind him, sombre, anxious, fearing to ask questions.

Jesus stopped under olive trees and said we should rest. The
lads stretched out, finding softer patches and small tufts of grass
on the stony ground, and smooth stones to prop their heads. Jesus
went on. I gave him a few minutes and then followed. I found
him in a tight grove of trees, holding on to an overhead branch,
resting his forehead against its trunk. He was praying in husky
half sentences, in a voice that was full of desperation and fear.

I put a hand on his shoulder, but he shrugged me away. This

distress was something he'd meant no one to see. He straightened up, pulling himself together. When I began to speak he put a hand over my mouth. 'Say nothing . . . Unless it's something I haven't heard from you already.'

He dominated me and I didn't speak. But it was as if there was an exchange between us, a silent one. I was telling him again that what he was doing was suicide, and unnecessary. He was repeating that it was the will of the Father.

Stubbornness you could call it, this determination not to back off and save himself. But probably it would be fairer to call it loyalty — loyalty to his followers, but more than that, to himself, to the God and the cause he had spent most of three years preaching. He had challenged the authority of the Temple and asserted his own. If the challenge and the assertion were to seem serious, he couldn't now run away.

He took a deep breath and gripped my shoulder. 'I want it to be over quickly. Finished. So . . . Let's get on with it.'

I moved aside to let him pass, and followed him back to where the others were resting. He gathered us around him and offered another little homily, speaking again as if he would soon be gone from us. It was a farewell. He asked us to repeat with him the prayer he'd taught us, and which we'd made our own. We did that, with a depth of feeling I could hear in all our voices.

Now he asked Simon Peter, James and John to go with him to another part of the garden, to pray with him while the rest of us kept watch. I was not invited, and felt it as a rebuff, but of course he was right. My prayers would have been to please him, not to please God, whose ear I'd never had, and whose very existence, even in those days, I allowed myself to doubt.

I don't think anyone went back to the tavern that evening, though for a time Bartholomew was missing. When he returned he had his jeweller friend with him, the one who had made him the new brooch. Most of us slept fitfully, or dozed, under the trees. Jesus was still praying with his three chosen ones when I heard voices, and saw lanterns crossing the stream below. I scrambled up and hurried out to the road. I could hear them calling to one another, up through the trees, across the zigzag lines of the path, as they climbed the slope. The 'wanted man' had been seen at the inn with his followers, and then leaving it in the direction of the gardens.

I rushed back and found him once again among the disciples. I broke in on what he was saying, grabbing him by the forearms – from which, I suppose, comes the story that I kissed him to signal which of our group was the prophet of Nazareth. 'They're coming,' I told him. 'If we scatter into the trees . . .'

He shook his head, still letting me hold him. 'No, Judas. I'm not running away.'

A moment later we were surrounded by Temple guards, Herodian militia, and one or two young Levites. Simon Peter, supported by James and John, tried to fight them off. Others of our group were already sliding away into the shadows. Bart's young friend, wearing only a loincloth, ran away towards the road. A militiaman made a grab to stop him, the loincloth came off, and he ran on, naked, vanishing into the night.

Jesus called the fishermen to stop resisting. Addressing the posse he asked, 'Why have you come for me by night, and with weapons, when you could have taken me in daylight at the Temple?'

They weren't there to argue. His hands were tied behind his back and he was dragged away. They were rough with him and he accepted punches to the ribs and slaps around the head with grunts and sighs, making no protest.

In a moment I found myself alone in the garden. The disciples, all except Simon Peter, who was following behind the posse, had run away. I hesitated, fearful, and then, inspired by Peter's courage, hurried after him. I saw something on the ground, shining. It was the brooch Bartholomew's friend had made. I picked it up – and I have it still, my only memento of that event.

I caught up with Peter and we followed at a distance, down the path to the bridge over the stream and up again, towards the city. We were soon at the Temple. Still following, we climbed a flight of stone stairs, walked through a courtyard, climbed more stairs. A broad corridor brought us to double doors opening on to a large apartment. We were stopped by guards and told we couldn't enter.

Peter took a seat on a bench. I stood at the door, craning to see what was going on. Inside, in what appeared to be a public room lit by torches around the walls, high priests and scribes were assembling. I imagined some of them at least to be members of the Sanhedrin. There was a familiar face among them. It took me only a moment to confirm that it was my uncle.

I approached the guards again. I pointed him out to them, named him, explained that he was my father's brother. 'He would not object to my being there,' I assured them. When they hesitated I added, in my best accent, 'He wishes to speak with me when this matter is concluded.'

They looked at one another for confirmation, and let me pass.

I took a place at the back. The high priest, Caiaphas, watched but didn't speak while Jesus was arraigned for inciting disorder, dishonouring the Temple, and making false and blasphemous claims for himself and against the authority of the priesthood.

Jesus said nothing.

Caiaphas took over. 'You are Jesus of Nazareth?'

Receiving no reply, he said, 'You rode into Jerusalem on an ass. You were hailed as "Son of David", the Messiah. You encouraged this blasphemous welcome.'

Jesus was silent.

Caiaphas quoted the prophecy. '"Fear not, daughters of Sion: behold your new King comes, riding on a young ass."'

Jesus said, 'That is the prophecy. Is riding an ass therefore forbidden?'

'You pretended to be its fulfilment.'

'It's you who speak of the prophecy. I rode the ass.'

'Are you King of the Jews? Are you the Messiah?'

Jesus shook his head slightly. 'These are your words.'

'What did it mean when you said, "Before Abraham was, I am."'

'It meant the soul exists beyond time.'

'Your soul, Jesus of Nazareth?'

'My soul. And the soul of man.'

'Did you say you would tear down the Temple and rebuild it in three days?'

'What I said was spoken openly in the Temple and in public places. If it was wrong, why did you not arrest me then, in front of my supporters?'

One of the guards, standing behind, slapped him across the back of the head. 'Answer the question.'

'We have witnesses,' Caiaphas said.

'If you have witnesses,' Jesus said, 'you will prefer their answers to mine.'

Caiaphas said, 'I ask you one last time. Are you the Christ? Are you the Son of God?'

Jesus looked at him, and around the room. The light of the torches flickered over him and in his eyes, which I thought were brave but not fearless. 'These are your words,' he said again. 'But I tell you this – you will see the Son of Man, who sits at the Lord's right hand, come down through the clouds of heaven, and you will know the truth of what I have said, and the consequences of what you do to me.'

My heart leapt at the courage of it. How wonderful if only it had been true! How superb if he knew it was not and said it anyway!

Caiaphas' smile was cold. He was satisfied. He turned to the members of the Sanhedrin. They consulted briefly, in murmurs, nodding their agreement, before he turned back to face the accused.

'Jesus of Nazareth, we are agreed that your blasphemies deserve only one punishment, and in the morning we will put you before the Roman prefect, His Excellency Pontius Pilate, who has the power to impose it.' He nodded to the guards. 'Take him away.'

I made a move towards my uncle but he turned quickly and disappeared into a back room with others of the council. I had seen his eyes on me already. In appearance I was like my father (and, indeed, like him), and I suppose he'd heard of my association with the prophet of Nazareth. It seemed he wanted nothing to do with me.

I passed the night with Simon Peter, wandering the empty streets, finding corners and doorways in which to catch some sleep. We two, destined, it seems, to be known as the denier of Jesus and his betrayer, spent those hours keeping watch, asking ourselves whether anything could be done to save him, while the other ten, who have earned no such bad report, or none that I've heard here in Sidon, made themselves scarce. Some must have set off immediately, walking overnight, back in the direction of our home territory. It was what I'd wanted Jesus to do.

Recently I asked Ptolemy about this. What had he done after Jesus' arrest? He said it had been necessary to go into hiding. 'We were all in danger. None of us was safe. And if Jesus was going to die, we were destined to be the bearers of his message. We had to make sure some of us lived to preach another day.'

How excellent, I thought, to have the best of reasons for self-preservation. But that was unfair. There was nothing they could have done to save him.

I said, 'So you were not present at the crucifixion?' Of course I knew he was not.

'Simon Peter was there,' he said. 'And possibly one other of our brotherhood.'

'One other?'

He nodded, and began feeling beside his chair for his walking stick. This was the kind of questioning I'd noticed he tried to avoid. His narrative of those events was so carefully shaped to suit his message, he didn't like requests for details that might spoil its outline or blunt its point.

'Who was the other?'

'The other?'

'Of the disciples. At the crucifixion. You said there was another.'

He shook his head. '*Might* have been. It's never been confirmed.'

I said I'd heard it was Judas of Keraiyot.

'I'm certain that's not true,' he said, though he looked anything but certain. When I was silent he added, 'Judas, you remember, killed himself.'

'Of course. I'd forgotten.'

Long ago Andreas
taught us: 'The Greek
wants Reason,

'the Jew looks
for a Sign.' Is there
a Sign in the fall

of the holy
city, that our race
should abandon

its thirst for a
Messiah, its hunger
for Zion?

Honour the stones
and let them lie
where they've fallen.

Listen to wind
and wave, the language
of seasons,

and let God die
of old age, untroubled
by our prayers.

CHAPTER 21

IN THE MORNING SIMON PETER AND I WASHED UNDER A FOUN-
tain and drank from it. We had no food and no money, but since
none of us, so far as I knew, had used the rooms booked in the
tavern, I thought it wasn't too much of a risk to go back there
and ask for something to eat. The innkeeper was puzzled that
the rooms hadn't been slept in, but he was not unfriendly, and
gave us a good breakfast. He hadn't heard of Jesus' arrest. I gave
an unsensational account of it, as if I thought it was only a
routine matter. The high priests, I explained, had objected to
something in Jesus' preaching. They were sending him on to be
dealt with by the Roman prefect.

At the mention of the prefect the innkeeper shook his head.
That, he told us, was not good. Pontius Pilate was brutal, and
he liked people to see that he was – that's why he conducted
his courts on a public terrace in front of the Antonia Fortress.
'It scares the shit out of us and makes us behave ourselves. They
say he's homesick for Rome, he hates Herod and the priests he
has to deal with, and he takes it out on us.' He nodded, pulling
a comical, dour face. 'And he loves the scourge. It's his morning
exercise.'

When Peter and I got to the fortress there was already a crowd
gathering in front of the terrace. About the middle of the morning

Caiaphas appeared, accompanied by others of the priesthood. Jesus was brought out. Eyes down, he looked tired, bruised, dirty and unhappy. He'd been stripped of his robe and sandals, and was bare to the waist. I felt such a pang for him I wanted to call out that we were there, but my courage failed.

Pilate kept everyone waiting. He arrived flanked by armed guards flashing with polished metal, accepted the salutes due to him as representative of Rome and the emperor, and took the judgement seat. The entry accomplished, he wasted no time, and few words.

'I have investigated this matter,' he said, addressing Caiaphas, but raising his voice so the crowd could hear. 'I have even taken the trouble this morning to call in the tetrarch of the Galilean region, Herod Antipas, currently visiting us here in Jerusalem. The tetrarch — no lover, I may say, of would-be prophets who are the vermin of his region — has agreed with me about this Nazareth person . . .' He stopped, looked to an official who bent down to whisper the name in his ear. I felt that this was part of the act, and that he probably knew the name perfectly well.

'About this Jesus of Nazareth,' he went on, 'who has, as we understand it, a ready turn of phrase and a piercing voice, but little else to recommend him. He is a worthless and deluded vagrant, but hardly a felon deserving more than a scourging — which I am myself ready to deliver.'

He smiled as he said this, pointing languidly, without turning, back over his shoulder to where a centurion stood to attention carrying the scourge as if it was the sceptre of office, its silver-inlaid handle lying over his heavy, tanned forearm, its leather thongs, each with barbs that flashed in the sunlight, hanging down towards the floor.

Pilate looked to the high priest as if for acquiescence, though I doubt he expected he would get it. Some kind of struggle for ascendancy was going on between these two. I could feel it, and that Jesus was its present occasion, without understanding exactly what was at stake.

'With respect, your honour,' Caiaphas said, 'this Jesus of Nazareth has blasphemed against the Temple and the authority of the priesthood. The people will not be satisfied.'

Pilate smiled again. It was an unpleasant smile. I wondered whether there were circumstances in which he could smile warmly, and doubted it. He appeared to give the matter some thought – or to wish to give that appearance.

'Let's say, then, that the sentence is death.' There was a stir of approval from the crowd. Pilate turned his smile outward like a cold beam over the gathering. 'Ah the appetite for blood – how dependable it is!'

He turned again to the high priest, and continued, still keeping his voice up, as if acting in a play. 'At this festival of Passover, as you know, High Priest, I am obliged to release one condemned man and return him to the people. Apart from the two highway robbers, who are of no consequence, two have been condemned by these sessions – Barabbas, the rebel, and now Jesus of Nazareth, the blasphemer. I propose to release the blasphemer. He will be scourged and set free.'

Now the murmurs were of discontent. 'Crucify Jesus,' someone called. 'Free Barabbas.'

It was taken up by the crowd. 'Crucify Jesus, free Barabbas. *Crucify Jesus, free Barabbas.*'

Pilate held up his hand, and the chant died away. 'This is your king, Jews, and you don't want him?'

'No we don't,' came a heavy voice from the crowd.

'You can have him,' another called, and there was laughter.

'With respect, your honour,' Caiaphas said, 'this man is not the king of anything. He is a carpenter's son from the provinces.'

'And who', Pilate asked, 'is Barabbas that you should want him released? Isn't he the murderer – a rebel against Rome?'

'He is a troublemaker, your honour, that is true. Not a worthy man, but not a blasphemer.'

Pilate snapped. 'Not a questioner of your authority, you mean.'

Caiaphas' reply was subtle. 'It is your authority, your excellency, and that of Rome, which have been challenged by this "King Jesus". Who has kingdom over the Jews if it is not our Emperor Tiberius? I say if one must be released to the people, it would be strange indeed if it should be he who has offered such a challenge.'

He looked to the crowd and they began to chant again. 'Crucify Jesus, free Barabbas. *Crucify Jesus, free Barabbas.*'

Twisted sideways, hunched uncomfortably in his chair, Pilate chewed a troublesome thumbnail, frowning at the crowd over the top of his hand. It occurred to me that he might have condemned Jesus to death only so he could reprieve him. This would mean he didn't have to reprieve the rebel, Barabbas, the one he wanted out of the way.

The chanting went on. He must at that moment have decided this was one battle he would have to concede. Abruptly he heaved himself up and stood, hands on hips, glowering, angry, intimidating. He held this posture until the silence was complete.

'It is not for the representative of Rome's greatness to split hairs with you, High Priest. If that is what Jerusalem wants, Jerusalem shall have it. Barabbas will go free and Jesus of Nazareth will die.'

There was a rumble of satisfaction from the crowd. Pilate

turned and snatched the scourge from its bearer. With no warning he swung it over his head and the barbed thongs struck Jesus across his bare back. The pain and shock of the blow pitched him forward into the dust. As he lifted himself to his knees a second blow struck. The sound he made was as much a gasp of astonishment as a cry of pain. Astonishment *at* the pain – that was how it seemed, as if at that moment, as the blood sprouted from the score of wounds torn in his shoulders, he was entering a searing world entirely new to him.

A third blow hit, and a fourth. The crowd was counting, '*Three. Four.*' In the gap between the blows I heard Jesus' voice, gasping, 'No, please . . .'

He was on hands and knees. '*Five.*' A fifth blow, and he had fallen again. Pilate hesitated in order to rub his upper arm. It looked as if a sixth was intended but as the '*Six*' was chanted he stopped, threw the weapon back to its guardian, and turned to the crowd, not concealing his contempt. 'Your king has received *my* punishment, Jews. My soldiers will deliver yours. Enjoy your Passover.'

He turned and swept away, followed by guards and officials. Jesus was on his feet again, staggering, his back wet with blood, his face with tears. Soldiers surrounded him. He was led through the crowd, who jeered, '*King of the Jews. King of the Jews.*'

'Save yourself now, prophet of Nazareth,' someone called.

'I have a toothache. Please cure me, miracle man.'

And a voice, not amused at all, but full of hate: 'Desecrator of the Temple. Death is what you *deserve.*'

Jesus vanished into the crowd and when I next saw him he was being hustled along the street in the middle of a group of twenty or more soldiers and beside a wooden cross which at that moment someone else, a burly citizen, was being made to carry. The soldiers, always bored and hating the local population, had amused themselves tormenting him. On his head they'd placed a wreath, or a crown, made of twisted rose stems, pushed down hard so the thorns were causing his brow and scalp to bleed. Stuck into this was a crude notice I wasn't close enough to read but which, I was told later, declared this was 'Jesus of Nazareth, King of the Jews'.

I lost him again. The streets were busy now, and many people, seeing that a crucifixion was about to happen, were following the soldiers and the condemned man.

I was distressed and wanted not to see the execution, but knew I had to. At one point my courage failed and I turned off into a crooked little backstreet and let the crowd surge on without me. I crouched in the dust. I tried to pray and knew I was not listened to. I recited the prayer Jesus had taught us to say together and found some comfort in it, though the comfort brought tears.

My pain was unimportant, but the imagination is a powerful and remorseless taster of every sensation, and while it was happening to Jesus in the hands and the feet, it was happening to me in the head – so powerfully it's as if I look back and remember the day I was crucified and expect to find I have the scars.

I don't know how long I remained there, a muttering weeping young man looked at by solemn-eyed urchins who had stopped playing to stare at me, and by women out on their balconies, shaking mats and hanging out washing.

When I set off again it was the tail end of the crowd I joined. We went, by the Damascus Gate, out through the city wall on the opposite side from the Mount of Olives and on to a main road, turning from that to a minor one that climbed a small hill I now know to be Mount Calvary. At the top I could see the three crosses, already upright in their prepared slots, already bearing their human fruit. People were standing about in the sun, talking, watching, some grim or thoughtful, many quite relaxed, enjoying themselves. There were men selling water, fruit juice and sherbet drinks by the cup; others offering small cinnamon and honey cakes. These executions were meant to terrorise us, and did, keeping us all subservient to the Roman power. But you could see that few there were thinking they might one day have to spread their hands to accommodate the imperial hammer and the imperial nail. I wonder how many lived to see the recent siege, and died the same way.

As I got nearer I could see Jesus on the middle cross, naked, writhing, groaning, his head rolling from side to side, squeezing his eyes shut so the tears ran out and streaked the blood smearing his cheeks. He was still wholly alive to the pain, and the sight of his feet, one over the other on a small platform, with a huge nail driven right through them, I could stand to look at only once.

I felt anger, the anger of frustration and despair. How could he have done this to himself? How could we, his friends, have allowed it? My anger was most of all with myself, because I'd seen what was coming, but had not been strong enough and clear enough in confronting him. I'd failed to save him from himself, or (if you prefer) from the almighty sadist, maker of heaven and earth, whose son he imagined himself to be.

I searched the crowd for our companions of the road. Of the disciples only Simon Peter was there, rock-like, grim, frowning up at the crosses as if they represented a puzzle he was determined to solve. The sisters Mary and Martha were standing not far from him. Mary at just that moment seemed to lose control, breaking into loud wailing, throwing her head back, tearing at her clothes and slapping her face. Martha, also tearful, tried to calm her. Mary Magdalene was close by, dry-eyed, and with an expression I couldn't read.

Two highway robbers had been nailed up before Jesus, one on either side of him. They too were conscious, suffering, and their families were weeping and calling to them. There were also the mockers, one calling to Jesus to prove himself as the famous miracle worker by coming down from the cross. 'Don't keep us waiting, Jesus,' he boomed. 'Do your stuff. Show us what you're made of. You'll be home in time for dinner.'

All I wished for in the hot hours that followed was for it to be over; for Jesus to be dead. Crucifixion could last a long time. I'd heard of strong men remaining alive three days. But I was also hearing people in the crowd, regulars at such events, saying that, because it was the eve of the Sabbath, the deaths would be hastened – that the Temple authorities would take it amiss if the bodies were still in sight after sundown. That meant, usually, the breaking of the legs – something that gave me a peculiar horror. But in fact, in Jesus' case, it was done with a spear.

It was in the middle of the afternoon and a cloud had come across the sun. I'd stayed close to the crosses. Sometimes, early on, I'd thought Jesus had seen me and recognised me. I hoped he had; that in his tormented consciousness he'd known the friend of his boyhood was there. Later, the blood on his face was so covered in flies I couldn't read his expression, but I knew he was still conscious because the writhing and the groans, though less frequent, continued. And then, taking us by surprise, he arched his spine, strained against the nails, threw his head back and shouted, 'Lord God in heaven, why have you forsaken me?'

It was torn out of him, a cry of protest, the last full-throated utterance of that remarkable voice I still hear in my head and in my dreams. It's how I know there's no God. If there had been one, and He had ordained this end for His faithful son and servant, He would at that moment surely have died of shame. Or perhaps there was a God and He did indeed die, and what we've been left with is a memory, a rumour, a shadowy recollection of what once was, carried about the world by the Ptolemys and the Pauls (another Jesus-sect passer-through this region), the travelling salesmen of the numinous, the divine, the eternal, the extinct.

The spear was pushed into his heart slowly, with deliberation, one might say with love, as if the Roman soldier was acknowledging that when you kill the Son of God you must make a proper job of it and show respect. It seemed to take for ever for the thing to go in, from tip to haft, gleaming as it vanished, and for ever for it to come out again, smeared, gory, the shine gone. Blood and a pale fluid followed it, out into the light. Jesus took in a deep gulp of air, held it, and expired with it, saying something I didn't catch. He was dead. I thanked God (because there was no one to thank) that it was over.

The soldiers were keen to get the bodies down, to be rid of them and get back to their barracks. While Jesus was still being lowered, Martha, having calmed her sister, herself became hysterical, shrieking at the centurion in charge, trying to rush at him and hit him with her fists. He held her at arm's length, remaining calm himself, trying to soothe her. He was middle-aged, pockmarked, gnarled, the survivor, probably, of many campaigns and many crucifixions. He spoke to her in broken Aramaic patched with Greek, saying what was meant to be something like, 'We're only doing our job, lady. We don't enjoy these things, but the law has to be upheld.'

Martha heard the sympathy in his voice, her rage turned to tears and she collapsed, sobbing, into her sister's arms.

Mary Magdalene came to speak to me; greeted me, in fact, as if I had been the mourner at a funeral and she a representative of the bereaved family. I had the impression that she was acting on Jesus' behalf; that she might say, 'Thank you for coming.' I saw again that expression I'd noticed at a distance and hadn't been able to interpret. Her eyes were shining. She was not unhappy. She was exalted.

My anger came back. I remembered a conversation when I'd wanted her to help me persuade Jesus to go back to Galilee, and she'd said his destiny might be to die. 'You're pleased?' I said. I pointed at the crumpled naked bleeding white body in the arms of the sweating Roman soldiers. 'He's dead. You're satisfied with that?'

She was unnaturally calm. 'He's dead. He will live again.'

When my frown, my anger, didn't abate she explained more clearly, as to a child. 'Jesus will walk the earth again. You'll see, Judas.'

I couldn't speak. I had to turn and walk away. When I'd calmed myself and came back, a man was explaining to the three women and to Simon Peter that he had permission from the Roman authorities to take the body. He was a wealthy trader who had heard Jesus preach and had been persuaded of his divinity. He came originally from Arimathea, but lived now in Jerusalem. He'd had a tomb made for himself, a sepulchre carved in rock in his garden in the city. It would be a fitting place, he said, for the body of the prophet, and he would make another for himself so that one day, in death, he would lie beside the great Jesus of Nazareth.

Like Mary Magdalene he seemed to be in a kind of rapture. His servants, who had brought linen and spices, and a litter for the body, were waiting to take it to the sepulchre, where they would anoint and wrap it. The women, Mary, Martha and Mary Magdalene, would go with them to assist and to see Jesus laid to rest.

I watched them carry him away. 'Jesus is dead.' I repeated this to myself. His disciples, all but two of us, had run away. The whole enterprise was over. Whatever we'd thought we were doing, whatever Jesus had thought he was going to achieve, had led only to pain, tears and this needless and gruesome execution. I reminded myself how he had urged us, when we felt we were not welcome, to 'shake the dust from our feet' and move on. That's what I had to do now. I had to restart my life. And in the shorter term I had to think how, with no money, I was going to get out of the city and make my way home.

This might have been difficult. I suppose I would in the end have swallowed my pride and gone to my uncle but, as it happened, I didn't have to. As I made my way back through the Damascus Gate two men ranged up on either side of me. They were Temple guards. I felt fear, a sinking in the stomach. Was I under arrest?

They didn't say so, but they spoke as if they had authority and were issuing orders. One said, 'Your uncle needs to speak to you.'

'At once,' said the other. 'We'll take you there.'

I didn't argue.

I stayed several days with my uncle, and although he was, as I'd thought when I met him as a child, inclined to be snobbish and self-satisfied, he was not without a sense of humour, and enough like my father to make me want to treat him with respect. He, in turn, was inclined to be indulgent, seeing me, I think, as a well-brought-up young man who had taken a wrong path, though for reasons he assured me he could understand. This was because he imagined that, as a follower of Jesus, I must be profoundly religious. He understood, he told me, how a young person such as myself, concerned for spiritual wholeness and truth, could sometimes expect too much of established religion and its priesthood, and so could find himself following false prophets who promised heaven and earth and could deliver neither.

I let him rest in this misreading of my character. He was my means of escape, and what – apart from being thrown out penniless into the street – could have come of confessing that I not only failed to believe that Jesus was the Son, I was failing even to believe in the Father?

He knew that I had watched the crucifixion and that I was distressed, and he was not so insensitive as to show satisfaction at the death of my friend. But it was not difficult to see he thought Caiaphas had scored a great victory over the Roman prefect in having Jesus crucified instead of Barabbas; and when I told him, that first evening, that a wealthy businessman was going to inter Jesus in a sepulchre somewhere in the city, he said at once, 'That can't be permitted.'

I asked who would prevent it. 'This man has authority from the prefect.'

My uncle smiled and nodded. 'Of course,' he said. 'That's it, then. Nothing to be done.'

But it was clear he didn't – not for a moment – think there was 'nothing to be done'. And when I heard, two days later, that the stone had been rolled away from the mouth of the tomb in the night, and that the body was gone, I knew this must be the work of the Temple priests and the Sanhedrin – or must have been done at their behest. It's one of the ironies of the story, as I look back on it, that this piece of grave robbery by the priesthood, intended to prevent a cult of Jesus growing around the site of his burial, had (from their point of view) the worse effect of fostering the much more powerful myth that he had risen from death.

Of course his followers 'saw' Jesus after the crucifixion. I'm always hearing stories of these sightings, which were many and various. He was seen near the tomb, he was seen in Galilee, he was seen on the road to Emmaus – sometimes by one, sometimes by three, once, even, by five hundred. He was changed, he was unrecognisable, he was the same, he was unmistakable. He talked, he was silent. He told one person not to touch him, another to finger his wounds. Ptolemy tells his faithful crowds a moving story (hearsay, of course) of Jesus, dressed in white as at my wedding, rising into the sky, taken up into heaven by the Father – growing smaller as he ascended until he was just a point of light, fading and vanishing.

I too saw Jesus after his death. In those first few days, especially, while the memory of the crucifixion tormented me and kept me awake at night, I saw him in the street, caught sight of him in crowds, heard his voice coming from an open window – just as I'd seen and heard Judith after her death. I still see them in dreams – both of them, though never together. Our dead are always with us. But they are not alive. That's the nature of being dead, and it's best we accept it.

As the days went by my grief caught up with me and replaced my anger. My uncle was sympathetic. He bought me new clothes and gave me money – not a small amount either. He was generous. He suggested I travel and take time to recover. I took his advice and came, after many small adventures, to Tyre, and from there, after many more, including the lightning strike that burned the ox cart containing all my worldly goods except a

wallet and a brooch, I arrived at this lovely village on the sea
just south of Sidon, where I met and married my second wife.
But that is another story.

> Today there's
> rain. It will nourish
> my orchard garden.
>
> Hector is
> out in it, pretending
> he's a soldier.
>
> I can see a
> boat bringing its
> catch to the jetty.
>
> Electra will
> be there to buy fresh
> fish for supper.
>
> Why am I
> weeping? It was all
> so long ago, and
>
> things take their
> course no matter what
> we do, and time heals,
>
> they say. Maybe
> it's myself I weep for,
> not my friend,

but the grief
seems real. Anyway,
I'm glad of the rain.

CHAPTER 22

LONG AGO I THOUGHT THE JESUS STORY ENDED WITH MY friend's death on the cross, but it seems not. As the years go by, and as evangelists of the cult pass through, it becomes clear that the story flourishes like Arabian whispers, changing and growing over time and distance. Divinity proved by 'miracles', and a promise of eternal life at the cost, merely, of 'belief' – these are irresistible terms in a world full of poverty, misery, pain and death. Bart and his fellow 'Christians' (as I've noticed lately they begin to call themselves) always find doubters and mockers; but equally they find ready ears, converts everywhere, every day. It's a strange thought that the name once mine, Judas of Keraiyot, goes forth to the west and to the north, to wherever it is these new disciples take it, to be known, as long as the story goes on being retold, as betrayer of the Son of God. I'm glad to have left them, the name and the identity, behind, in favour of Idas of Sidon, Idas the Greek, Idas the poet.

I am at last to be rid of my house guest. Whatever it is (the will of God, he would say) stirs Ptolemy and directs his next move has spoken. With his ever-dutiful attendant Reuben, he plans to be on the road in the morning. I had my daughter-in-law prepare us a farewell meal – a last supper, I called it, but not to him. I have, on the whole if not entirely, enjoyed having him with me, and now I will enjoy having him gone.

Theseus joined us, and we sat at a table out on the terrace under the palms, watching the bats flit over silently against a sky that, for some time after the sun was gone, didn't lose its velvet-black blueness. When I spoke of it, Ptolemy told us how much he missed colour from his world, but then couldn't resist the preaching habit, and put an end to the sympathy he'd evoked by saying that the colours of heaven, which he saw more clearly since his blindness, were infinitely more rewarding.

I told him that when I was young my visions and dreams of heaven had been colourless, and now, as an old man, I accepted the logic of that.

He asked what was its logic.

'Since nowhere is colourless,' I said, 'heaven is nowhere. It exists only in imagination.'

He smiled and drummed his fingers on the table. 'Logic clearly has its limits.'

'And faith, unlike anything else in our experience, has none.'

We'd eaten well and were still drinking wine, which loosened my tongue. 'I've got used to calling you Ptolemy,' I told him. 'But to me you're really Bartholomew.'

'I was Bartholomew.'

'Yes,' I said. 'And I knew you then.'

In the long silence that followed his dead eyes hunted for me, as if I might be hiding from him among the vines in some dim corner of the terrace. 'Your voice . . .' he said.

'You know it?'

'It's like a voice I've known.'

'It *is* a voice you've known.'

He was silent again, perhaps letting the particular timbres repeat inside his head. I knew he'd puzzled over this before.

I said, 'We travelled the roads together.'

He sat very still.

'With Jesus.'

His own voice was quiet, low-pitched, even fearful, as he asked, 'What was your name?'

'My name was Judas.'

His face showed he knew it was true. This was the knowledge his ears had given him and he'd rejected all the time he'd been in my house. Now, hearing me affirm it, he couldn't bring himself to accept it. He needed it to be untrue. 'That's not possible,' he said.

'Judas of Keraiyot. Yes, it's so.'

'No.' He shook his head, frowning fiercely. 'You died.'

'Are you sure?' I'd heard him preach about the suicide of 'Judas the betrayer', even claiming he remembered seeing my body cut down from the very fig tree Jesus had cursed.

'Yes,' he said. 'I'm sure.'

'Then I must have risen from the dead.'

He stood up. One hand went to the cross he wore around his neck, the other patted the air until it found Reuben's shoulder.

I said, 'You believed it of Jesus. Why not of Judas?'

He gave whatever signal it was that set Reuben in motion, and followed him to the door, where he turned. 'You should have told me this before inviting me to stay.'

'You should have told me you were Bartholomew.'

'Damn you,' he hissed. 'You always had an answer, even when you had nothing to say.'

'You feel you've been tricked,' I said. 'Or trapped. I'm sorry, Bart. I thought I was doing you a favour.'

He said quickly, coldly polite, 'I'll be gone in the morning. I thank you for your hospitality.'

He was so pale and tense with anger, I laughed. 'Shouldn't I be the angry one? Haven't you gone about the world maligning me as the betrayer of Jesus?'

He wagged a finger at me. 'I won't discuss this, Judas. You've deceived me.'

'By living? You expect me to have died for your comfort? To make your Jesus story less untrue?'

His frown became fiercer, more concentrated, and at the same time his face seemed to clear, as if only now there was something he understood. 'I know you,' he said. His eyes rolled upward in his head, showing the whites. 'You were with us all that time and we didn't know who you were. But *he* knew. Must have known. That was his strength against you, and now it will be mine. I don't fear you, Judas. My strength is in knowing the truth.'

He was holding his cross in front of him, shaking it at me. With great ferocity he said, '*You are the Devil.*'

I'm afraid I laughed again, which may only have made him feel more certain. Isn't it said the Devil has a lot to laugh at? 'Why not?' I said. 'If Jesus is the Son of God, why shouldn't Judas be the Devil? And he and I went to school together – think of that!'

He stood in the doorway, quivering with his 'recognition', which he was not now going to give up. I could see him working it out. If I, Judas, was the Devil, wasn't it perfectly possible I might 'die', 'kill myself', and reappear like this, to tempt and torment the followers of Jesus? I didn't altogether dislike the idea. It was a new theology and gave me a certain status – very much below Jesus, of course, but a significant player in the metaphysical drama. I felt honoured in a way.

These were the things I wanted to say to him; things I would once, in my younger, more combative days, have said. But the old man has learned to curb his tongue and keep his best jokes to himself. I was thinking, rather, that it was sad we should part on such a sour note, and maybe it didn't have to be so.

'Bart, old friend,' I began, taking a step towards him – but the fierce expression remained, and he pushed the upheld cross at me as if he believed it would fell me if I got too close.

'Jesus protect me,' he prayed, rolling his dead eyes up towards the heavens.

He was not going to let me be just a man – a smart bastard, a sceptic, but a friend. I was the Devil, and he was on guard.

And then I remembered some news I'd heard from that Jewish family, refugees from Bethphage, who'd arrived the day after the camel drivers. It was something they'd been asked to take as a message to any of the Jesus cult met along the way. I'd been saving it – hadn't passed it on to Ptolemy because I'd known it would upset him even more than it upset me, and the right moment hadn't presented itself.

'Listen to me, Bart.' I said it in a crisp, no-nonsense tone, and he listened. 'There's more news from Jerusalem – something sent especially for you and your friends. It came when you were preaching and I haven't told you. Haven't had the courage . . . It's about the sons of Zebedee.'

'James and John.' As he said their names he took a half-step towards me. The cross was still there, held up, but tilting down, not thrust at me so aggressively. 'You're going to tell me . . .'

He stopped, and I finished his sentence. 'They're dead. Yes, I'm afraid they are.'

He nodded. 'Of course. If they were there, I knew they'd fight.' He approached me.

'James was killed fighting,' I confirmed.

'And John?'

I didn't know how else to say it. 'He was crucified.'

He winced. Tears sprang to his eyes. He let the Devil hug him, and even half returned the embrace.

We stood like that for some moments. Theseus, who had watched and listened to it all, drifted discreetly from the room, pointing up the hill to signal that he was on his way home. Reuben studied the patterns in my son's mosaic tiling that decorated the floor.

'Go to bed, Bart,' I said at last. 'I'll be up before you in the morning. We'll give you a good breakfast before you hit the road.'

He nodded, mumbled thanks. He seemed small, but courageous at that moment. He patted the arm of the Devil Judas, and allowed himself to be towed away, blind, into history.

> This morning he
> leaves and I'll give him
> the brooch his friend
>
> the jeweller made,
> lost in that scuffle
> in the garden.
>
> Fitting, it seems,
> that a blind man
> should seek the light –
>
> as that a man
> with eyes should look
> to the horizon.

Our friend was
not the Messiah, nor
will there be one.

This is the truth
I write. It will not
hurt you. Grasp it!

DATE DUE

C.K. STEAD

Mansfield

'C.K. Stead is challenging, fun, urbane and brilliant. Read him'
Spectator

Spanning three years in the life of the writer Katherine Mansfield during the First World War, this novel follows the ups and downs of her relationship with Jack Middleton Murry and her struggle to break through as a writer. As her brother and lovers are drawn into the conflict, Mansfield becomes more and more determined to write the "new kind of fiction" which she feels the times demand.

While sticking scrupulously to what is known about Mansfield's life and her friends (a cast that includes D.H. and Frieda Lawrence, Bertrand Russell, Dora Carrington, Lytton Strachey, Aldous Huxley, T.S. Eliot, Lady Ottoline Morrel and Virginia Woolf), this extraordinary novel takes the reader beyond biography into the mind and emotions of its subject. It is a sharp, subtle and appealing portrait of the person of whose work Virginia Woolf wrote: 'It was the only writing I was ever jealous of.'

'Stead's style is crisp and cool, always lucid, sometimes comically witty, and also capable of powerfully vivid description'
London Magazine

'The most consistently lyrical portraitist'
Independent on Sunday

VINTAGE BOOKS
London

BY C.K. STEAD
ALSO AVAILABLE FROM VINTAGE

☐	**Mansfield**	0099468654	£7.99
☐	**The Secret History of Modernism**	0099447061	£6.99
☐	**All Visitors Ashore**	1860469361	£6.99
☐	**Talking About O'Dwyer**	1860468365	£6.99

FREE POST AND PACKING
Overseas customers allow £2.00 per paperback

BY PHONE: 01624 677237

BY POST: Random House Books
C/o Bookpost, PO Box 29, Douglas
Isle of Man, IM99 1BQ

BY FAX: 01624 670923

BY EMAIL: bookshop@enterprise.net

Cheques (payable to Bookpost) and credit cards accepted

Prices and availability subject to change without notice.
Allow 28 days for delivery.
When placing your order, please mention if you do not wish to receive
any additional information.

www.randomhouse.co.uk/vintage